GILDA JOYCE
The Ghost Sonata

also by

Jennifer Allison

Gilda Joyce,
Psychic Investigator

Gilda Joyce
The Ladies of the Lake

GILDA JOYCE
The Ghost Sonata

JENNIFER ALLISON

DUTTON CHILDREN'S BOOKS

30359 1992

DUTTON CHILDREN'S BOOKS
A division of Penguin Young Readers Group

Published by the Penguin Group
Penguin Group (USA) Inc., 375 Hudson Street, New York, New York 10014, U.S.A.
Penguin Group (Canada), 90 Eglinton Avenue East, Suite 700, Toronto, Ontario, Canada M4P 2Y3 (a
division of Pearson Penguin Canada Inc.) • Penguin Books Ltd, 80 Strand, London WC2R 0RL, En-
gland • Penguin Ireland, 25 St Stephen's Green, Dublin 2, Ireland (a division of Penguin Books Ltd)
Penguin Group (Australia), 250 Camberwell Road, Camberwell, Victoria 3124, Australia (a division of
Pearson Australia Group Pty Ltd) • Penguin Books India Pvt Ltd, 11 Community Centre, Panchsheel
Park, New Delhi - 110 017, India • Penguin Group (NZ), 67 Apollo Drive, Rosedale, North Shore
0745, Auckland, New Zealand (a division of Pearson New Zealand Ltd.) • Penguin Books (South
Africa) (Pty) Ltd, 24 Sturdee Avenue, Rosebank, Johannesburg 2196, South Africa
Penguin Books Ltd, Registered Offices: 80 Strand, London WC2R 0RL, England

This book is a work of fiction. Names, characters, places, and incidents are either the product of the
author's imagination or are used fictitiously, and any resemblance to actual persons, living or dead,
business establishments, events, or locales is entirely coincidental.

The publisher does not have any control over and does not assume any responsibility for author or
third-party websites or their content.

CIP Data is available.

Published in the United States by Dutton Children's Books,
a division of Penguin Young Readers Group
345 Hudson Street, New York, New York 10014
www.penguin.com/youngreaders

Designed by Irene Vandervoort

Printed in USA • First Edition

ISBN 978-0-525-47808-9

1 3 5 7 9 10 8 6 4 2

"After silence, that which comes nearest to expressing the inexpressible is music."

—ALDOUS HUXLEY

CONTENTS

Prologue ∞ 3

1 The Nightmare ∞ 5

2 The Piano Lesson ∞ 7

3 A Dubious Plan ∞ 14

4 Bad Omens, Good-luck Charms ∞ 24

5 Fear of Flying ∞ 29

6 Turbulence ∞ 40

7 The Arrival ∞ 45

8 Wyntle House ∞ 48

9 The Drawing of Numbers ∞ 56

10 The Apparition ∞ 63

11 The Ritual ∞ 70

12 The Holywell Music Room ∞ 80

13 The Disaster ∞ 95

14 Julian's Performance ∞ 101

15 Dead Man's Walk ∞ 108

16 The Wandering Children ∞ 116

17 The Haunted Melody ∞ 122

18 Professor Sabertash and the Tarot ∞ 125

19 The Voice ∞ 129

20 A Visit from a Stranger ∞ 138

21 Professor Sabertash ∞ 147

22 The Clue in the Bookshelf ∞ 156

23 The Five of Swords ∞ 159

24 An Icy Message ∞ 165

25 The Sight-Reading Competition ∞ 168

26 The Page-Turner ∽ 176

27 The Stranger ∽ 186

28 The Alice Trail ∽ 193

29 Julian and Jenny ∽ 199

30 Port Meadow ∽ 203

31 A Clue in the Graveyard ∽ 209

32 The White Rose ∽ 217

33 Mrs. Choy and Mrs. Chen ∽ 223

34 The Breakthrough ∽ 226

35 The Finalists ∽ 234

36 Substitute Ghosts ∽ 237

37 The Accident ∽ 244

38 Dr. Cudlip and the Baffling Case ∽ 246

39 Beneath the Black Water ∽ 256

40 The Message ∽ 260

41 A Tormented Soul ∽ 266

42 A Disturbing Discovery ∽ 271

43 A Drop of Poison ∽ 276

44 The Ghost in Gloucester Green ∽ 281

45 The Last Sign ∽ 287

46 Art and War ∽ 291

47 The Final Round ∽ 299

48 Sequins and Sabotage ∽ 308

49 The Ghost Sonata ∽ 317

50 "Curiousity Killed the Cat" ∽ 320

51 Professor Waldgrave's Confession ∽ 324

52 The Aftermath ∽ 332

53 The Winners ∽ 340

GILDA JOYCE
The Ghost Sonata

I suppose none of this would have happened to us
if we hadn't traveled to Oxford, England--to a
land where eccentric scholars ponder the great
questions of life while safely nestled within
their Gothic walls and dreamy gardens, to a city
of antiquity, where ghosts haunt the winding back
streets, silent cloisters, and damp hallways of
elite colleges.

My best friend, Wendy Choy, hoped to distin-
guish herself in an international piano competition. I simply dreamed of traveling overseas to
escape a tedious week of school, a seemingly endless Michigan winter, and the humiliation of an
unrequited ninth-grade crush. I pictured myself
snacking on tea and scones while practicing my
English accent. I would impress college dons and
students alike with my penchant for using British
sarcasm and slang, not to mention my lively collection of interesting hats. Together, Wendy and
I would bask in the warm glow of applause following her piano performances.

Naturally, I was also prepared to test my psychic skills in a land where nearly every old
hotel, pub, and college library has a ghost
story--a tale of some lonely apparition appearing

to the sleep-deprived student or drunken reveler in the wee hours of the morning.

I was prepared for all of these things.

I wasn't prepared to feel helpless as I watched my best friend experience a disturbing change. Nothing in my Master Psychic's Handbook had prepared me to watch the most reliable person I know become the victim of the most unusual haunting I had yet encountered.

The Chinese have a saying: "If you believe it, there will be, but if you don't, there will not."

But what about people like Wendy, who do their best to remain rational—even a bit skeptical—and who nevertheless find themselves haunted by an unwelcome ghost?

The English have a saying when calamity strikes: "Put the kettle on; we'll have some tea."

But I needed more than tea to help unravel a haunting on foreign soil. I needed every ounce of the expertise and psychic intuition I had developed in my career as Gilda Joyce, Psychic Investigator.

1

The Nightmare

Wendy Choy saw two shadows in the room. She heard the clinking of knives—metal scraping against metal—then a tearing sound, as if someone were ripping cloth or gauze to make bandages.

"Hilp me wheel the tray over hiere. Make sure everything is sterile, okay? Good, good." The familiar voice had a Russian accent. "How are you feeling, Windy?"

"I don't know. Sss——" For some reason, Wendy couldn't find the word she wanted to speak.

"Don't worry; it will be quick," said the voice. "We need to make a few adjustments."

Someone flipped a switch, and an overhead light revealed a grand piano on top of which shiny objects were spread upon a tablecloth. As Wendy looked more closely, she saw scissors, knives, scalpels—an assortment of surgical instruments lined up very symmetrically, like rows of piano keys.

"No——" Wendy breathed. "N——" Her brain screamed the word, but it seemed that her voice no longer worked. Her teeth clenched. She felt paralyzed. She couldn't articulate the word no. She couldn't move or speak.

In the light, she saw two faces peering over the table of instruments—a wrinkled, wizened face with raccoonlike eyeliner and next to her a round, moonlike face, the face of a little girl. Two hands picked up scalpels and began to cut.

Wendy awoke suddenly to discover a spiral notebook embedded in her cheek and a puddle of drool on top of her biology textbook. She had dozed off while studying in the school library, and she was late. It was after four o'clock, and her mother would already be sitting in the parking lot, waiting to drive her to her piano lesson.

As she hastily gathered her belongings and stuffed them in her backpack, Wendy sensed the disquieting residue of the nightmare she had just experienced. She couldn't quite recall the details, but she felt as if she had just received an ominous warning.

2

The Piano Lesson

Waiting outside the front door of her piano teacher's house, Wendy clutched her sheet music and did her best to stifle the feeling of trepidation that often preceded her lessons.

"Windy! Come een; come een!" A petite, exquisitely dressed woman threw open the door and beamed at Wendy, her deep-set eyes framed by heavy, black eyeliner and a web of wrinkles.

Mrs. Mendelovich spoke with a Russian accent. She wore an ornate red scarf around her neck, and her silvery hair was slicked back tightly in a French twist, her perpetual hairstyle. She walked gracefully, with poker-straight posture, reminding Wendy of an aging ballerina.

Mrs. Mendelovich had converted her living room into a piano studio where two full-grand pianos filled the room like black racing cars in a garage.

"I haf wonderful news," Mrs. Mendelovich declared as Wendy sat down at one of the pianos.

Wendy immediately felt nervous.

"Windy, my darling, your audition was a success! You haf been chosen to travel to Oxford, England, to compete in Young International Virtuosos Piano Competition!"

Wendy felt dizzy, as if she were suddenly peering down at Mrs. Mendelovich from a tightrope. The words "international virtuosos piano competition" seemed to soar with too much importance.

"Are you happy?"

"I guess."

Wendy imagined how her parents would respond whey they learned the news. Her father's face would turn ever-so-slightly pink. He would come close to breaking into a huge, sloppy grin—a smile he would quickly control with a more appropriate, humble appreciation. Her mother would slyly post information about the competition next to her manicure station at the Happy Nails Salon so she could tell her clients all about her talented daughter who is "one of the best young piano players in whole country! Going to England!" Her parents would be thrilled. They would also nag her incessantly during the next few weeks to make sure she practiced enough.

"Wish to win," Wendy's mother would say.

"Play that spot again," her father would say, eavesdropping on her practice sessions. *"Sounds messy there. Do over. No, no. Still not right. Here, listen to how Lang Lang plays on this CD. You do enough times, you can be perfect, too."*

Wendy's father greatly admired the pianist Lang Lang, and he often enjoyed reminding Wendy how Lang Lang gave his first public recital at age five; how Lang Lang and his father had shared a tiny, cramped apartment and endured much suffering for the sake of Lang Lang's music studies in Beijing; how Lang Lang was so grateful to his family—his father in particular—

that he allowed his father to perform with him in concert at Carnegie Hall.

"But Dad, even if I make it to Carnegie Hall someday, you won't be able to perform with me because you won't take any music lessons."

"Too late for me," said her father. "Too old now. Point is that Lang Lang is a great boy. A great son."

"Sorry to be such a disappointing daughter."

"You will surprise me," he said. "There is greatness in you. Your mother and I have sacrificed much, and someday you will make us very proud."

"Ming Fong and Gary weell also compete," Mrs. Mendelovich continued, shaking Wendy from her reverie. "I am so ploud of all my very best students!"

Ming Fong was also in ninth grade, and her mother, Mrs. Chen, worked with Wendy's mother at the salon. Because the workplace friendship between the two women masked a thinly veiled competition, Wendy constantly heard about Ming Fong's achievements. Ming Fong made straight A's ("not a single A minus! Only A pluses!"). Ming Fong never wasted time watching television. Ming Fong always helped her parents cheerfully and expressed humble gratitude. Unlike Wendy, who was born in America, Ming Fong had come to America only a few years ago, but her English was excellent and she constantly helped her parents communicate with hospitals, schools, employers, and the Department of Motor Vehicles. Of the two girls, Wendy had won more piano competitions, but Ming Fong was hot on her heels, often placing second. It bothered Wendy that she often caught Ming Fong watching her, as if observing her behavior and calculating something—striving to either imitate or undermine the object of her ambition.

"Wow," said Wendy, feeling at a loss for words as she imagined traveling to England with Ming Fong, Gary, and her piano teacher. "All three of us qualified for the competition?"

"They found the audition tapes of my students superb. This is gleat, gleat honor for me as well, being your teacher."

Wendy sighed and tried to smile. She felt a great sense of honor and a greater sense of dread.

After her lesson, Wendy sat on Mrs. Mendovich's front porch, waiting for her mother to pick her up. A slate-gray January sky glowered overhead. Wendy watched as two young girls wearing parkas dragged a sled down the icy sidewalk, followed by a small dog. For some reason, she envied both the girls and the dog.

Wendy pulled her cell phone from her backpack and dialed Gilda's number.

"Gilda Joyce here."

"Why do you answer the phone that way? You know it's me calling."

"This is my business phone, Wendy. For all I know, it could be a client looking for help with a haunting. Anyway, I'm kind of busy right now."

"What are you doing?"

"Watching a rerun of *Saved by the Bell*."

Wendy wished she could sit down next to Gilda with a bag of potato chips and do absolutely nothing except watch a simpleminded television show that she had already seen several times before. Gilda always had multiple projects in the works, but she somehow also managed to prioritize things like watching television and reading books that had nothing to do with school. Of course, Gilda's grades were far less consistent than Wendy's straight-A average.

"If you can believe it," said Wendy, feeling reluctant rather than excited to share her news, "I got into that piano competition I was telling you about."

"The international one?"

"I'll be going to England in just a few weeks."

There was a moment of silence at the other end of the line because Gilda was so excited, she jumped up from the couch and began to pace back and forth. "No way."

"Way."

"Then why aren't you jumping up and down and screaming? Wendy, this is *awesome*!"

Wendy wished she could share Gilda's enthusiasm. For some reason, she felt a lump rising in her throat—a strange homesickness. It reminded her of the feeling she had on the first day of summer camp.

"You are so lucky!"

"It isn't luck; I spent the whole year practicing."

"That's true; you kept practicing even though I did the best I could to thwart you." Gilda often called during Wendy's scheduled practice times to tell her what was on television or to encourage a "mental health" break. Occasionally, she turned up at Wendy's house uninvited and offered her services as a "live studio audience."

"Wendy, I can't wait! You know how I've always wanted to go to England!" Gilda's many career goals currently included plans to become a novelist who lived in either a cramped, dimly lit London apartment or a grand English manor house filled with ghosts. Her published books would all be based on the bizarre and extremely dangerous mysteries she solved in real life.

"Gilda, I don't think this competition is going to provide free airfare for friends of mine who want to come along for the ride."

"You can't possibly go without me, Wendy. That would just be *wrong*."

"Believe me, I wish you could go, too. I just doubt your mom is going to pay for a plane ticket and hotel on such short notice. In fact, I doubt my parents will even be able to afford the trip right now; I'll be stuck traveling with Mrs. Mendelovich, Gary, and Ming Fong."

"I'll think of *some* way to get there," Gilda insisted. "If you're going all the way across the pond, you're going to need my help."

"Why would I need your help?"

"You don't understand the English and their ways."

"And you do?"

"I read novels, Wendy. I know all about tea and crumpets and bangers and mash, and all that stuff. For example, when you're in England and you need to find an elevator, you say, 'Where's the lift?'"

"You're right. I can't possibly compete in a piano competition without knowing about English elevators and the history of tea and crumpets."

"You'll also need someone to cheer you up between practice sessions. You know how grumpy you get."

Wendy stood up because her mother's car was pulling into Mrs. Mendelovich's driveway. "Gilda, if it makes you happy to pretend you're traveling to Oxford with me, go right ahead." Secretly, Wendy reflected that if there was anyone who *could* find a way to get herself to England on short notice, it would be Gilda.

3

A Dubious Plan

As Wendy practiced her scales and arpeggios, she did her best to ignore Gilda, who sat on the Choys' living room couch. Gilda, in turn, was doing her best to ignore the stack of untouched homework that sat next to her. Instead, she flipped through several books she had found at the library with titles like *A Photographic Tour of Oxford Colleges* and *"Spotted Dick": An American's Guide to British Language.*

"Get this, Wendy. In England, if you want to say that someone is totally crazy, you say, 'She's gone doolally!' or 'She's gone dotty and barmy!' And if you want to describe something that's way too girlie and cutesy, you call it 'twee'!"

"Good words to know when I'm hanging out with you," Wendy muttered as she continued to progress through her scales in a series of major keys.

"And listen to this, Wendy. If you feel like you're going to throw up, you could say, 'Stand back, mates; I think I'm to park a custard!' Isn't that *great?*"

"Lovely. I can't wait to puke like an English person." Wendy began running through the minor keys.

"I can't wait to start talking this way," Gilda continued, half speaking to herself. "I can just see us in England—slurping tea, drinking warm beer, eating scones and clotted cream, driving on the wrong side of the road..."

Wendy abruptly stopped playing. "What are you talking about, Gilda? For one thing, we aren't old enough to have our licenses, and for another thing, you just told me yesterday that you missed the deadline for that study-abroad program you were thinking of. Why do you keep talking as if we're actually both going to England? At first it was cute, but it's beginning to seem like you're just in denial." Wendy turned back to her series of scales.

"There's more than one way to get to England, Wendy. I'll figure something out." Secretly, Gilda had to admit that Wendy had a point. At the moment, she had no feasible way of getting permission to leave school for a week, not to mention the expense of traveling overseas. But as she skimmed through photographs of medieval architecture with soaring spires, college students laughing in dim pubs, cobblestone streets lined with lampposts, and picnics in rose gardens, Gilda felt certain that she was meant to go to Oxford for some reason. *It isn't fair that Wendy gets to go and I don't*, she thought. *Wendy doesn't even seem excited!*

"Wendy, don't you even want to take a look at these pictures? Can you believe you'll be in Oxford in a matter of days? You are so lucky!"

Wendy turned around on the piano bench to face Gilda. "Look, I'm not going there to slurp tea and stuff my face with clotted cream. I'm actually scared out of my mind. Just look at this!" Wendy thrust a piece of paper at Gilda—the competition rules and guidelines. "I don't think you realize how much pressure these competitions are, Gilda."

FIFTH ANNUAL YOUNG INTERNATIONAL VIRTUOSOS PIANO COMPETITION

Congratulations! Based on your outstanding audition tape, you have qualified to compete in the Young International Virtuosos Competition!

Five years ago, internationally renowned pianist Eugene Winterbottom decided to create a new opportunity for talented young pianists to launch their careers and gain international exposure, and the first Young International Virtuosos Competition was held at Oxford University. Since then, the competition has been held in Prague, Paris, and Stockholm. This year's competition returns again to the United Kingdom, to be hosted by the music faculty of Oxford University.

PERFORMANCE REQUIREMENTS
At the time of their audition, performers must demonstrate an ability to perform music from four major artistic eras—a work of baroque music, a classical work, an impressionistic or Romantic piece, and a work by either a late twentieth-century or a contemporary twenty-first-century composer. A list of acceptable composers and

compositions is available. In the first round of the competition held at Holywell Music Room, two works from eras of the pianist's choice must be selected for performance. The event is open to the public.

The Sight-Reading Test:
The first-place winner of the Young Virtuosos Competition will demonstrate well-rounded, professional-level skills. For that reason, a sight-reading test is also part of the competition, and abilities to quickly learn music are factored into judging decisions.

Finalists:
Finalists will perform one of their selected compositions for an audience at the Sheldonian Theater. Tickets will be sold to the public for this event.

Page-Turners:
* The competition organizers will make every effort to provide a page-turner for the sight-reading portion of the competition if needed, but availability is not guaranteed.

JURORS

Rhiannon Maddox
Born in Wales, Professor Maddox studied at the Royal Academy of Music in London, where she now teaches. Much in demand both as a recording artist and as a performer with major symphony orchestras across Europe and in the United States, Professor Maddox is known for

her experimental and boundary-breaking approach to piano performance, and she often includes works of pop music and jazz in concerts that feature more traditional classical works. She has collaborated and recorded with a broad range of musical artists, from famed cellist Yo-Yo Ma to pop star Madonna.

NIGEL WALDGRAVE

Professor Waldgrave completed his studies at the Royal Academy of Music in London and made his concert debut on the London stage after winning the Leeds Competition. Professor Waldgrave retired from the concert stage following a hand injury and has subsequently become a respected music historian and critic. He is the author of numerous books, including *Playing with Purity: Staying True to the Masters* and the popular pet-care book *A Cat's Music Companion.*

EUGENE WINTERBOTTOM

Founder of the Young International Virtuosos Competition and an internationally renowned performer, Winterbottom's performances and recordings of Rachmaninoff, Ravel, and Chopin piano concertos have been celebrated with both popular and critical acclaim. He is also known for his unique approach to piano pedagogy; his master classes and workshops are highly sought-after.

Professor Winterbottom will adjudicate the final round of the competition.

PRIZES

The winner of the competition will receive a concert engagement with the London Symphony Orchestra. The winner will also receive a five-thousand-pound cash prize.

*Under special circumstances, accommodations and travel expenses may be provided for competitors who wish to bring their own page-turners due to special needs. A request to the competition organizers must be submitted in advance.

As she read about the competition, Gilda felt annoyed that her mother was right—the day *had* finally come when she actually regretted giving up piano lessons. Everything about the competition sounded magical and exciting: she loved the sound of places like Holywell Music Room and the Sheldonian Theater. If only *she* were the one who could play the piano brilliantly! Gilda imagined herself amazing English audiences, then meeting people like Rhiannon Maddox and Eugene Winterbottom for tea and scones following her performances.

"My knees went weak when I heard your performance," Eugene Winterbottom would say.

"Brilliant!" Rhiannon Maddox and Nigel Waldgrave would declare. *"And to think you only started playing piano a few months ago!"*

"Wendy, I think this competition sounds amazing," said Gilda.

"It sounds scary."

"You've done this before, Wendy. You *always* do well."

"Everyone always assumes 'Wendy *always* does well.' What about the one time I *don't* do well?"

"When that one time happens, we'll just pretend we don't know you."

"You're beginning to annoy me right now, you know that?"

"Wendy, you know you could sit up there and play nothing but 'Twinkle, Twinkle, Little Star' and I'd still think it was fantastic."

Wendy sighed. "That doesn't make this less scary, Gilda."

Gilda didn't understand Wendy's fear. Ever since elementary school, Wendy had played piano in the school talent show and accompanied the choir and instrumental soloists. She did all of this without making any mistakes—at least not any noticeable ones. Sometimes she disappeared for a weekend, and afterward, a new, framed certificate from a competition she had won would appear on the bulletin board in her bedroom. To Gilda, Wendy's musical abilities seemed like an inevitable part of her best friend's being. It was hard to imagine why she would be afraid of playing in front of others when all of her efforts seemed to bring success.

Wendy began a series of angry, impatient-sounding arpeggios—difficult four-interval exercises Mrs. Mendelovich had prescribed to strengthen Wendy's weak fourth fingers.

Gilda turned back to the Young International Virtuosos Competition information and noticed something in the guidelines that triggered a delightful tickle in her left ear—her personal psychic signal that *something interesting* might be about to happen: "Under special circumstances, accommodations and travel expenses may be provided for competitors who wish to bring their own page-turners due to special needs..."

"I've got it Wendy!" Gilda shouted over Wendy's arpeggios. "I just figured out how I can go to Oxford with you!"

Wendy stopped playing and regarded Gilda impatiently. "How?!"

"Meet your official page-turner: Gilda Joyce!"

Dear Dad:

Get this: I tagged along to Wendy's piano lesson today, and I actually managed to convince Mrs. Mendelovich that I should be Wendy's page-turner!! I think it was my familiarity with Professor Nigel Waldgrave's scholarly book <u>Playing with Purity</u> that impressed her. (I did some research in advance.)

"Waldgrave believes that Bach must be played very dry—no pedal whatsoever," Mrs. Mendelovich said, probably testing my knowledge.

"I totally agree with him," I replied. "I loathe wet playing."

I told her I've been helping Wendy stay on track with her practice schedule, and that I would help keep her disciplined and motivated while we're overseas--kind of like a personal trainer. (I don't think

Wendy appreciated that comment much.)
Anyway, Mrs. Mendelovich actually called
the competition organizers right away to
ask if I could be Wendy's special page-
turner, and as a "special favor" to her,
they actually said yes!!!

Break out the tea and scones! Break out
the umbrellas and gum boots! I'm going to
England—to Oxford University!!

PACKING LIST:

1. Passport
2. Handbook of English Slang
3. Pink umbrella
4. Assorted frocks and jumpers (dresses and
   sweaters)
5. Knickers (English underwear!)
6. "Gum boots" (or "wellies")—for hiking
   through the rainy, sheep-crowded countryside
7. "Tainted Royalty" outfit: color-
   coordinated pillbox hat, jacket, and
   skirt; strand of pearls, stiletto pumps,
   and fishnet tights
8. Arm-length white gloves (for me) and
   pair of hot-pink gloves for Wendy to
   wear backstage
9. Giant fake-diamond cocktail ring

10. "London Mod" outfit: wig, white tights, white go-go boots, black-and-white checked minidress, white lipstick, "Twiggy-style" false eyelashes
11. "English Wedding" hat with wide brim and plume
12. "Mysterious Traveler" hat with black, eye-concealing netting
13. Cat's-eye sunglasses (for on-the-go disguises)
14. Makeup kit
15. Tiara and selection of evening gowns and wigs for concert performances
16. Typewriter
17. <u>The</u> <u>Master</u> <u>Psychic's</u> <u>Handbook</u> (of course!)

4

Bad Omens, Good-Luck Charms

Wendy walked alone, following a narrow cobblestone street lined with row houses. She gradually became aware of a steady clicking sound—the echo of footsteps from a short distance behind. She walked faster, and the pace of the stranger's footsteps also accelerated. *Someone is following me*, she thought in a rush of panic.

Wendy whirled around to face the person trailing her, but the street was empty. In the yellow lamplight, shadows shifted in the doorways and alleys. She turned to continue walking and felt a dull ache in her stomach as the sound of footsteps immediately resumed.

Faint strains of piano music wafting from a building just ahead gave Wendy a sense of hope and relief. *I must be getting close to the practice rooms*, she thought. Hearing the chaotic tangle of scales and arpeggios, she felt reassured that other people must be nearby; she wasn't completely alone on the dark street after all.

But something was wrong: the piano music seemed too eerily familiar. Wendy realized she was listening to fragments of the very pieces she would perform the next day at the competition.

She found herself wandering through a hallway lined with practice rooms, and was surprised to find them all empty, their doors left open with only upright pianos and vacant piano benches inside.

The door of the last practice room in the hallway was closed. Wendy approached the room, then stood on tiptoe and peered through the small glass window in the door. A boy sat at the piano inside, practicing Mozart's D Minor Fantasy—a piece Wendy also planned to perform. Something was odd: it seemed that his hands weren't quite moving in time with the notes he played. Wendy felt a deep foreboding—the sense that some awful truth was right before her eyes—something she didn't want to let herself acknowledge.

He's dead, a voice told her.

He turned to look at her through the small glass window in the practice room door. Her heart sank as he waved to her.

As usual, Wendy awoke from the dream feeling that something—or *somebody*—was nearby, waiting for her. She buried herself under the covers, then threw them off with an abrupt violence, as if hurling the blankets at the shadowy nightmares that lurked in the corners of her immaculate bedroom. She swung her legs over the side of her bed and rubbed her eyes, trying to scrub away a burgeoning headache. With her chin resting on her fists, Wendy stared at her open suitcase on the floor. The suitcase was packed with neatly folded clothes and stacks of piano music. Wendy seemed transfixed by the luggage, as if it were a window through which she could view some interesting scene from her future. *I'm flying to England tonight*, she told herself. *By tomorrow morning, I'll be far from home, riding in a bus from London to Oxford.*

She knew she should feel happy and excited, but instead, she found herself wondering why her nightmares seemed to occur more frequently as the date of the piano competition approached. Anxiety dreams before a big performance were nothing new to Wendy: there was the familiar dream that she had accidentally walked onstage naked; the dream that her hands suddenly became paralyzed; the dream that the piano keys made no sound when she pressed them down; and the dream of sitting on the piano bench and discovering that another competitor had left gum on the seat. But the dreams she had been having lately were different—more disturbing and more *real* than any nightmare she had experienced before. *What if they're actually bad omens?* Wendy wondered. *What if they're signs that something terrible might happen to me?*

"So lazy!" said Mrs. Choy, interrupting Wendy's trance. "Nine o'clock and still in bed!" Standing in Wendy's doorway, she held a long, red silk dress on a hanger.

"Mom, our flight is a red-eye, and I probably won't get any sleep tonight."

Mrs. Choy held out the dress. "You wear this dress in the show. Lots of luck!" Mrs. Choy considered herself a thoroughly modern woman, but she still maintained several ancient Chinese beliefs and superstitions. One of these was her certainty that the color red would help bring luck and keep away evil spirits. As a result, red decorations and pieces of art were tastefully placed throughout the Choys' neat, uncluttered house—wall hangings, fans, figurines of dragons and frogs. A strong believer in feng shui principles to increase the flow of "positive energy" in her home, Mrs. Choy also placed green "money plants" in strategic locations and avoided all angular shapes and sharp objects.

Wendy eyed the dress skeptically. It reminded her of a Chinese wedding gown. "I don't know, Mom. . . . It seems a little too Chinese for England."

"Nothing wrong with Chinese. Red for good luck."

"Thanks for the vote of confidence."

"To win, you need luck. You win, you get five thousand pound. You lessons not cheap!"

Wendy was well aware that the winner of the competition would receive a cash prize and the opportunity to perform with a major orchestra. She also knew that both her parents worked overtime in jobs they didn't particularly like to make this sort of opportunity possible for her, and she accepted as a fact the idea that she owed them some significant success as payment for their sacrifices. If only she could win something big, like the competition at Oxford University—something her parents could tell their friends about—she would prove herself *worthy*.

"Mom," said Wendy, "I might *not* win. This is an international competition. That means there could be lots of kids there who are better than me."

"Always someone better. You *work* harder."

"There are other people who work just as hard."

"Don't be afraid to win."

Wendy feared something much scarier than winning—something nameless that she couldn't even articulate. Her mother couldn't possibly understand the deep unease that had been creeping into the corners of her mind, so there was no use trying to explain.

"Okay, Mom," said Wendy, simply wanting the conversation to end. "I'll take the red dress." *But I probably won't wear it*, she thought.

5

Fear of Flying

Gilda and Wendy sat near their gate at the British Airways terminal, waiting for the boarding of flight nine to be announced.

"You haven't said anything about my travel attire." Gilda wore a black dress, lace-up black-leather boots, and a hat with netting that half-concealed her eyes. She felt very mysterious in the clothes, as if she were a traveling spy.

"I like the hat," said Wendy. "The net over your face kind of reminds me of dead bugs on a windshield, though."

"That's exactly what my brother said."

"See?"

"He has even less fashion sense than my grandmother."

Nearby, Mrs. Mendelovich paced back and forth as she spoke in Russian on her cell phone, gesturing dramatically.

"I wonder what she's talking about," Gilda whispered.

"She's probably yelling at her husband because he forgot to run an errand or something," said Wendy. "She always does that during my piano lessons."

Sitting across from Gilda and Wendy were Ming Fong and Gary. Ming Fong's childish clothes and diminutive body made her look younger than her fourteen years. Her hair hung in a ruler-straight bob just below her moon-shaped face. Gary was a plump boy dressed in uncomfortable corduroy pants. He sat with a book of music open, tapping out the fingering of a composition and quietly humming to himself.

"Did you practice today, Wendy?" Ming Fong asked.

"Not much," said Wendy.

Ming Fong's eyes narrowed slightly. "*How* much?"

"A couple hours, I guess. I ran through all my pieces."

"I practiced four hours. I usually practice at least five."

"Good for you," said Wendy, with thinly veiled annoyance.

"Wendy doesn't need to practice," Gilda interjected. "She's naturally talented."

Ming Fong fixed Gilda with a stare, as if she were calculating something in some computerlike portion of her brain. "Wendy will probably win the whole competition," she declared with sudden forced cheer. "Wendy *always* wins."

Wendy squirmed. It was a compliment, but for some reason, she felt as if she had just been jinxed.

"Of course Wendy will win," said Gilda. "She can practically play Rachmaninoff's Third Piano Concerto with her toes. Besides, Wendy and I have big plans for that five large in prize money."

Ming Fong's mouth became a small, flat line.

"*Gilda* has plans for the prize money," said Wendy.

"What would you do with the five thousand pounds?" Gary looked up from his music, suddenly interested.

"First, we'll take a trip to Paris and update our wardrobes.

Then we'll probably travel through Europe, followed by a cruise," said Gilda.

"Whatever's left over will go into our college funds," Wendy joked.

"Community college, of course," Gilda added.

"Devry University."

"Speak for yourself."

"I don't get it," said Gary. "Are the two of you playing duets together in the competition or something? Why would you split the prize money with Gilda, Wendy?"

Wendy grinned. "That's actually a very good question. I mean, shouldn't the person who's doing the *performing* get all the money?"

"We're splitting it because I'm Wendy's official page-turner for the sight-reading competition," Gilda explained.

"Clearly you deserve half the prize money."

"Why does Wendy get her own page-turner?" Gary asked.

"She has special needs," Gilda blurted before Wendy could reply.

"Wendy's learning disabled?"

Wendy snorted at this comment, and Ming Fong burst into surprisingly manic laughter. "Learning disabled!"

"It's not funny," said Gilda, feeling, for some reason, that Ming Fong was laughing way too hard. "'Special needs children' is actually what they call learning-disabled kids in England."

Ming Fong and Gary were suddenly confused, unsure whether Wendy did, in fact, have "special needs."

"Anyway," Gilda continued, "I'm kind of like Wendy's personal trainer as well as her page-turner, right, Wendy?"

"Completely wrong."

"That's why Mrs. Mendelovich asked me to come with her to England." Gilda eyed Mrs. Mendelovich, who was now gesturing even more broadly as she wandered farther away from her students.

"Gilda wanted a cheap trip to England," said Wendy. "That's why she's here."

"Don't forget getting out of school for a week." With a twinge of dread, Gilda remembered that her suitcase included a stack of books and homework assignments her teachers had piled on "so you keep up while you're away." Her English teacher, Mrs. Rawson, had been particularly grumpy about Gilda's request for a week away from school in the middle of February and had given Gilda the extra assignment of keeping a detailed travel diary. Because her teacher had obviously expected a horrified response to this work, Gilda had done her best to cringe and look nauseated. Secretly, she thought it was the first interesting homework Mrs. Rawson had ever assigned.

Gary looked at his watch. "Aren't we supposed to be on the plane by now? The flight must be delayed."

As if on cue, a flight attendant's voice blasted over the loudspeaker. "Passengers on British Airways flight number nine, please note we have a delay due to a mechanical problem. Our mechanics are working to resolve it. We expect a delay of at least fifteen minutes."

Throughout the room, passengers shot each other looks of

exasperation and trepidation. "Mechanical problem? *That* doesn't sound good," they joked ruefully.

Wendy felt an unpleasant, light-headed sensation. Everything around her seemed slightly blurry, paler than normal. She felt queasy as she noticed a red-haired girl and her mother staring at her from across the room with a little too much interest.

"I'm surprised they actually *told* us it was a mechanical problem," said Gary. "Everyone's first thought is, 'Oh no! This plane is going to crash!'"

"It isn't going to crash," said Gilda confidently. "I would have gotten a psychic vibration if it was."

"Really?" Gary looked interested. "You mean, you always know when a plane is going to crash?"

"Just the planes I'm on." Secretly, Gilda felt a rush of anxiety. Gilda wasn't at all sure she *would* know if the plane was going to crash. She simply felt certain that it would be far too mean a cosmic joke if, on her very first trip to England, her plane actually took a nosedive.

Gilda noticed that Wendy's face had taken on a greenish hue. "Hey—what's wrong?"

"I have a bad feeling about this."

"Wendy, we both know that flying is probably safer than driving around in Detroit."

"It's just—last night I had this horrible dream." Wendy hesitated. She twirled a lock of hair around her finger, then examined the ends of her hair for split ends. She still felt that talking about the dream might make the disturbing images too real and powerful.

"A dream about *what?*"

Wendy sighed. "Well, I was alone, walking down a street. It was lined with a bunch of row houses and weird buildings, and then the next thing I knew, there were a bunch of practice rooms filled with pianos."

"So it's about the piano competition."

"Wait—I'm not finished. I realized that someone I saw in one of the rooms—someone who was sitting there playing the piano—was actually *dead.*" Wendy's voice cracked a bit on the word *dead.* She simply couldn't bring herself to describe the way the boy had waved at her with an eerie recognition. For some reason, this was the scariest part. It was an image that held some crucial significance, but its meaning was something she would rather not know.

Gilda felt a tiny tickle in her ear. A faintly cold sensation radiated through her spine.

"Creepy," said Gary.

Ming Fong simply observed Wendy with an intense, expressionless interest.

"So, what do you think it means?" Wendy asked.

Gilda thought for a moment. She believed that her own dreams sometimes contained psychic messages or warnings, and there was definitely something very eerie about the dream Wendy had just described. However, Gilda wasn't at all sure how to interpret it, and she didn't want to make Wendy feel more scared than she already was.

"Wendy, how did you *feel* when you were having the dream?" Gilda had read that one of the important elements of analyzing a dream was to consider the emotions evoked by the images.

"I felt kind of alone, I guess—scared that something terrible was going to happen to me."

"Hey, why don't I read your tarot cards?" Gilda suggested. "Maybe we can get some clue about what that dream means."

Throughout the winter, Gilda had been expanding her psychic skills by studying a book called *The Mystery of the Tarot*. She had even begun reading fortunes for friends and acquaintances during her lunch period at school, just to add some excitement to her school day. In addition to what she regarded as the uncanny accuracy of her fortune-telling, Gilda also found tarot card readings to be a great way to start conversations with people who had previously ignored her. So far, her only big error had been an attempt to make a boy named Craig Overcash (for whom she had harbored a crush for almost two years) believe that he would "soon have a new, strikingly attractive girlfriend who has psychic abilities." Craig did find a new girlfriend, but she didn't have psychic abilities. More importantly, she wasn't Gilda.

Wendy wrinkled her nose. "What if you give me a bad reading? Then I'll feel even worse."

"I don't give bad readings." Gilda rummaged in her backpack and pulled out her tarot cards. *The Mystery of the Tarot* advised keeping the cards "wrapped in a purple silk scarf and facing east," but Gilda kept hers wrapped in a leopard-print scarf and stuffed in her backpack. She handed the deck to Wendy.

"Now shuffle them and think about a question or problem."

Wendy shuffled the cards. She glanced up and again noticed the red-haired mother and daughter placidly staring at her, as if she were a television show they were watching. She squelched a strange urge to stick out her tongue at them.

"Are you thinking about your question?" Gilda asked.

Wendy nodded. As she moved the cards back and forth with her quick, lithe fingers, she thought about the dream and wondered what it meant. She wondered who would win the piano competition and whether she would perform well. She thought of her mother offering her the red dress: *wish to win.*

"Okay," said Gilda. "Now hand me the cards."

Gilda stood up and fanned out the cards on her seat. "Pick a card."

Wendy tentatively drew a card. Ming Fong and Gary leaned closer to watch.

"Now place your first card face up on the chair so we can see it."

Wendy flipped the card to reveal an image of a young man sitting up in bed. He held his head in his hands in a hopeless attempt to dodge nine swords that soared swiftly through the air, directly toward his body.

"See?" Wendy whined. "This is what I was talking about!"

"That kind of looks like a bad card," said Gary.

"There aren't 'bad' cards. The cards are just a mirror to show you what forces are at work in your life."

"Swords flying at you looks bad," said Gary.

"Wendy's first card represents her current situation in life. You picked the Nine of Swords, Wendy, which means that fears are hanging over you, and you may be having sleepless nights."

"It looks like she's going to be stabbed," said Ming Fong.

"Please draw your next card, Wendy."

The second card featured a picture of a monstrous-looking devil with large webbed wings and curly horns.

"As I was saying," said Wendy. "I would *hate* to get a bad reading."

Secretly, Gilda had to admit that this was one of the worst readings she had seen in some time. Nobody wanted to get the Devil card.

"Does that mean she'll become possessed or something?" Gary asked.

"*Bleaaaaaagh!*" Wendy did her best horror-film imitation of a girl possessed by demons.

"Yikes!"

Gilda sensed she was losing control of the reading. "Gary, you can't be so literal. The Devil card usually just means Wendy might be feeling trapped by something—maybe by another person—maybe by something else in her life."

Wendy leaned back in her chair and crossed her arms. "Okay, that's enough fun at my expense."

"Come on, Wendy. Just finish the reading."

"I'm done."

"But the next card will give you something important to ponder."

"The next card better give me something nice to look forward to for a change." This time, Wendy reached for the opposite end of the fanned cards. The card she drew depicted a skeleton riding a horse and waving a black flag. On the ground beneath the horse's hooves was a corpse.

All four of them stared silently for a moment.

"Wow," Wendy whispered, suddenly at a loss for wry comments and jokes.

Gilda knew that drawing the "Death card" didn't necessarily meant that an actual death was predicted. All the same, there was always something unnerving about the image of that skeleton riding a horse. You couldn't help but feel stirrings of dread when you drew the Death card. Gilda noticed a cold sensation in her hands. What, exactly, did this card mean? What if Wendy's dream really did mean that some disaster was imminent? She reminded herself of one of the rules from her *Mystery of the Tarot:* "Try not to alarm the person for whom you're interpreting the cards," the book's author urged. "Try to put a positive spin on the reading. Never say things like, 'It looks like you don't have long to live,' or 'Some dire calamity may soon befall you and your loved ones.'"

"What we have here is the cute little Death card." Gilda did her best to speak in a cheerful tone of voice. "It doesn't necessarily mean that Wendy—or any one of us—will die soon. It might simply mean that something is coming to an end or changing."

Maybe your winning streak is coming to an end, a mean voice in Wendy's head whispered. *Maybe you aren't up to any of this at all.*

"To be honest, I'm getting a little freaked out," Gary admitted. "Do you think we should tell someone about these tarot cards?"

"'Excuse me, Mr. Airplane Pilot,'" said Wendy in a self-mocking tone of voice, "'we just did a tarot reading, and now we're scared this plane is going to crash!'"

"But what if this is our one chance to say something?"

Gilda suddenly wished she hadn't offered to do the tarot card reading for Wendy after all. Gary had a point; if the cards were a warning about the flight, they *should* say something. "This plane *isn't* going to crash," Gilda declared, hoping that by saying the words with enough certainty she could make them true. She was going to England, by jingo, and no tarot card reading was going to stop her. "And Wendy, you still have one last card to draw."

"You've got to be kidding me. There's no way I'm drawing another card after these three."

"But the last card is the one that tells you what you're supposed to *do* about the whole situation. It could put the other cards in a positive perspective."

"Now boarding British Airways flight nine for London Heathrow Airport," a smooth voice announced over the loudspeaker. Mrs. Mendelovich waved at them from across the room. There was no time left; they had to board the plane despite Wendy's disturbing tarot cards.

Gilda scooped up her tarot cards, and the four students grabbed their backpacks and joined Mrs. Mendelovich in line.

Wendy again felt light-headed as she followed the red-haired mother and daughter down the dim, carpeted ramp leading to the plane.

6

Turbulence

Gilda and Wendy shot each other horrified looks when they realized they weren't seated together on the plane: Gilda was wedged between Gary and Ming Fong, and Wendy's ticket had her seated across the aisle, next to Mrs. Mendelovich.

"Wonderful!" Mrs. Mendelovich declared. "I seet next to Windy!"

Pointing at Mrs. Mendelovich, Gilda mouthed a silent command to Wendy: *"Ask her to switch seats!"*

"I CAN'T!" Wendy whispered in reply.

"Cheeildren!" Mrs. Mendelovich stood up in the middle of the aisle, drawing the attention of everyone in the surrounding seats along with that of her students. "I want to teell you something—how very ploud I am of you today. You are my stars. You haf made me so ploud." A tiny tear trickled through her black eyeliner into the folds of her skin. "You haf plepared and plepared and plepared. Soon you will walk onstage, seet down to play, and—my God! Pearfect." Mrs. Mendelovich grabbed Wendy's hand for emphasis. Wendy stiffened, and Mrs. Mendelovich gave her hand a little pat. "Each of you—like my own cheeildren—that is how ploud I am. I tell people: these three—the best I haf taught. The best! And maybe—one of you will ween." She addressed these last words to Wendy, who suddenly wore a glazed expression.

Gilda wished she were sitting closer to Wendy so she could make a joke about "weening the competition."

Gilda now understood Wendy's conflicted sense of fear and admiration for her teacher. Mrs. Mendelovich's big personality was both intoxicating and smothering. At the same time, Gilda found herself wishing that she were a more genuine part of this group—a true competitor rather than a lowly page-turner. What would it feel like to have somebody be that intensely "ploud" of something you had accomplished?

"So, you are all ready for England?" Mrs. Mendelovich asked the group. "You haf copies of your music, and scores all numbered for the judges? You haf your pajamas and underwears and toothbrushes?"

Everyone nodded and stifled giggles at the word *underwears*.

"If not—too late now!"

Gary and Ming Fong laughed a little too uproariously at this comment.

Mrs. Mendelovich was asked to sit down because a flight attendant had just begun to describe the safety features of the aircraft. Each of Mrs. Mendelovich's students watched with rapt attention as the flight attendant talked about "floating devices" and "oxygen masks." Gary actually scribbled some notes with a pencil.

As the plane took off, Gary and Ming Fong both pulled down their serving trays and opened music books that were virtually black with complex little lines and dots of notation. Gilda watched as they tapped their fingers on top of their plastic serving trays, pretending to play invisible pianos. Clearly, neither Gary nor Ming Fong was going to offer much conversation during the long flight.

"You missed a few notes there." Gilda elbowed Ming Fong as she speedily drummed out the fingering of the Chopin "Ocean Étude."

"No—no missed notes."

Gilda pointed at Ming Fong's music. "Right there, that patch of squiggly bits was a complete mess."

"Those are thirty-second notes, not squiggle bits. No mess— all right notes."

"Ming Fong, I saw your middle finger move right when it should have moved left."

Ming Fong frowned intensely at her music.

"Gilda's kidding, Ming Fong," said Gary.

"I was completely serious." Gilda couldn't help thinking that a big, juicy fight with Gary and Ming Fong might liven things up and make the time go faster. "Ming Fong was missing notes by the basketful."

"Crazy Gilda!" Ming Fong donned her headphones to listen to a recording. This put a quick end to the whole conversation and the possibility of an entertaining argument.

Gilda peered across the aisle at Wendy, who was listening with an unintentionally nauseated expression as Mrs. Mendelovich described the quirks of one of the competition judges: "Professor Waldgrave, he is genius, but leetle crazy in the head," Mrs. Mendelovich declared. "He loves nobody but his cat!"

Gilda wished she could switch seats with Wendy. Mrs. Mendelovich probably had lots of interesting stories about musicians who were "crazy in the head," and that would at least be more interesting than being stuck between Ming Fong and Gary.

It was difficult to hear Mrs. Mendelovich over the drone of the plane engine, so Gilda decided to eavesdrop on an English couple directly behind her instead. *Maybe I'll pick up some observations for my travel diary*, she thought. Gilda had decided to make her diary as lively and interesting as possible for Mrs. Rawson, who had never been overseas in her entire life.

"I couldn't believe the portion sizes Americans have at restaurants," the woman was saying. "I'd be a size one hundred if I stayed over here much longer. Absolutely ginormous amounts of food!"

"No wonder they're so fat with those 'all-you-can-eat' restaurants," said the man.

Gilda peeked over the edge of her seat to catch a glimpse of the couple. She noticed with satisfaction that both the man and the woman were slightly plump.

TRAVEL DIARY—ENTRY ONE
<u>English Tourists Frightened by American Appetites:</u>
English folk who visit the States are both awestruck and revolted by the ginormous amounts of food eaten by the average American at each meal. To the English, it is considered "ginormous" to visit the salad bar more than three times, or to eat both an entire steak and an entire pie all at once. They fail to realize that the typical American needs an

extra layer of fat to survive the long, cold winter in an environment where food may suddenly be scarce.

TEAM MENDELOVICH FLIES "ACROSS THE POND":
Team Mendelovich begins its journey to the Young International Virtuosos Competition with great foreboding, following a disturbing tarot card reading for team member Wendy Choy. So far, no calamity has befallen any member of the group, but the night is still young. . . .

Wendy did her best to pay attention to Mrs. Mendelovich's stories, despite the unusual sensation of pressure in her head and a roaring in her ears like the sound of ocean waves. Was that the sound of her own blood pulsing through her body? She was intensely and painfully aware of being alive—aware of the fact that her fragile body was suspended in a clunky man-made machine thousands of miles above the ground. *Maybe this is how it feels when you know you're going to die at any minute*, Wendy thought. She watched Mrs. Mendelovich's lips moving and her expressive hands gesturing excitedly, and felt an intense desire to flee her surroundings. The problem was, there was nowhere to go.

Wendy gasped as the plane suddenly hit something with a loud *BUMP!* Everything shook violently, and the passengers around her collectively caught their breath.

The plane dropped abruptly, as if its ability to fly had been a mere dream—as if gravity had just remembered to pull the ridiculously precarious metal container filled with people down, down toward the earth.

7

The Arrival

TRAVEL DIARY:

Following a gut-wrenching flight through stormy skies—a flight that nearly resulted in several custards being parked throughout the plane—Team Mendelovich arrived in England looking bleary-eyed and feeling unwashed. There was a moment when everyone truly thought the plane was going to crash. Naturally, the four of us couldn't help thinking about that ominous tarot card reading I did for Wendy only hours before.

As it turned out, the plane bumped and careened through the thunderclouds until we landed on the runway. Finally, we are here in London, squinting into a gray, caffeine-deprived morning and grateful to be alive.

Personal Note:

Trying to sleep when you're stuck between Ming Fong and Gary is no picnic! Ming Fong kept poking me and whispering that I was "snoring softly." I replied that she was "killing me softly" with her nonstop pretend piano playing. Then, every time I started to doze off, Gary's warm, plump knee would sneak over into my space and nestle against my leg. Some people have a serious problem keeping their knees and elbows to themselves.

Arrival at Heathrow Airport:

Team Mendelovich is questioned with the utmost suspicion as we proceed through customs. This might be due to Mrs. Mendelovich's heavily accented declaration that: "We are Americans, here to ween the Young International Virtuosos Competition!" Gary's briefcase receives a close inspection for potential hazardous materials or weapons. Hidden amongst his music and sharpened red pencils, the customs officials discover a Star Wars action figure and a Daredevil comic book.

Observations of English Folk:

Mrs. Rawson, if you were here, you would see that the English resemble most other humans, although a few still have webbed feet and the remnants of small dorsal fins from the days when this island nation was completely submerged by water.

Along with such forms of transport as scooters, roller skates, and unicycles, the English have perfected the art of riding buses (they call them "coaches") and ingeniously, these vehicles actually have two floors for passengers— "double decker" for twice the fun! A coach ride means one thing to the Englishman or woman—a grand opportunity for a picnic. When riding the coach, expect to be surrounded by the furtive rustling and sundry odors of fast-food containers, foil-wrapped burgers, and sausage sandwiches.

<u>The Arrival in Oxford:</u>
Team Mendelovich arrives in Oxford—the land of dreaming spires, wet umbrellas, and bicycles ridden by trendy students and starchy old ladies alike. Hip, hip horray! We made it to Oxford alive!!

8

Wyntle House

Rolling their suitcases along in weary silence, Gilda, Wendy, Gary, and Ming Fong followed Mrs. Mendelovich from the bus station at Gloucester Green, down Walton Street, and past the imposing stone walls of Worcester College toward Wyntle House—the guesthouse where they would be staying in Oxford. In the early-morning quiet of the city, their suitcases rumbled loudly against the sidewalk.

Walking under a sky so low it seemed that she might reach up and touch the gray, hanging clouds, Gilda reflected that the morning felt lonely, but in a strangely good way. In her imagination, the bleak, dreary weather gave the day an appealing "murder mystery" atmosphere. After all, here she was in England—about to have an adventure—far, far away from the tedious lives of people like Craig Overcash and his disappointing girlfriend. Gilda decided that she pitied them. She imagined that she was an English detective who had been invited to visit Oxford to solve a difficult case. Her name was Penelope Stunn.

Gilda glanced at Wendy and noticed the pinched expression on her face. "What's the matter? You aren't still thinking about that tarot card reading, are you?"

"Not exactly. You know that weird feeling you get—like when you feel like you're reexperiencing something that already happened?"

"You have déjà vu?"

"Everything here looks so weirdly familiar to me."

"Maybe you're just remembering a picture you saw in a brochure."

Wendy shook her head. "It's different than remembering a picture." She had the overwhelming feeling that she had actually *been* in Oxford walking down this very street before.

"Hey, maybe you're having a memory of a past life." Gilda wasn't sure whether she actually believed in reincarnation, but she liked the idea that people might have more than one chance at life—an opportunity to try out different identities. "Maybe you were English in one of your former lives," she suggested. "Maybe you were a scholar here at the university during the Dark Ages!"

"Probably why I remember this paved road and the sidewalk and these little cars so clearly—from my life here during medieval times."

Gary and Ming Fong seemed deaf to this discussion of past lives. Their blank, exhausted expressions concealed vague terror at finding themselves in a foreign country where they would have to play the piano at the best of their abilities in a matter of hours.

Mrs. Mendelovich, in contrast, was energized by her arrival in Oxford. When the plane landed, she had quickly powdered her nose, grabbed her purse, and practically danced through the airport toward customs. As she clipped along in her high-heeled, sling-back shoes, it seemed that the closer she got to the piano competition, the more energy she had.

The group followed a long row of terraced Victorian houses with tall, pointy roofs, until they reached one with a mauve awning from which a basket of wilted pansies dangled next to a sign for WYNTLE HOUSE.

Mrs. Mendelovich rapped on the door, and a small dog inside the house immediately responded with loud, yapping barks. A moment later, a bleary-eyed elderly woman opened the door and peered at the group. "I expect you're the piano people, then?"

"I am Mrs. Mendelovich, and these are my students," Mrs. Mendelovich declared with exaggerated formality. "We are here from America for Young International Virtuosos Competition!"

"Right. I'm Maggie Luard. Come in; we've been expecting you." Mrs. Luard spoke with a hoarse, deep voice that was nearly as low as a man's. She didn't seem particularly impressed with the notion of a group of young American pianists coming to stay at Wyntle House.

I bet musicians and scholars from all over the world turn up at her doorstep every week, Gilda thought. *Maybe she lost interest in them years ago.*

As the group entered Wyntle House the tiny, yipping dog broke into more high-pitched, joyous barks. Mrs. Luard didn't seem to notice as the dog released a tiny trickle of pee on the carpet.

"If you need anything, just ask me or my son, Danny, who works here with me. I wish there was a piano here in the house, but I imagine they'll have you set up with practice rooms in the colleges. Now, I hope you lot are feeling energetic, because most of your rooms are at the very top of the stairs on the fourth floor, and there is no lift. Miss Piano Teacher, your room is a bit lower—on the third floor." Mrs. Luard handed everyone their room keys. "The front door is most often open during the day, and breakfast is served from seven o'clock in the morning. You can have a full English breakfast or just help yourselves to milk, juice, and cereal downstairs."

Heaving their luggage up a few steps at a time, the group climbed a seemingly endless series of narrow staircases. Gilda marveled that each time she was certain that they must have reached the top floor of the house, she discovered yet another, more narrow flight of stairs cloaked in worn, mauve carpeting.

When they reached the third floor, Mrs. Mendelovich hurried to unlock her room. "I must leave now to attend a meeting of piano teachers," she said. "Remember, don't be late for drawing of numbers at the Music Faculty Building! Please, walk together and look at maps!"

Gilda realized with happy surprise that they might be very much on their own in Oxford. They had only just arrived, and Mrs. Mendelovich was already trusting them to find their way through the city independently. Not only that; Gilda would have her own room in the guesthouse with her very own key! *This trip might be even more exciting than I imagined*, she thought.

Mrs. Mendelovich disappeared into her room, and the four young people continued trudging up the last flights of stairs.

"I guess you girls won't need to do your butt crunches this week," Gary joked, huffing as he heaved his suitcase up the remaining steps.

"Some of you boys still need to do some, though," Wendy mumbled.

"What did you say, Wendy?"

"Oh, nothing."

"Butt crunches!" Ming Fong blurted a bit hysterically, apparently feeling liberated in the absence of Mrs. Mendelovich. "Crunchy butts!"

Gilda turned to look down at Ming Fong, who was several feet behind on the staircase. "Ming Fong, don't forget we're here representing the United States, so we need to help our country's bad reputation by behaving with some decorum. Oh, and remember to curtsy when you meet English people next time."

"What does 'curtsy' mean?" Ming Fong asked.

"People don't curtsy unless they're meeting royalty, do they?" Gary asked.

"Gary, it's most important that *you* curtsy whenever you meet new people here in England as well. Every English boy must have a proper curtsy."

"What is 'curtsy'?" Ming Fong repeated.

"It's like a special kind of bowing," Gilda explained, "only much cuter."

"Oh," said Ming Fong thoughtfully. "We curtsy before we play piano in England?"

"No," said Wendy sharply. "Taking a bow is plenty."

"Oh, I get it. Gilda is silly again," said Ming Fong. "Crazy Gilda!"

On the fourth floor, Gilda opened the creaking door to room

number twelve. She found a single bed; a tiny sink and mirror; a small, drafty window with old curtains that resembled dish towels; a tiny television; a kettle for making tea; a writing desk; and a wooden dresser. There was also a bookshelf crammed with novels left by previous guests, along with a handful of Oxford guidebooks and some textbooks with titles like *Linear Geometry* that looked very dry. The mauve carpeting was stained and both the attic ceiling and the floor were slanted. Gilda felt chilled, as if thin, ghostly fingers of air had just crept through a crack in the old window and slipped under her clothes. All in all, it was a tiny, depressing room in a decaying old house, but Gilda didn't mind because it was exactly the kind of sparse, lonely room that Penelope Stunn would choose to stay in while she worked to solve her murder case.

Gilda immediately opened her suitcase, placed her manual typewriter on the desk, and rolled in a piece of paper to begin the next installment of her travel diary.

Sitting on her bed in room number nine, Wendy could not match Gilda's enthusiasm for Wyntle House. She knew that, above all, she should be grateful that she had some privacy; she easily could have been stuck sharing a room with Ming Fong. But something about the room felt unlucky—possibly even dangerous. At home, Wendy often challenged her mother's penchant for strategically positioning furniture and placing "good-luck objects" in various corners of the house. "Seriously, Mom," she would say, "how can putting an object in a particular spot actually affect your life?"

"Energy flow," her mother always replied. "Flow of good or bad energy. For example: sharp object pointing at you—very bad, like knives."

It was easier to be skeptical at home. Alone in England, she found the feng shui nightmare of her room in Wyntle House genuinely disturbing. She was painfully aware of the sharp rectangular shapes of virtually every object in the room pointing at her like daggers, the unfavorable placement of the bed, the sickly light blue and white colors that surrounded her on the curtains, bedspread, and wallpaper. The room seemed to be extending an invitation to bad luck.

Wendy opened her suitcase and unfolded the red silk dress her mother had given her. It clashed vibrantly with the demure, drab room. Suddenly overwhelmed by homesickness, Wendy found silent tears welling up as she thought of her mother innocently offering a red dress as a good-luck charm. Her mother had no clue that her daughter might literally be traveling into a nightmare.

I want to go home, Wendy thought. The idea surprised her in its simplicity. For a brief moment, it seemed almost possible. After all, there might still be time to avoid the doom that might be awaiting her here in England. She could simply call her parents, ask them to change her return ticket, and her mother would pick her up at the airport. At home, she would be safer from the nightmares—from the unknown force that seemed to be hovering near her, drawing closer with each day.

Wendy imagined the phone conversation that would ensue if she actually did call her mother.

"Mom? It's me."

"Wendy? You okay?"

"I'm . . ." She wouldn't be able to talk. She would burst into fresh tears.

"Wendy! You in trouble?"

"I—I want to come home."

A long silence would follow.

"Mom? Are you there?"

"Wendy! What is problem?"

"I want to come home."

"Win competition first; then come home."

"I'm just so homesick, or something. Nothing feels right."

"I raise a crybaby? Be strong! Wish to win! Fong not call her mother and say, 'Waa! Want to go home.' Ming Fong is brave. I raise a crybaby."

"You don't understand. I feel like I might actually be in danger."

"Stay in practice room where you belong, and be safe. Wear good-luck charms."

No, there was no way around it. Wendy decided she would simply have to be brave and face her nightmares on her own.

The Drawing of Numbers

Gilda and Wendy walked down St. Aldate's Street, past the soaring spires of Christ Church College and finally to the modern stone building that housed Oxford University's music faculty and practice rooms.

A white-haired man greeted them at the door and pointed to the Dennis Arnold Hall, where the drawing of numbers would take place.

The room buzzed with anxiety and excitement. Students, teachers, and parents glanced at one another, subtly attempting to discern who might pose the most serious competition. Gilda observed some bespectacled, rumpled-looking boys and a group of girls who dressed in neat skirts, Mary Jane shoes, and little cashmere gloves—girls who wore their long hair slicked back in ponytails and who clutched their music books to their chests. *Probably English boys and girls*, she told herself. There were also a few girls who slouched at the back of the room wearing low-slung jeans tucked into knee-high boots, as if they had just strolled into the Music Faculty Building from a day of shopping on High Street. A small group of exuberant boys speaking in boisterous Italian wore tracksuits, as if ready to warm up for an athletic event. Gilda spied Mrs. Mendelovich at the front of the room, enthusiastically embracing a plump balding man who kissed her on both cheeks.

Several people eyed Gilda with unconcealed curiosity because her netted "travel hat" was impossible to ignore. *They probably think I'm an eccentric English pianist*, she thought. A lanky teenage boy whose dark, shaggy hair framed his strikingly pale face slouched against a wall and watched her with particular interest.

Gilda smiled brightly and cracked her knuckles. "Can't wait to get up there and play me Rach Three!" she declared loudly in what she hoped was a Yorkshire accent. She knew Rachmaninoff's Third Piano Concerto was supposed to be among the most difficult works for the piano.

"What do you think you're doing?" Wendy whispered.

"I'm psyching out our competition."

"You're acting *weird*. Everyone's staring at you."

"They're just freaking out because I mentioned the Rach Three."

Wendy didn't have a chance to reply because a frumpy woman who stood at the front of the room, suddenly commanded everyone's attention.

"I want to welcome everyone to the fifth annual Young International Virtuosos Piano Competition!" she announced. "My name is Frieda Heslop; I'm a fellow of New College, and one of the organizers of this year's competition. I must say, we're very pleased indeed to have the competition return to Oxford University this year, and I trust you will have an inspiring experience in this very musical city. We are very pleased to have two eminent musicians as our jurors: Professors Nigel Waldgrave and Rhiannon Maddox. They may offer some brief verbal suggestions and comments following your first performance in the tradition of a master class—something that I think you'll all find beneficial. Finally, the famous Professor Eugene Winterbottom will also be one of our judges in the final round. As you well know, the standards to qualify for the competition are rigorous, so if you've made it here, you should already give yourself a nice pat on the back."

Gilda gave Wendy an ironic little pat on the back, and Wendy rolled her eyes.

"And as the teachers in the room should be aware, the judges are not given the names or nationalities of performers until the conclusion of the competition. You will now draw a number, which you will keep for the preliminary and sight-reading rounds of the competition. Ten finalists will redraw prior to the final round, which will be held in the Sheldonian Theater. The number you draw will determine the order of performers and, of course, your performance times. So—fingers crossed, and hope for your lucky number!"

Polite murmurs rippled through the room as Professor Heslop picked up a straw hat that was resting upside down on one of the grand pianos. "When I call your name, please come to the front of the room and draw your performance number from the hat."

Gilda and Wendy watched as a series of piano students walked to the front of the room, drew a piece of paper from the hat, and then walked back to their seats with inscrutable expressions.

"Try to draw a high number," Gilda whispered. "That way, they'll remember you at the end of the competition. But not *too* high, otherwise, the judges will be bored and might not be listening anymore. Oh, and whatever you do, don't draw number one. Whoever draws number one can forget it."

"Thanks," said Wendy drily. "You're a huge help."

"If you concentrate on the number you want, you might actually get it."

"Ming Fong Chen!" Professor Heslop announced.

Ming Fong skipped to the front of the room and squeezed her eyes shut tightly as she reached into the hat, reminding Gilda of a child playing a silly game at a birthday party. She opened the piece of paper with extreme seriousness and walked slowly back to her seat.

"Maybe she drew number one," Gilda whispered.

"Wendy Choy!"

Wendy sauntered to the front of the room and drew her number. She didn't look at the folded piece of paper until she returned to the back of the room and stood next to Gilda. When she opened it, her face wore the same pale, pinched expression Gilda had observed earlier that day.

"What's the matter?"

Again, Wendy had a very disturbing feeling of recognition, as if she were being pulled toward something she couldn't resist.

Gilda elbowed Wendy. "Let's see it!"

Wendy handed Gilda the piece of paper. The number 9 was clearly written in black ink.

Gilda stared at Wendy. "You've got that feeling again."

Wendy nodded. "But I have no idea why."

Gilda squinted at the number and noticed a distinct tickle in her left ear. *Something about the number nine is significant*, she thought. *But what is it?*

Closing her eyes, Gilda concentrated on the number nine. An image entered her mind—a door with a number on it. Gilda visualized herself walking toward the door and opening it. Her eyes flew open when she realized she was picturing Wendy's room in Wyntle House.

"Hey!" Gilda declared, a bit too loudly, causing several teachers and students to shush her. "It's your room number, Wendy!" she whispered excitedly. "Your room in Wyntle House is also number nine!"

Wendy pulled her room key from her pocket and realized that Gilda was absolutely right; her room was number nine.

"Are you impressed? My psychic skills are really improving."

"Maybe it's just your memory that's improving. Anyway, that's not such a huge coincidence, is it?"

Gilda suddenly remembered something else: *Wendy drew the Nine of Swords during her tarot card reading.* Gilda was about to share this revelation but then decided to keep this piece of information to herself; the tarot card reading was still a sore subject. "It's probably just a coincidence," said Gilda. "Unless—"

"Unless what?"

"What if there's something weird about your room in Wyntle House?"

"Like what?"

"I have no idea. Just let me know if you notice anything odd, okay? And make sure you lock your door at night."

"Thanks for being so reassuring."

"Jenny Pickles!" Professor Heslop called from the front of the room.

For a brief moment, bad omens were forgotten. Gilda and Wendy gaped at each other with bug-eyed glee at one of the most hilarious names they had ever encountered in real life.

"Jenny Pickles!" Gilda whispered. "Can you believe it?"

Gilda and Wendy craned their necks to catch a glimpse of Jenny Pickles, and were both disappointed when a perfectly normal-looking red-haired girl walked briskly to the front of the room, her long curls bouncing. She was actually quite pretty. She also looked distinctly familiar.

"Hey, she was on the plane with us," said Wendy. "And I think that's her mom over there." Wendy pointed to a plump woman whose carrot-colored hair exactly matched her daughter's. With a flash of annoyance, Wendy remembered how the two of them had stared at her as they waited for their flight.

"There's no way that girl can win the competition," Gilda whispered. "Can you imagine how the concert announcements would look? 'Come see the London Symphony Orchestra—featuring Jenny Pickles!'"

"Thank you very much indeed," said Professor Heslop, after the last numbers had been drawn. "Please don't forget to check the performance time for your number, which is posted in the lobby here in the Music Faculty Building. Remember—please arrive *early* at the Holywell Music Room for your performance tomorrow. Finally, very best of luck to all of you in the first round of the competition!"

As the musicians mingled and gathered their belongings, Ming Fong bounded toward Gilda and Wendy.

"What number did you get, Wendy?"

Wendy showed her the number nine.

"Hey, I have number *eight*!"

Gilda and Wendy both wondered the same thing: was the close proximity of Ming Fong's and Wendy's numbers an eerie omen, or was this simply a meaningless coincidence?

"Gary drew seven, and I told him I want to follow him. So funny I get the number I want! We get to wait backstage together!"

"Great." Wendy didn't attempt to feign enthusiasm.

"*So* glad I didn't draw number ten, Wendy. Then I would play *after* you, and that would be bad because you are always so perfect." Ming Fong fixed Wendy with an intense stare. "I know you will be the best player tomorrow."

"I'm not perfect," said Wendy, once again feeling that she had somehow been jinxed even though Ming Fong's words had been a compliment.

10

The Apparition

I can switch rooms with you, if you want." Gilda and Wendy sat on Wendy's bed, watching a singing contest for couples who performed amateur duet versions of rock and pop songs.

"Why? What's wrong with *your* room?"

"Nothing. I just thought you might feel safer if you weren't staying in room number nine."

Wendy sighed as she picked up the remote and clicked off the television. "I can't let these superstitions get to me, Gilda. I'm supposed to be a rational person."

"Just because you have a gut feeling you can't easily explain doesn't mean you aren't a rational person, Wendy."

"It just bugs me that I have no idea what this feeling *means*." Wendy clutched her knees to her chest and chewed on a lock of hair. "Maybe it's all just performance anxiety or culture shock or something."

"That's possible. I mean, your parents are from China, but you've never been out of the States."

"Neither have you."

"I went to Canada with my dad once, so I was more prepared for this experience."

"Canada doesn't count. You can drive there in your car from Detroit."

"That's such a stereotypical American attitude. You don't even recognize Canada as a separate foreign country."

"You know what I mean," said Wendy, twisting another lock of her hair and pausing to gnaw on it as if she were a small animal attempting to chew through a rope. "Going to Canada isn't like going overseas."

"Stop chewing your hair, Wendy. Didn't you ever hear about the girl who died from doing that?"

"Here comes one of your urban legends."

"When they did the autopsy, there was a hair ball the size of a meteorite in her stomach."

"Thank you for the disgusting image. Anyway, my *point* was that there must be some *reasonable* explanation for this weird feeling I keep having."

Wendy was used to participating in Gilda's investigations from a distance, from which she could offer objective advice while remaining slightly skeptical of the whole project. She hated the notion that she was now becoming an irrational, weak person. She certainly never expected to be in the role of someone who needed Gilda's help—the kind of person who needed protection from some invisible, potentially sinister force. *This feeling I keep having isn't based on anything real*, Wendy reminded herself. *The tarot cards don't mean anything, and drawing the number nine was just a little coincidence.* "Look, I'd better get some sleep," she said, determined to finally put an end to her first day in England. "The competition starts really early tomorrow."

"Okay," said Gilda. "Knock on my door if I'm not up by eight, okay? I want to get up early so I can walk with you to the competition. Don't forget—I'm right across the hall if you need me."

Wendy stood up and picked up her toothbrush. "I'll be fine."

"Gary is right next door, too," Gilda added. "I'm sure he'd be up for a slumber party. Maybe he'd even let you play with his Luke Skywalker action figure if you ask nicely."

"Good night, Gilda." Wendy gave Gilda a little shove out the door. "Don't oversleep, because I'm leaving early tomorrow."

When she returned to her room, Gilda felt as if she had crashed into a wall of fatigue. She knew she should put on her pajamas and brush her teeth, but she suddenly felt too chilled to function, as if she were fighting a case of the flu. *I'll just lie down and get warm for a minute*, she told herself. Without turning out the dim overhead light or changing into her pajamas, she kicked off her shoes and crawled under the thin duvet cover.

Gilda huddled under the covers and listened to the gurgling and rumbling of pipes and the hissing of radiators in the old house. *It's like being trapped inside the digestive system of an old, gassy person*, she thought. Through the thin walls, she heard Gary blowing his nose, followed by water running noisily into the bathtub. She squeezed her eyes shut and tried to block out the sound of splashing, trickling water.

Despite the noisiness of the house, Gilda quickly drifted into sleep and dreamed that she was turning pages as Wendy performed her piano music. The odd thing was that the two girls were in motion, as if they were riding on the back of a truck—as if the piano itself were a kind of vehicle. As Wendy played faster, the piano moved faster, until Gilda had a giddy sense of terror; they were in danger of losing control.

"Slow down," said Gilda.

"You missed the turn!" Wendy snapped angrily.

Gilda turned the page, but it was too late. They suddenly lurched forward into a deep ditch and crashed down into what seemed to be a bottomless pit.

Gilda awoke to the unpleasant sound of water trickling through a pipe in the wall. She peered at her surroundings through half-opened eyes and found herself gazing into a face. It was a boy's face, and it seemed to be watching her from a few feet above the ground. Then, the face gradually dissolved like an image being erased from a strip of film.

As if hypnotized, Gilda watched the spot where the face had been. *Did I just see a ghost?*

Despite her many experiences receiving messages through dreams, séances, and automatic writing, Gilda had never actually seen a ghost before.

Gilda sat bolt upright in bed. "Who's there?" she whispered aloud. There was no answer. She squinted into the dim light, but the face did not reappear.

Gilda was about to run to Wendy's room to tell her what she had seen, but then she reminded herself that the first round of the competition was the next morning. She knew Wendy hated being awakened in the middle of the night.

Gilda stood up and decided to type a report of her experience instead:

```
To: Gilda Joyce
From: Gilda Joyce

Re: Oxford, UK GHOST-SIGHTING REPORT--
PSYCHIC INVESTIGATION NEWS FLASH!!!

A transparent face was observed suspended
in the air, hovering over my bed. The
apparition appeared to be a boy's face,
but it was difficult to tell. Was this a
hallucination caused by jet lag--some kind
of waking dream? Or was it a real ghost??
     This house is very old, so it's plausi-
ble there could be a ghost in just about
every one of the guest rooms.
     Note to self: ask Mrs. Luard if she's
noticed any spirit activity in Wyntle
House.
```

Gilda stopped typing and listened. The house was perpetually noisy in the night: every few seconds she heard sighing, creaking, and gurgling sounds that might be old pipes or shingles loosening in the wind—or something far stranger. Now more fully awake, she felt her heart beating faster and a prickling sensation in her limbs.

Leaving the dim light on, Gilda practically dove back into her sagging bed and pulled the covers up to her chin. Again, she thought of running to Wendy's room but resolved to let her best friend get some sleep the night before her competition.

Wendy sat down, adjusted the piano bench, and placed her hands on the keys. Something was wrong: she couldn't remember the opening notes of her first piece—the "Gigue" of the Bach French Suite in G Major. She glanced into the audience and saw her parents sitting at her mother's manicure table, surrounded by tiny bottles of blood-red nail polish and watching with hopeful, fearful anticipation. Wendy closed her eyes and tried to concentrate, but something blocked her memory of the first measures of her music. Instead, she could only remember a single musical phrase—a simple melody in A minor.

Play it, someone urged her. She began to play the notes she heard in her mind, and when she looked up again, she saw her parents' crestfallen faces.

Wendy suddenly awoke to the sound of real piano music—a simple, sad melody that reminded her of a folk song. The music came from somewhere in the house, possibly in a room right next to hers. Or was it coming from a floor below?

Who's practicing at this time of night? Wendy wondered, still half asleep and feeling lulled by the lyrical, melancholy mood of the music. *Maybe that's why I incorporated that music into my dream.*

Then, as she became more lucid, Wendy felt a shiver of fear. *Hadn't Mrs. Luard mentioned there was no piano in Wyntle House?*

She pulled the covers over her head and hugged her knees to her chest. Abruptly, the music stopped.

Wendy lay in the darkness with her heart pounding, listening to a thick silence punctuated by the eerie hissing of the radiator. She wanted to run across the hallway to ask whether Gilda had also heard the music, but she somehow couldn't make herself throw off the covers, expose herself to the chilly air, and step into the darkness of the hallway by herself. She had no idea what, exactly, she was afraid of, but she had the distinct feeling that somebody might be waiting for her in the hallway.

Wendy lay awake long into the night, listening to every groan and creak of the house, wishing that she could somehow forget her fears and drift into sleep.

11

The Ritual

Rain drummed upon the windowpanes and wind whistled across the roofs of terraced houses. Gilda glanced at her travel alarm clock and thought she must still be dreaming. How could it already be 8:15 A.M.? Why hadn't her alarm gone off, and why hadn't Wendy knocked on her door? *Maybe Wendy decided to leave extra-early to practice before her performance*, Gilda reasoned. *Still, she could have at least tried to wake me up.*

Shivering, Gilda sprang out of bed, grabbed a towel, and hurried into the hallway. She discovered Jenny Pickles exiting the bathroom, her wet, red hair wrapped in a towel turban.

"That bathtub in there is totally deesgustin'," Jenny declared. "I'd rather be hosed down in the backyard."

"I thought it looked pretty grotty," said Gilda, who was surprised to hear Jenny speak with a slight Southern accent.

"Grotty?"

"That the English way of saying 'gross.' I'm Gilda, by the way." Gilda extended her hand with a businesslike friendliness, and Jenny raised her eyebrows with amusement.

"Nice to meet you, Gilda. I'm Jenny."

"You're Jenny *Pickles*." Gilda couldn't resist an opportunity to say the name Jenny Pickles. "I remember you from the drawing of numbers."

"My mom wants me to start using a stage name."

"I think Jenny Pickles is a great name. It's very unique."

"And damn silly, too. You're from Michigan, right?"

Gilda nodded. "I think we saw you at the Detroit airport."

"Yeah, my mom and I just moved up to Detroit this year." Jenny squinted at Gilda. "I think I saw your friend—that Asian girl—at a piano contest in Grand Rapids this year."

"You saw Wendy Choy at a competition?"

"That's right—Wendy Choy. She was awesome! Well, I'd better go make myself purdy if I'm going to turn up on time for my performance."

"Jenny—"

"Yes?" Jenny paused on the steps.

"This sounds weird—but have you noticed anything *strange* in this house since you've been here?" Gilda decided she might as well find out whether any other ghosts had been spotted in the guesthouse.

"Hell, yeah."

Jenny counted items on her fingers as she spoke: "Creepy bath and shower, weird button to flush the toilet, breakfast of eggs and sausages that look like they're going to crawl off your plate—"

"I mean, have you noticed any *other* strange things?" Gilda decided it was best not to tell Jenny about the vision of a boy she had seen—at least not yet. She had learned during the past year that once people *expect* to see ghosts, they often start seeing them everywhere.

"What *sort* of strange things?"

"Jenny! What the hell are you doing piddlin' around up there? Your hair rollers are hot!"

"Coming, Mummy!" Jenny rolled her eyes and tried to fake an English accent at the sound of her mother's loud, twangy voice from the floor below. "Sorry, Gilda; I'd better get moving before my hair dries looking like the Bride of Frankenstein or my mother has a coronary fit. She believes that '*hair* is the key to success.'"

"Your mother is absolutely right. In fact, I was just about to give myself a quick perm before I head down to the competition."

Jenny snorted with laughter and bounded down the steps to fix her hair.

Gilda entered the grotty bathroom and found that the floor was cold and wet. A sheer, flimsy curtain fluttered over a drafty window, forcing bathers to expose their naked bodies to the walled gardens below as they climbed into the shower.

Gilda normally wasn't the squeamish type, but the combination of slimy white lime scale, black grout, and a crumbly rusty-brown substance that surrounded the edges of an ancient tub perched on porcelain feet made her feel a new kinship with people who rarely bathed.

If you can face a ghost, you can face a dirty bathtub, Gilda told herself.

She turned on the shower pump and discovered that the handheld shower head attached to the bathtub didn't work. There was no way around it; she would have to take a bath. Gilda took a deep breath, climbed into the tub, and stuck her head under the running water. She gasped, realizing that the water flowed from a single spout in two separate streams—one boiling hot and the other freezing cold. She shampooed hastily, braced herself for the simultaneous onslaught of hot and cold water as she rinsed, then hurriedly wrapped herself in a towel, shivering in the chilly air.

Gilda scurried back to her room and hastily grabbed her "London mod" outfit, pulling on the white tights and boots and the checked wool minidress. She didn't have time to dry her wet hair, so she quickly pulled her hair back in a ponytail and stuck the large, plumed hat on her head instead. She grabbed her coat, umbrella, and shoulder bag and ran out the door.

Gilda assumed Wendy had already left, but she nevertheless paused to rap on her door just in case. "Wendy? You in there?"

Gilda was surprised to hear rustling from inside Wendy's room, followed by the sound of objects clattering to the floor. She heard Wendy's voice. "Crap! You've got to be kidding me!" Something else toppled over. "Ow!"

"Wendy? What are you doing?"

Wendy opened the door angrily, and Gilda was taken aback to see her standing in her pajamas with tousled hair and puffy eyes. One thing was for sure: she did *not* look like someone who was about to perform in an international piano competition.

"It's all over," she said. "I'm completely doomed."

"Why aren't you dressed? I thought you were supposed to be at Holywell Music Room by now!"

"Why didn't *you* wake me up?"

"I overslept, that's why. I thought you had already left!"

"Well, I obviously overslept, too. I must have turned off my alarm in my sleep or something." Wendy picked up a book of music and hurled it across the room as if she were an angry toddler. Then she sat down at the foot of her bed and covered her face with her hands.

Gilda had never seen this side of Wendy, who was almost always in control of her emotions. *Maybe Wendy's big secret is that she throws a little tantrum before every one of her piano competitions*, Gilda thought. *Maybe her parents have to stuff her into the car kicking and screaming before her performances.*

"Look, Wendy, we have to get moving. You can still make it."

"No, I can't!"

"Now don't your knickers in a twist, luv; we just need to find you a frock to wear and then we can shove off." For some reason, Gilda felt that an approximation of a northern English accent was best suited to the stressful occasion.

"Stop talking in that accent, please."

Gilda opened Wendy's wardrobe and found all of her clothes neatly folded or hanging from hangers. "Hey, how about this little red number?"

"Gilda, there's no point. I knew I was jinxed!"

Gilda turned to face Wendy with hands on hips. "Wendy, you flew across an ocean to play for these people, so there's no way you're going to miss this just because you're running a little late this morning. Now—just throw on your clothes, curl your eyelashes, and get your butt down to the concert hall!"

"You don't understand. I can't do it."

"Why not?"

"There's this whole *thing* I'm supposed to do before I perform."

"Thing? What kind of thing?"

"Just a bunch of stuff I do for luck. Kind of a ritual."

"You do a *ritual*?" Wendy had never mentioned this before. *Maybe you never really know your friends until you travel to England with them and stay in a decaying, haunted house*, Gilda thought. "So . . . what does this ritual involve?"

"A bunch of things. It takes some time. I have to shampoo my hair and eat exactly a half a bowl of Cheerios . . ."

"Why *half* a bowl of Cheerios?"

"I don't know why. It's just something that works for me. See? I knew you would just think I'm weird."

Wendy's ritual involved washing her hair in strawberry-scented shampoo while tapping the fingering of her piano music on her scalp, eating exactly half a bowl of Cheerios with her lucky spoon, brushing her hair twenty times on each side, then closing her eyes and visualizing her entire performance from beginning to end. She had carried out the ritual ever since she won her first competition. Objectively, she knew that winning a competition had nothing to do with the half bowl of Cheerios she had consumed that day or the strawberry scent of her long hair, but the repetition of as many of the details as possible of that first winning morning reassured and calmed her on the day of a performance. And the truth was, it did seem to bring a kind of luck; she had won many competitions since that day.

"Wendy, I don't think you're weird at all. I just think you're crazy."

"The thing I love about your jokes, Gilda, is that they're so well-timed. It's like you can tell I'm just sitting here wishing that someone would make fun of me as my entire life falls apart."

"Come on—my brother was just telling me about this baseball player who has a ritual of eating nothing but chicken on the day of a big game because he's sure it helps him win."

"What happens if he *doesn't* eat chicken?"

"I don't know. I guess he loses the game."

"That really helps me."

"Wendy, we both know your ritual is not what makes you able to play the piano brilliantly, okay?"

"Maybe not, but it makes me *believe* that I can play."

Gilda thought for a moment. "Look, maybe you can do *part* of your lucky ritual. There isn't time to wash your hair and all that, but why don't I run downstairs and fix you a bowl of cereal while you get dressed? I bet Mrs. Luard has some English cereal like Weetabix or Shredded Hedgehog Crisp, or something."

"What about my hair?"

"Just brush it."

"I'm supposed to *wash* it!"

With a surge of frustration, Gilda grabbed Wendy's strawberry shampoo from its perch on the wardrobe and thrust it in Wendy's face. "Wendy, stop acting like a spoiled child star. This bottle of pink chemicals does not hold the key to your piano performance, okay? It makes you smell like a cough drop anyway."

"It smells like strawberries."

"Well, today you're going to pretend you're English royalty, and go without bathing or shampooing."

"I bet Prince William takes showers."

"I'm talking about the queens of the olden days," said Gilda, absentmindedly sticking Wendy's bottle of strawberry shampoo into her shoulder bag. "We'll just squirt some perfume on you like they did during the Elizabethan era when nobody bathed." Gilda remembered reading in a history book that Queen Elizabeth I used to bathe once a year with a stick of butter. "Now—I'm going to head downstairs to get your cereal. When I come back, I expect you to be dressed. Okay?"

Wendy sighed. "Okay."

As she turned to leave Wendy's room, Gilda noticed something unusual on the floor. She stooped to pick it up, and when she flipped it over, she felt an icy sensation in her stomach. She stared at the object for a minute, trying to absorb its significance. It was a tarot card—the Nine of Swords. The frightening thing about the presence of the card on Wendy's floor was that it was from a completely *different* deck of cards than the one Gilda owned. The image on this version of the Nine of Swords featured the enormous numeral 9 and the word *despair* looming over a darkened landscape. A lone, shadowy figure walked amid nine swords piercing the dry earth. The picture had a moody, nightmarish quality. It was as if some phantom had read Wendy's future during the night, leaving behind a cryptic, bleak verdict.

"Wendy," said Gilda cautiously, "you didn't buy a deck of tarot cards yesterday, did you?"

"When would I have time to buy tarot cards?" Wendy grabbed a wool sweater from her wardrobe and hurriedly pulled it over her head.

"Just wondered . . ." Gilda didn't want Wendy to see the card before her performance, but it was too late because Wendy was already peering over her shoulder.

"Where did *that* come from?"

"I just found it here on your floor. It seems like someone slipped it under the door."

Gilda and Wendy contemplated the mysterious card. Worse than the gloomy picture on the Nine of Swords was the realization that someone had purposefully placed it under Wendy's door with the hope that she would discover it on the first morning of the competition.

"It seems like a warning of some kind," said Gilda.

Wendy nodded and grew very pale, remembering the music she had heard in the middle of the night. For some reason, she didn't want to tell Gilda about it yet. She still hoped it had all been an unusually vivid dream.

"Don't worry about this now, Wendy."

"Easy for you to say."

"I'll figure out what this means. You just finish getting dressed, and I'll run downstairs and grab a couple muffins or something to take with us."

Outside the door to Wendy's room, Gilda pulled out her journal and quickly scribbled some notes to herself:

Psychic Investigation Notes—First Morning of the Competition:

The Nine of Swords turns up on Wendy's bedroom floor in Wyntle House. Is this further evidence of a haunting, or did someone purposefully leave the tarot card to upset her? I suppose it could have been left by another competitor—someone who wants to undermine Wendy's confidence or scare her. If that's the case, I'd say that Ming Fong is a likely suspect, although it could be Gary or just about anyone else around here....

On the other hand, I've read in my <u>Master Psychic's Handbook</u> that there have been cases of poltergeists that left messages in the form of scribbled notes on mirrors and walls or even words carved into stone. Some were able to cause mysterious changes in photographs. I suppose it's possible for a ghost to leave a tarot card for someone to find. Either way, it's very strange!

12

The Holywell Music Room

Holding their umbrellas to shield themselves from a steady, monotonous drizzle, Gilda and Wendy walked quickly through Gloucester Green, past rows of buses, an assortment of pizza and kebab shops, and a handful of touristy pubs. They made their way to Broad Street, where Gilda felt compelled to pause and peer up at a row of giant sculpted heads that perched on the semicircular gate surrounding the Sheldonian Theater. With square beards and wide eyes shaped like giant olives, they seemed to gaze above the street as if they were gods who could see some distant future event.

"I think they're supposed to be Roman emperors," Wendy said, remembering something she had read in a guidebook.

"They kind of look like those guys we used to see when my dad took us to the Harley-Davidson convention in Detroit."

"Gilda, come on! I'm late enough as it is!"

The girls hurried on to Holywell Street, where the narrow road was lined with terraced houses painted a variety of pastel colors—white, blue, lime green, pale pink. Just ahead were the high, stone walls of New College. Weary-looking students emerged from an arched doorway that reminded Gilda of the entrance to a castle. They pulled on backpacks, jumped on bicycles, and sped down the street, presumably in search of coffee at one of the cafés.

Gilda and Wendy stood on the sidewalk in front of the Holywell Music Room—a simple white building with two arched windows that seemed to peer at the girls with a surprised expression.

Wendy suddenly wished she could make herself much smaller—the size of a mouse that could scurry away in the gutter or hide in a corner of the building until the competition was over.

"We made it!" Gilda glanced at her watch, relieved that Wendy still had fifteen minutes before her performance time. Then she realized that Wendy seemed paralyzed by the sight of the Holywell Music Room.

"I can't do it," Wendy whispered.

"Wendy, what is your deal? This isn't like you at all."

"Did you know this place is like one of the oldest concert halls in the whole world?"

"It is?" To Gilda's eye, the building looked less antiquated than the medieval architecture of many of the college buildings.

"I mean, it's one of the first places ever built just for performing music—with no other purpose."

"Well, *your* purpose is to play music. So let's go, okay?"

"What business do I have playing in the Holywell Music Room, where so many great musicians have performed? I'm just a kid from Detroit who can't even wake up on time."

"Should I get out my violin, or do you want to have your self-pity party without music?"

"Without music."

"Wendy, first of all, you've practiced just as hard as those people of olden times did—probably harder, since they had to spend so much time powdering their wigs. For another thing, you're unshowered and heavily perfumed, just like they were. Besides, they were all drunk or insane in those days anyway."

"They were *not* all drunk or insane."

"Come on, Wendy. Just picture everyone in there naked and wearing eighteenth-century wigs, and you'll be fine."

Gilda grabbed Wendy's hand and practically dragged her up the steps leading to the building entrance. As they walked through the door, Wendy heard the sound of familiar music— the Chopin Ballade No. 3—a happy, horsey-sounding piece that, in the current performance, sounded frantic. "That's Gary playing," Wendy whispered.

Mrs. Mendelovich rushed toward them from a backstage hallway. "Windy! Thank God!"

A young woman who was handing out brochures at the entrance to the concert hall shot Mrs. Mendelovich a warning glance, pressing her finger to her lips.

"I was worried you got lost," Mrs. Mendelovich said in a slightly lower voice. "Thank God you are here."

Professor Heslop appeared. "Is this number nine?"

"This is Windy Choy—one of my stars."

"And she is performer number nine, is she?"

"I'm number nine," said Wendy.

"Numbered score for the judges?"

Wendy handed Professor Heslop photocopies of the music she would play. Each bar of music was marked with a number in case the judges wanted to point to a specific phrase in their comments.

"Yes, well, I'm afraid Wendy won't have time to practice on the warm-up piano. You'll have to go straight to the backstage waiting room, Wendy."

"But she must warm up!"

"Mrs. Mendelovich, I'm afraid there just isn't time. Wendy is late. Follow me, please, Wendy."

Mrs. Mendelovich grabbed Wendy's hands and pressed them in a prayer position between her own. "Windy, I know you weell make me ploud. You are champion."

"I'll try," said Wendy meekly.

Gilda wondered if Wendy was going to need someone to give her a shove onto the stage after the events of the morning. "Professor Heslop," she said, "is it okay if I wait backstage with Wendy?"

"The backstage waiting area is only for performers," Professor Heslop replied curtly.

"Professor Heslop," Mrs. Mendelovich interjected, "Geelda is our page-turner, and I would like her to wait with Windy."

"I suppose I can make an exception for *you*, Mrs. Mendelovich." Professor Heslop eyed Gilda's hat with disapproval and then turned to lead Gilda and Wendy to the backstage waiting room.

"Just don't distract me, okay?" Wendy whispered. "My concentration is completely off as it is."

"How could I distract you? I'm here to *help* you concentrate, Wendy."

They entered a small backstage rehearsal room filled with

music stands, a harpsichord, and an upright piano. Two other competitors waited there—Ming Fong and a boy who observed Gilda and Wendy with frank interest as he tilted back precariously on two legs of his chair, bracing himself against the harpsichord with one hand to keep from toppling over. He wore a white T-shirt and a worn leather jacket and jeans, as if affecting the style of a very young Marlon Brando. His black hair was disheveled, and he had none of the usual accessories of a young classical pianist waiting backstage for a performance—no marked-up music score in his lap, no mittens on his hands. Gilda felt certain that she recognized him from *somewhere*. Then she realized it was the boy who had observed her from across the room during the drawing of numbers. For some reason, she felt herself blushing under his gaze.

Ming Fong turned to give Wendy a prim little smile, then glanced up at a large clock on the wall with eyebrows raised as if saying: *You're late!*

She almost seems happy that Wendy's late, Gilda thought suspiciously.

Both Wendy and Gilda took note of Ming Fong's girlish dress trimmed with lace, and with a broad sash that tied behind her back in a giant bow. It looked like the kind of dress an antique doll might wear. As a final touch, she positioned a large red silk flower in her hair that matched the enormous crimson mittens she wore on her hands to keep her fingers warm.

"She looks like Alice in Wonderland," Gilda whispered cattily, wanting to distract Wendy, who seemed to be oddly fixated on the flower in Ming Fong's hair.

Wendy nodded, but she was actually wondering why the

red flower in Ming Fong's hair bothered her so intensely. Somehow the flower seemed to be mocking her—declaring victory in advance.

Secretly, Gilda had to give Ming Fong some credit for dressing with what she could only hope was a competitive strategy: the childish dress was ridiculous but memorable: it made her look much younger than her fourteen years. *Either she's completely clueless*, Gilda thought, *or she's trying to give the judges the impression that they're watching a child prodigy.*

Gilda glanced at Wendy and found herself wishing that she had at least brought a feather boa to drape around Wendy's neck to add some color to the drab, black skirt and gray woolen sweater she had hastily selected. Then Gilda remembered the pair of arm-length pink gloves she had stuffed in her bag.

"Here, Wendy." Gilda pulled the gloves from her bag. "Put these on to keep your hands warm."

Wendy eyed the hot-pink gloves. "Thanks, but I'm not going to the prom right now."

"But these look nicer than those boxing mitts you're wearing. You need some color."

"Shush!" Professor Heslop gave the girls a warning glance, and the boy who was watching the two of them grinned.

Wendy opened the music for her Bach French Suite, turned her back to Gilda, and began tapping the fingering of the notes inside her mittens.

Gilda decided to observe Ming Fong, who sat with a collection of Chopin compositions opened on her lap and a pair of headphones on her ears. Burning to ask Ming Fong about the tarot card Wendy had received, Gilda impulsively tapped her on the shoulder. Ming Fong turned to peer at Gilda with distant eyes, as if she had just been called out of a daydream. She reluctantly removed her headphones.

"Hey, Ming Fong," Gilda whispered. "Does this look familiar to you?"

She handed Ming Fong the tarot card she had discovered on Wendy's floor and watched her expressionless face closely.

"One of your tarot cards?"

"It isn't mine," said Gilda. "This one is different."

"Scary picture," said Ming Fong. "Spooky."

"Have you seen this before?"

Ming Fong shook her head.

"Are you sure? *Someone* left it under Wendy's door."

Ming Fong eyed Wendy, who sat with mittened hands covering her ears in an attempt to concentrate on her music. "Wendy looks scared."

"She isn't scared," said Gilda defensively. "We just wondered who gave this to her."

"Scared," said Ming Fong, turning back to her music. "That card looks like bad luck."

"What are the two of you talking about?" Wendy peered over her shoulder at Gilda.

"Nothing." Gilda hastily stuck the tarot card back in her bag. She had to admit that Ming Fong wasn't acting particularly guilty. *Maybe she's just a good actress*, Gilda thought. She was about to ask Ming Fong a few more questions when the boy sitting across the room grabbed his chair and shuffled closer to the three girls, drawing both Ming Fong and Wendy's attention.

"Reading fortunes, are we?" he asked. "Any luck for me?"

Wendy reached over and pinched Gilda. It was her sign that she thought a boy was cute. Gilda took another look at the boy and saw that his ears stuck out a little, his nose was a bit crooked, and his skin was very pale—almost translucent. His blue-gray eyes were a striking contrast to the floppy, eye-grazing layers of his black hair. He had dimples when he smiled. She pinched Wendy back much harder.

"Ow!"

Professor Heslop approached the group. "Excuse me. This is a serious international competition," she whispered. "I don't know how you do things in America and China, but here in England, we show respect for the performers onstage by keeping quiet during a competition."

"I'm English, actually," said the boy. "And I know for a fact that we show as little respect for performers as possible in this country."

Professor Heslop wasn't amused. "Quiet please, the lot of you; or I will have to ask you to wait outside in the rain. I have to go check on the front entrance now, and I expect you all to behave yourselves."

The group fell silent until Professor Heslop was out of earshot.

"In America, we just throw greasy McDonald's hamburgers at the stage throughout the whole performance," Gilda whispered. "It's our way of showing appreciation. How do you do things in China, Wendy?"

"We throw chopsticks and raw fish."

"Shh!" whispered Ming Fong loudly. "Be quiet! I don't want to wait outside in the rain." Ming Fong put her headphones back on.

"Bit of a Bossy Britches, isn't she?" said the boy.

"Tell me about it. Ming Fong drives us crazy."

"No." The boy pointed a thumb at the door through which Professor Heslop had just exited. "I meant Heslop."

"Oh, yeah. A real gorey granny."

"You mean 'granny gore.' All crotchety and grumpy."

"I prefer 'gorey granny.'"

He looked bemused. "You don't often hear an American trying to talk like a Scouser."

"I'm not trying to 'talk like a Scouser.' This is how I *always* talk." Grateful that she had studied her *Handbook of English Slang* so carefully, Gilda remembered that Scouser referred to the slang used in the city of Liverpool where all the great "oldies" songs by the Beatles originated.

"I'm from those parts. Well, I'm actually from a little toilet of a village up north called Crawling."

"Sounds charming."

"Oh, it is. Nobody's heard of it. So—what are you playing?"

Gilda wished that she was actually competing in the competition so she could talk to this boy about her music. "I'm playing the Rach Three," she whispered.

His eyes grew wide. He actually looked scared. "Seriously?"

"Just kidding, unfortunately. I'm actually Wendy's page-turner and manager. And my name is Gilda."

"Nice to meet you, Gilda. I'm Julian."

Gilda shook his hand, reflecting that most of the boys she knew at school never offered to shake hands with a girl. His hand felt warm and noticeably well-developed, as if his hands were older than the rest of his body.

"So, Wendy has her own manager?"

"That's right."

"Sounds like she's got it sorted."

"She's extremely sorted." Gilda noticed Julian eyeing Wendy with interest and felt a possessive urge to redirect his attention before Wendy jumped into the conversation. "Wendy's had some problems adjusting to a foreign country, though," Gilda added.

"Can't blame her," said Julian. "It's bloody gloomy this week."

"Plus, she overslept this morning, so she's in a really gormless mood."

"She doesn't look gormless."

"Excuse me." Wendy peered over her shoulder at Gilda. "Do the two of you mind not talking about me when I'm sitting right next to you?"

"I'm Julian." Julian extended a hand to Wendy.

As Wendy shook Julian's hand, they heard a rush of polite applause from the concert hall following the conclusion of Gary's performance.

"Thank you, performer number seven," a man's voice projected over the diminishing clapping.

"That must be Professor Waldgrave," Wendy whispered.

"It was a technically adept performance," Professor Waldgrave continued from the performance hall, "but you must keep a steadier tempo and maintain more *control*. It was as if you were riding a horse that got away from you and you had no sense of where the music was going to end up. And speaking of music—let's *play* some next time, shall we?"

A murmur of surprised, sympathetic laughter welled from the audience. Gilda couldn't help but feel sorry for Gary.

"Ouch," Julian whispered.

"Omigod, I'm toast," Wendy muttered.

"Wendy, you play better than Gary," said Gilda. "Professor Waldgrave has a point; Gary's performance was kind of boring."

"What I meant about that comment," Professor Waldgrave continued from the performance hall, "is that you must think about *color*. It was as if your entire performance was colored in shades of brown. I felt as if I were watching a young child scribbling with a single brown crayon. And if the performance had a scent, it would be smelly."

"Bollocks!" a woman's voice piped up.

Julian snorted with amusement.

"I beg your pardon?"

"Your comments are far too harsh, Nigel."

"That must be the bizarre Professor Maddox," Julian whispered.

From the backstage room, Gilda, Julian, Wendy, and Ming Fong sensed a tense silence descending over the audience in the concert hall; it was surprising to hear the two judges voicing such blunt and public disagreement with each other.

"We have to keep in mind the difficulty of this piece. There were some quite lovely moments, and he played with great confidence. Fine job, performer number seven. Just try to find that little spark that really gets your audience excited."

A jolt of adrenaline surged through the backstage room as Professor Heslop hurried through the door and gestured to Ming Fong that it was time for her performance. Ming Fong removed her mittens, placed her music on her seat, and stood with her thin arms folded across her chest and hands wedged in her armpits. In her feminine dress she looked even more diminutive than usual, like a fragile doll.

Gary emerged from the concert hall. His round face looked flushed.

"Good job, Gary," said Gilda and Wendy politely.

"Sounded like old Waldgrave gave you the verbals, mate," said Julian.

Gary looked confused. "He said I didn't play music."

"Maybe add more dynamics next time," Wendy suggested.

"If there is a next time." Gary looked dejected.

"How's the piano out there?" Wendy asked. One of the things she dreaded about piano competitions was walking onstage to play on a completely unfamiliar instrument.

"Kind of stiff. It's cold in the room. The acoustics seem great, though."

Gilda had intended to ask Gary if he knew anything about the tarot card that had turned up in Wendy's room, but the topic seemed impossible to broach right after Gary had been humiliated onstage.

"Good luck, Ming Fong," said Gary glumly.

Ming Fong nodded but didn't look at Gary. She was already in another world—the world of her own performance.

"Good luck, Wendy," Gary added, even more forlornly.

"Thanks, I'll need it."

"I'd stay and watch you, but I should probably go practice." Gary hesitated, as if hoping that Wendy would beg him to stay.

"Don't go practice, mate!" said Julian. "You should celebrate. There's a whole town out there full of meat pasties and college girls!"

Gary smiled uneasily. "I should really practice my sight-reading before tomorrow. I'll see you guys later."

"Performer number eight will play the Bach C Minor Prelude and Fugue from the 'Well-Tempered Clavier' followed by Chopin's 'Ocean' Étude," Professor Heslop announced.

With iron-straight posture, Ming Fong walked onstage toward the piano. A moment later, a barrage of staccato sixteenth notes burst from the stage like machine-gun fire.

Ming Fong played with such effortless speed, efficiency, and perfection, the music almost didn't seem human. Something about her playing made Gilda think of steel parts moving quickly down an assembly line to be hammered and drilled by little robots. Her performance was at once mechanical and beautiful: it was as if Ming Fong had transformed from a little girl wearing a frilly dress into a tiny factory of sound that exploded with streams of brilliant sparks and silvery smoke.

"Bloody 'ell," Julian breathed. "She has fingers."

Gilda was alarmed when she looked at Wendy: her face had the pale, clammy appearance of someone who might get sick at any moment.

"Here, you need to breathe!" On impulse, Gilda reached into her handbag, uncapped Wendy's bottle of strawberry shampoo, and thrust it under Wendy's nose.

Wendy took a deep breath.

"Now—just relax."

"Omigod, I've never been this nervous in my life. I feel like I'm going to be sick."

Gilda wondered if she should have brought a barf bag for

Wendy, just in case. "Whatever you do, don't park a custard onstage, Wendy."

"Thanks. Big help."

"Just picture the judges in their knickers," Julian suggested. "That Waldgrave is a loony sod anyway."

A burst of applause followed Ming Fong's performance.

"Thank you, performer number eight," said Professor Waldgrave after the applause died down. "Now, I have to be very frank with you . . ."

People in the audience held their breath. Was Professor Waldgrave ruthless enough to destroy the spirit of the tiny girl who sat at the piano wearing a pretty red-and-white dress—a girl who played faster than a speeding bullet?

"I loved it," said Professor Waldgrave.

The audience released a sigh of relief tinged with disappointment. After all, it had been more *interesting* to watch Gary receive harsh criticism.

"It was crisp, accurate, perfectly pure playing. I believe Mr. Bach would have liked your interpretation of the music."

"She's better than me," Wendy whispered. "I don't know how it happened just in the last month, but she somehow got better than me."

Gilda grabbed Wendy by the shoulders and gazed directly into her eyes—a gesture she had seen Wendy use when trying to get her little brother's attention when he misbehaved. "Listen to me, Wendy. Don't worry about Ming Fong right now. You're only competing against yourself, okay? Just focus on your own game out there." Gilda felt as if she had turned into some kind of athletic coach. "Now—just close your eyes, take a whiff of your strawberry shampoo, and try to think about your own music."

Wendy closed her eyes. Music came to her, but there was a problem. *It wasn't the music she was supposed to perform.* It was as if some music virus had entered her mind—an alien composition that was attaching itself to the crucial brain cells containing her competition music. Bach and Mozart were being replaced by a simple, melancholy theme in A minor—music she had heard somewhere, but *where?*

Then, with a surge of nausea, Wendy remembered the music that had pulled her out of sleep in the middle of the night. *No,* Wendy told herself. *Please don't think about that.* She tried to focus on the Bach French Suite—the first piece she would play—but for some reason, she was having a hard time remembering the opening melody.

Something is wrong with me, Wendy thought.

Ming Fong practically flew from the concert hall into the backstage waiting room, her face illuminated by a brilliant smile. Professor Heslop congratulated her warmly—something she hadn't yet done for any other performer—then signaled Wendy to prepare to walk onstage.

"I'll go watch you from the audience," said Gilda.

Wendy nodded mutely. Gilda noticed that her hands shook slightly as she removed her thermal mittens.

As Gilda made her way toward the performance hall, she had the uneasy feeling that she had never in her life seen Wendy so scared.

13

The Disaster

The performance hall of the Holywell Music Room resembled a horseshoe-shaped indoor amphitheater. Rising up from the stage floor were a semicircular series of red, curving benches from which the audience peered down at the performers below. Two gilded, octopuslike chandeliers hung from the high ceiling, and organ pipes decorated with floral designs perched just above the stage.

Gilda made her way up the steps and found a spot in one of the upper rows just as Professor Heslop stepped onstage to announce Wendy's performance selections. From her seat, Gilda could see the bald spot in the middle of Professor Nigel Waldgrave's thinning auburn hair. Bizarrely, a fat orange cat perched on top of the music score in front of him. Gilda remembered Mrs. Mendelovich's comment: "He loves nobody but his cat!" *Professor Waldgrave must REALLY love his cat if he can't even leave it behind while he judges a piano competition*, Gilda mused.

A striking woman with dark curls literally springing from her head and pointing in several different directions at once, Professor Rhiannon Maddox was dressed from head to toe in somber black. Her pointy, lace-up boots made Gilda think of a witch's costume for Halloween. She and Professor Waldgrave sat with their bodies turned sharply away from each other as they scribbled notes to themselves.

As Gilda watched groups of college students and gray-haired ladies who had wandered into the concert hall and were peering down at the piano below with bright, self-satisfied expectation, she suddenly felt intensely nervous for Wendy. Something about the position of the piano on the ground floor below made it look exposed and vulnerable, and she realized for the first time that the task of performing for this audience at Oxford University was actually monumental—on par with walking a tightrope or getting shot out of a cannon at the circus.

Stay calm, Wendy, Gilda thought. *You can do this; you can do this....* Gilda closed her eyes and tried to use her psychic skills to send Wendy some luck.

As she walked onstage, Wendy felt strangely removed—as if she were watching herself from a distance as she approached the full-grand piano shining like black ice on the stage floor, its keys stretched in a wide, gap-toothed smile. Feeling far too aware of the eyes peering down at her from above, she sat down at the piano bench and twisted the creaking knobs to adjust its height. *Take your time,* Mrs. Mendelovich had told her a thousand times. *Listen for the music before you play.*

But nerves took over, and Wendy launched into the music too quickly. She watched with amazement as her hands moved through the fast, frantically joyful Bach "Gigue." Luckily, her fingers had a physical, completely unconscious memory of their own and they managed to breeze through the notes despite her sense that she was watching *someone else's* hands. Wendy marveled that her fingers could function so well despite her panic. At the same time, she was petrified that her hands would fail her at any moment. All it would take was a tiny gap—a single missed note—and the whole thing would fall apart.

Wendy breathed a sigh of relief as she concluded the Bach without a memory lapse or major stumble.

Her second piece—the Mozart D Minor Fantasy—was more simple and exposed than the fast-paced Bach. A mournful melody in the right hand alternated with chords in the lower register—like an orchestra that plunged the music into darkness before the return of a single, poignant voice. Mrs. Mendelovich had worked with Wendy to perfect every detail of this delicate, sensitive music, hoping that the piece would showcase Wendy's ability to play "at a more mature level." All the other kids would stick with music that featured what Mrs. Mendelovich called "big technique"; Wendy would stand out by demonstrating her more sophisticated artistry—her ability to control moments of silence as well as the notes themselves.

Usually, when Wendy performed the Mozart Fantasy, she heard her teacher's voice in her head, guiding her through the music—*"Soft here; steady!"* and *"Build now! Crescendo!"* But Mrs. Mendelovich's voice did not come to her this time. Instead, there was another voice she didn't recognize—the maddening intrusion of that dream-melody in A minor.

She missed a note. It wasn't a subtly missed note; the dissonant sound was like a sudden stab wound in the middle of the music. Wendy was so surprised, she actually stopped playing for a moment.

Oh no, Wendy! Gilda thought, struggling to keep from standing up in her chair and running to Wendy's aid. *Whatever you do, keep playing, keep playing, keep playing!*

A snowdrift of silence settled across the concert hall.

Where was she in the music? Wendy realized with horror that she was *lost*. She glanced into the audience and saw the judges watching her expectantly. Was it her imagination, or was a *cat* also sitting on the table watching her?

"I'm sorry," said Wendy, her small, clear voice carried by perfect acoustics up to the highest levels of the performance hall. "Would it be okay if I started over?"

Gilda couldn't believe what she was seeing. This sort of thing simply didn't happen to Wendy. Everyone knew that Wendy *never* caved under pressure. In fact, Gilda had come to regard Wendy as virtually invincible when it came to any kind of performance, whether it was a math quiz, a school talent show, or an international competition. She did her best to send Wendy a thought message: *Stay calm. Forget everyone is looking at you. You can do it; you can do it; you can do it. . . .*

Time itself seemed to stand still as Professor Maddox stood up and walked toward the piano holding the copy of Wendy's sheet music. The pointy heels of her witch's shoes hit the wooden floor like the beat of a steady metronome. The audience rustled and whispered in the upper benches as Professor Maddox pointed to the measure where Wendy had lost her way.

Wendy took a deep breath and lifted her hands to the keyboard again. This time, she made her way through to the end of the piece, but she felt as if she were the last person limping across a finish line in a marathon.

Polite, sympathetic applause welled from the audience. Gilda bit her fingernails on Wendy's behalf. What would Professor Waldgrave say to her after such a noticeable memory slip?

The judges looked at each other for a moment, as if sharing some private, sad memory. "Shall I go first this time?" Professor Maddox asked.

Professor Waldgrave nodded, covering his mouth with a tight fist.

"The Mozart is a deceptively difficult piece," said Professor Maddox. "You did remarkably well until you lost your way. Believe me, it happens to the best of us at one time or another."

Wendy attempted to smile ruefully. She wished that Professor Maddox wouldn't say nice things that made her want to burst into tears. *Don't cry, don't cry, don't cry,* she kept telling herself. It was bad enough to botch her performance. The only thing that would make it worse would be crying onstage in public.

"You have good technique and a very expressive playing style, but I didn't feel I was really hearing *you* playing, it was as if part of you was somewhere else. Try to tell a *story* with the music—convey some of your own feelings."

Somewhere behind Wendy's eyes a wall of tears was rising, threatening to leak out. So far, she held back what felt like an imminent flood.

It was Professor Waldgrave's turn to speak. "Try not to get so nervous," he said gruffly.

The musicians in the audience tittered.

"I'm serious," Professor Waldgrave continued. "Getting nervous means that you're thinking about *yourself* too much. Stop thinking about yourself, and start thinking about *Mozart.*"

"That was a bit rude," said Professor Maddox.

"Excuse me, Rhiannon; I'm not finished."

Wendy actually felt grateful for this hostile exchange; it surprised her enough to make her momentarily forget her imminent tears.

Gilda leaned forward, suddenly very curious about the relationship between the two competition judges. *They obviously loathe each other*, she thought. *But why?*

"In my opinion," Professor Waldgrave continued, "you should work on playing the piece the way *Mozart* would want it played instead of infusing it with adolescent emotion. But of course, Ms. Maddox and I disagree on that front, amongst others."

"Yes," said Professor Maddox. "We disagree completely."

"The Bach was quite good, actually," Professor Waldgrave continued, "but the Mozart needs work. You weren't listening to yourself as you played. Want to know a little secret that can teach you more than any piano teacher ever will?"

Wendy nodded and did her best to avoid glancing in Mrs. Mendelovich's direction.

"Two words. *Tape recorder.* You'll hear yourself and say, 'No, that *can't* be me. I don't sound like *that!*' Well, that *is* how you sound. So once you know how you *really* sound, you can start improving. Thank you very much, number nine."

"Thank you," Wendy murmured. She stood up and bowed apologetically.

As Wendy left the stage, she felt grateful for one thing: her parents had not been there to witness her public humiliation.

14

Julian's Performance

"Hey, wait! Wendy!" Gilda caught up with Wendy just as she slipped out the front door of the Holywell Music Room.

Wendy regarded Gilda with a stone-faced expression. "Thank God my parents weren't here."

"I'd like to see *them* get out there and play in front of all those people."

This only made Wendy more upset. She turned and sat down on the wet steps that led to the front door of the building, her head buried in her arms. Gilda sat next to her under a steady drizzle of rain that coated their hair and clothes with a fine mist. "Do you want my hat? I just remembered I left my umbrella inside."

"No. I don't want to wear your stupid hat!"

"None of this is the hat's fault, Wendy."

Wendy reburied her face in the crook of her arm.

"I know nothing I say right now will help," Gilda ventured, "but I honestly think the judges were seriously impressed with you. I mean, aside from that one little glitch—"

"You mean the gaping *silence* in the middle of the music?"

"But *before* that, I was watching the judges, and even Professor Waldgrave looked seriously *interested.*" This was actually true. Both professors had stopped scribbling with their pens and looked at Wendy as if they were genuinely intrigued with *something* about her performance.

"Well, it won't be enough to get me into the final round after this. I can't believe it's already all over."

"It's never over until the fat lady sings."

"Whatever that means."

"There's still the sight-reading competition tomorrow, and that could really bring up your score. Plus, I'll be right up there with you to keep you company and help you look good on-stage."

Wendy stared at the entrance to New College across the street, where a plump porter argued about something with a small group of tourists. "I can honestly say that I've never had nerves like that before in my whole life."

"Tomorrow we're going to set about five alarm clocks and get you up in time for your ritual, okay?"

"I'm not sure that was the *real* problem." Wendy dug through her music bag, found a wad of tissue, and blew her nose.

"Was it that tarot card that turned up in your room?"

"Maybe." Wendy hesitated, watching the tourists walk glumly down Holywell Street after being thwarted from entering the college. The porter retreated through the arched wooden door-way. "I was just wondering... did you hear anything strange in the house last night?"

"Like what?" Gilda felt a strong tickle in her left ear as she remembered the vision of the boy's face that she had seen in her room. She had purposefully avoided mentioning it to

Wendy before her performance, but now she wondered whether Wendy had also perceived something out of the ordinary.

"I heard piano music in the middle of the night."

"But Mrs. Luard said she doesn't own a piano."

"I know. And there was something really odd about the music," Wendy continued. "It seemed to shift around—almost like a piano was floating from room to room."

Gilda decided it was time to tell Wendy about the apparition she had seen. "Wendy, I think Wyntle House might be haunted." Leaning closer, she spoke in a low voice. "I didn't hear the piano music, but I'm pretty sure I saw a *ghost* in my room."

"You've got to be kidding. You saw a ghost and didn't rush into my room to tell me?"

"I thought you needed your sleep."

Wendy looked skeptical. "Are you sure you weren't dreaming—or seeing shadows on the wall or something?"

"Are you sure *you* weren't dreaming about the piano music? After all, you are in a piano competition and you're totally stressed."

"I was awake when I heard it."

"I was awake when I saw a ghost."

The girls were distracted by Mrs. Mendelovich's voice from the entranceway of the Holywell Music Room. "This is Ming Fong—my prize student!" Mrs. Mendelovich and Professor Heslop stood in the doorway with Ming Fong between them.

"She certainly performed brilliantly today," said Professor Heslop.

"How annoying," Gilda whispered, sensing Wendy's irritation.

Wendy shrugged. "I don't give a crap." But in truth, she did care. In all the years she had studied with Mrs. Mendelovich, she had never once let her piano teacher down. In fact, she had always played *better* at public performances than she did at her piano lessons. "Windy always rises to the occasion!" Mrs. Mendelovich always bragged. "Tough as nails! Handles pressure like a true concert soloist."

"Hey," said Gilda, hoping to distract Wendy from the awkward situation, "why don't we go do some sightseeing?"

"Not now," said Wendy, hurrying to stand up. "I'm going to go buy a tape recorder like Professor Waldgrave suggested. I want to know how I *really* sound."

"You sound great, Wendy. Let's go have some tea and scones."

"I just really need to be alone right now, okay?"

"But—"

Wendy abruptly fled down the steps just before Mrs. Mendelovich and Ming Fong approached, smiling and laughing. Ming Fong beamed with pride as she sprung open her black umbrella. Neither of them noticed Gilda sitting on the step or Wendy disappearing around the corner as they made their way toward Holywell Street.

Gilda walked back into the concert hall to retrieve her umbrella and discovered Julian onstage performing. As he concluded his first piece—Chopin's "Fantasie Impromptu"—and launched into Beethoven's "Pathetique" Sonata, Gilda found herself fascinated and unable to leave.

Julian's performance style was highly dramatic; he threw

away notes with big flourishes. Gilda loved the anxious, melo-dramatic, slightly *spooky* sound of the music by Beethoven, which reminded her of someone tiptoeing down a dark hallway where ghosts lurked in the corners. Then—suddenly—there was a chase scene, as if a ghost or monster were in close pursuit.

He seems to be having fun out there, Gilda thought. She noticed that Professor Maddox smiled happily as she listened. Next to her, Professor Waldgrave frowned and squinted through his glasses, as if shielding himself from Julian's exuberant perfor-mance. On the table, Professor Waldgrave's cat concentrated on licking between its splayed hind toes.

As Julian struck the last notes of the "Pathetique," the con-cert hall erupted into enthusiastic applause. "Encore!" some-one yelled, and giggles rippled through the room.

Professor Waldgrave scowled at the audience like an elemen-tary school teacher chaperoning a field trip. "Excuse me!" he said. "This is a *serious* piano competition, and that behavior is terribly common."

The room immediately fell silent.

"This was an expressive performance, but there was a bit too much cheap drama for my taste. Closing your eyes, staring at the ceiling, throwing your hands up in the air unnecessarily; it all went out with Liberace and wearing white sequined tuxedos."

"Not true," muttered Professor Maddox.

"May I finish, Rhiannon? As I was saying, I felt as if I were listening to the warped sound track of a bad silent film—a film with no story. It was too fast. And call me old-fashioned, but there were simply too many wrong notes."

What wrong notes? Gilda wondered. There had been a tornado of notes, and they had all sounded great. She stifled an urge to blow raspberries at Professor Waldgrave.

"I completely disagree," said Professor Maddox.

"How completely surprising."

"Beethoven's 'Pathetique' Sonata is one of the most overplayed classics in the repertoire, and this performer actually made me *want* to listen."

Julian's face opened into a hopeful smile. Professor Waldgrave gazed up at the ceiling with exasperation.

"You did miss lots of notes, and that was a little distracting sometimes," Professor Maddox continued, "but you understand how to communicate with your audience. You told a story with the music, and you made us want to listen to you."

Professor Waldgrave mumbled something inaudible.

"What was that, Nigel?"

"I believe the word he used was *rubbish*," said Julian from the piano.

The audience chuckled.

"Time's up, performer number ten," said Professor Waldgrave. "On to the next performer, please."

As Gilda watched Julian leave the stage, she pulled out her journal to scribble a quick travel diary entry for Mrs. Rawson. She wanted to make sure she gave her teacher as many educational, tantalizing, and creative details as possible about her trip, and Julian's music had suddenly inspired her to write:

TRAVEL DIARY ENTRY—English "Words-of-the-Day" for Mrs. Rawson:

1. <u>Gormless:</u> without gorm. Uninspired, boring, and lame. Many English folk loathe gormless people and things and will go to great lengths to avoid them. An appreciation for tire-size hats and feasting on vital organs, for example, can be attributed to the English avoidance of gormlessness.

2. <u>Knickers:</u> the preferred English undergarment. An English woman wouldn't be caught dead wearing "panties." Instead, she prefers the comfort of large woolen pantaloons or a tight rubber body stocking, called "knickers." When a person is upset, his or her knickers are said to be "in a twist," as was the case with Wendy Choy this morning.

<u>Personal note:</u>

I know this sounds shallow, considering the trauma Wendy just experienced, and the fact that I seem to have a serious haunting on my hands. But I can't help it: I think I have a little crush on that English boy, Julian. He's really cute in a funny-looking sort of way, and I like the way he talks.

<u>To do:</u>

Find a way to have a conversation with Julian!

15

Dead Man's Walk

Wait! Gilda!"

As Gilda headed toward Broad Street, she turned to see Julian walking behind her without a coat or umbrella, his hands stuffed in his pockets and his shoulders hunched in the rain.

"Can I share that very pink umbrella with you?"

Gilda felt jittery with the surprise of Julian's presence. "Oh—sure." She waited for him to catch up. "Here, want to carry it? You're taller."

Julian took the umbrella and held it over both of them. "I've always wanted a pink umbrella but never had the nerve to buy one."

"You're welcome to wear my hat, too."

Julian placed Gilda's hat on his own head. "Now I look like a real Oxford student. 'Oh, *this* hat?'" He mimicked a posh, lisping accent. "'Just something Mummy sent for me to wear.'"

Several passersby regarded Julian with interest and subtle approval, assuming he must indeed be an eccentric, theatrical college student.

"Your performance was great," said Gilda, immediately feeling that this comment didn't come close to capturing how much she truly admired the way Julian played piano. "I mean, you sounded amazing."

"You stayed to hear me play?" Julian looked genuinely flattered.

"At first I went back into the building because I forgot my umbrella."

"I should have known; I can't compete with a pink umbrella."

"But then I loved that spooky music you were playing, so I stayed to hear the whole thing."

"Spooky? Oh, you mean the Beethoven. Yeah, I guess it is kind of spooky. Old Waldgrave hated it, though."

"He's wrong."

"He's doolally and a nutter."

"Why is he so mean?"

"I have no idea, but I'm sure you've heard what everyone suspects—that all of his judging decisions are made by his cat."

"No way."

"I'm completely serious. If the cat purrs, you get a high score. If the cat puts its ears back and twitches its tail, then you can kiss your chances good-bye."

Gilda made a mental note to keep an eye on Professor Waldgrave's cat just in case there was any truth to this theory. What a scandal it would be if the winner of the Young International Virtuosos Competition was actually selected by a cat!

"So what do you think it means when Waldgrave's cat licks between its toes?" Gilda asked.

"I have no idea."

"That's what it did during your performance."

"That explains Waldgrave's critique, then. 'Toe-licking is far too expressive!'" He mimicked Professor Waldgrave's officious tone. "'We haven't seen toe-licking since the days of Liberace!'"

Gilda laughed. "I wonder if that cat really does make his decisions for him. I guess it's possible; my mom has a friend who claims she let her dog choose her boyfriend. She says it worked out better than usual."

"Thinking of trying that for yourself, are you?"

"We don't have a dog."

"Then I'll assume you don't have a boyfriend." Julian grinned mischievously, and Gilda was annoyed to feel herself blushing.

"I recently broke up with someone," Gilda fibbed. Being completely ignored by Craig Overcash could hardly be called a "breakup," but for some reason she wasn't about to let Julian know that she had never had a boyfriend in her entire life. She felt eager to change the subject. "So—why do you think Professor Maddox and Professor Waldgrave hate each other so much?"

"Lover's quarrel."

"You have to be joking."

"No joke. I reckon they snogged in one of the practice rooms, and then everything went sour."

"Ick. There's no way I can picture those two kissing."

"You can never tell. Some people go for the balding, grumpy professor type."

Gilda wondered whether the two judges had a relationship that went bad. *That would explain some of the cutting remarks*, she thought. "But if they're so mad at each other, how can they be fair judges?" she wondered aloud. "They'll always disagree with each other no matter what."

"Exactly. Which brings us to the fact that nothing's ever fair in the end, so there's no point caring too much about the whole thing."

Gilda was struck by how different this attitude was from the intensity with which Wendy, Ming Fong, and Gary viewed the competition. How could somebody with so much talent take such a nonchalant attitude toward the opportunity to win thousands of pounds and gain international recognition?

"You honestly don't even care whether or not you win?"

"I'm just doing this for a lark, really. My dad didn't want me to go at all."

"Why not?"

Julian shrugged. "My dad, he's glad I have a hobby that keeps me off the streets and such, but he doesn't see what it's all leading to—all this sitting at an instrument for hours. He was a musician himself—playing in pubs and all around town, and it never really came to much. He installs toilets for a living now."

"Oh." Gilda thought this sounded like one of the worst jobs anyone could have.

"It's odd. Sometimes I almost get the feeling that he'll actually be disappointed if I prove him wrong—if I show him that I *could* make a career of music."

Gilda remembered how her father had encouraged her to pursue her passion for writing, how he had given her the gift of his lucky manual typewriter before he died. He had never said anything like, *That's not a very practical career, Gilda. You'd be better off pursuing plumbing.* Of course, Gilda had no idea what her dad would have thought of her career as a psychic investigator. *That* interest had evolved only after his death.

"It was my piano teacher who actually convinced my parents to let me come down here and compete," Julian explained. "I'm staying with some of my teacher's friends who live nearby. Oh, and I'll definitely be beaten to death if any of my friends ever discover that I traveled to Oxford with Mr. Goodwin for a piano contest."

"There are some kids like that in my school, too. Only I'm not friends with them."

"In Crawling, you don't get to pick your friends; you just fend off attacks."

Gilda laughed, but she sensed a conflict in Julian—a hidden sadness. "For what it's worth, I think you could actually win this, Julian."

"Well, thanks for saying that."

"I *shouldn't* be saying that because I'm really rooting for Wendy. We've got big plans for the prize money."

"Send some of it in my direction, then. Wendy's quite good; the nerves got to her a bit, though."

"I know. I really should go try to find her and see how she's doing."

But Gilda didn't want to leave Julian. They passed a sea of student bicycles leaning against the stone walls of Lincoln College, then wandered into the Covered Market—an indoor market filled with flower stands, butcher shops, vegetable and fruit displays, bakeries, and small cafés. Outside the butcher shops, the smell of cold sausages permeated the air. Rabbits and pheasants hung from their feet with fur and feathers still intact. Julian pointed to a window display featuring THE WORLD'S OLDEST HAM!—a dried, shriveled piece of meat.

"I'd fancy a posh lunch," said Julian, staring at the dessicated ham.

"Me, too," said Gilda, suddenly realizing that she was very hungry. "I'm starved for something posh and gooey, like macaroni and cheese."

Julian laughed. "I was thinking more along the lines of something fancy and expensive. I've only got five quid at the moment, though, so I think we'll have to settle for Brown's Café here—unless you're secretly loaded with cash like any self-respecting American."

"Sorry, I left my millions in the States."

The two wandered into Brown's Café to order lunch. *This is almost like a real date*, Gilda thought, suddenly feeling self-conscious about the idea of eating with Julian. *I'm actually on a date with an English boy!*

Gilda and Julian ordered sandwiches at the counter, then found a small table at the back of the café. A portly man plunked himself down at the table next to them and gobbled a plate of sausages while reading a book entitled *A History of Gastronomy*. He picked up a plastic container of mustard and squirted it loudly, then blew his nose into his napkin with a trumpeting sound. At the same moment, a shiny button burst from the waistband of the man's trousers and skittered across the floor, drawing the attention of several diners. Red-faced, the man glared at the button, which now lay on the other side of the room. *It isn't that funny*, Gilda told herself. *Don't laugh!* Nevertheless, she snorted with glee as Julian grinned and kicked her under the table.

"I bet he teaches at the university," said Gilda, after the man hastily finished the rest of his sausages and left the café—not without giving Gilda and Julian a reprimanding glance.

"My guess is that he works in a secondhand bookstore," said Julian. "He *wanted* to go to school at Oxford, but he flunked his A levels. So he's spent his years reading all the dusty gastronomy books in the store instead."

"And he eats sausages for lunch every day," Gilda added.

"Except Thursdays. On Thursdays he eats tripe."

"I take it you like people-watching as much as I do."

"People are ridiculous," said Julian, "but at least they're entertaining."

"They're not *always* ridiculous."

"Believe me," said Julian, "most of them are ridiculous."

The rain had stopped by the time Gilda and Julian left the Covered Market. They wandered down busy Cornmarket Street, then to a narrow path that led into the private gardens of Merton College. Gilda was delighted to hear gloomy organ music from the college chapel intermingling with church bells in the distance.

"There's a shortcut here that leads to the Music Building," Julian explained.

Gilda followed him onto a straight walking path that divided a meadow with playing fields on one side from the college buildings on the other.

"I think this is called Dead Man's Walk," said Julian. "My teacher said they used to have funeral processions here."

At the end of the path, Christ Church Cathedral loomed like a Gothic castle, its spires soaring under a mixture of dark and sunlit clouds. Gilda was instantly intrigued with Dead Man's Walk: she had the sense that there must be hundreds of ghosts nearby—spirits that drifted silently down the streets and pathways, wandering to destinations that still existed from antiquity.

Something about the quiet, moody atmosphere of Dead Man's Walk made Gilda want to confide in Julian—to share something more meaningful about herself. "This probably sounds weird," she ventured, "but I think the guesthouse where Wendy and I are staying might be haunted. In fact, I'm pretty sure I saw a ghost on our first night here."

Gilda half-expected Julian to respond with a joke, but instead he became thoughtful. "I saw a ghost once," he said.

"You *did?*"

"I was never quite the same after that night."

As Gilda and Julian walked through Christ Church Meadow, Julian told his story.

16

The Wandering Children

A couple years ago," said Julian, "some of my mates bet me that I couldn't spend the whole night in the cemetery, so I decided to prove them wrong.

"We met in the center of town just before midnight. They handed me a flashlight and a blanket and vowed that they wouldn't play any rotten tricks; it was going to be a completely fair bet. We trotted past the darkened shops and the drunkards wobbling home, then down an alleyway and toward the old churchyard. The church is away from the houses and shops, surrounded by a grove of trees that were creaking in the wind. As we walked under the trees, I kept remembering this old poem my grandfather used to recite to spook us when we were walking at dark:

> *Ellum do grieve,*
> *Oak, he do hate;*
> *Willow do walk when ye travels late.*

"It's a poem about how trees have their own spirits. Elm trees can die of grief if they see another tree being chopped down. Oak trees can be dangerous and mean. But it was the part about the willow tree that always gave me the shivers—the idea that if you're walking alone at night, a willow tree might quietly uproot itself from the ground and tiptoe behind you. Every now and then you'll hear a *swish, swish, swish* sound. Then, just as you look behind, the tree sinks its roots right back into the ground. When you start walking again, it follows you, and gradually this begins to drive you crazy with fear.

"Anyway, in the dark, it all seemed quite plausible—trees tiptoeing around and such—but I had to put a brave face on, of course, and not share any of these thoughts.

"My mates trotted away laughing, leaving me all alone in the cemetery, which was just crammed with rotting tombstones, and I sat down on the cold, damp ground. I couldn't help thinking about how I was surrounded by dead bodies and bones—how all that separated me from them was a few feet of dirt. I nearly had a heart attack every time I heard the crackling of a twig or the hooting of an owl.

"By now I was frozen, and wished I had about three more woolen blankets. I couldn't tell if my eyes were just playing tricks, but all the shadowy tombstones were beginning to look like little people standing all around me. I turned off my flashlight because I didn't like seeing all the names on the tombstones, because knowing the names of all those corpses under the ground would make them too real, reminding me that they actually *were* people. I tried just sitting there with my eyes closed, but that was somehow scarier.

"So my teeth were clacking and practically jumping out of my jaw, and my bones were chilled. Then it started to spit down rain, and that's when I almost got up and left. But I remembered they had bet me twenty quid that I couldn't stay there, and of course I didn't want to lose that dosh. So I convinced myself to give it just another hour, thinking I would get used to everything and stop feeling scared.

"And that's when I saw it. Or—that's when I saw *him*.

"At first glance, it looked like a completely real, ordinary child who was just standing there in the drizzle. But the thing was—I knew he wasn't *supposed* to be there. I knew in my bones that this was not a normal little boy who just happened to climb out of bed and wander from the village into the cemetery in the middle of a rainy night.

"'Are you lost?' I called, just in case he really was a lost child. 'Where's your mum?'

"He didn't answer. Then I noticed that his clothes looked odd, somehow old-fashioned. He looked at me as if he recognized me—that gave me the chills—and then the strangest part happened. He vanished right into thin air.

"So I did what you would expect. I ran. Because I suddenly knew what I had seen. They say that all across England—probably even all over the world—there are ghosts of children who were murdered. They're called 'Wandering Children.'"

Gilda felt her scalp tingle at the spookiness of Julian's story. She also had to squelch an urge to pull out her *Master Psychic's Handbook* to see whether Wandering Children appeared in the index. "So what did you do next?" she asked.

"I went home and had a bath and a cup of tea."

"But—didn't you want to find out that ghost-boy's identity, maybe figure out what happened to him in the past? I mean,

118

maybe there was a reason he materialized in front of you. Maybe he was trying to send you a message!"

"He was trying to scare the pants off me."

"Ghosts don't really set out to frighten anyone, Julian. People just get scared because they're dealing with something they don't understand."

Julian looked annoyed. "Leave it to an American to spoil a good ghost story."

"Leave it to an English boy to go home and have *tea* after seeing a ghost."

"Leave it to an American girl to feel pointlessly superior to tea."

"Look, Julian, I didn't realize you were just telling me a *ghost story*. I thought you said this really happened to you."

"It *did* happen."

"Well, that's why I'm curious about the details." *I can't believe we're already getting in a fight when we haven't even had a chance to become boyfriend and girlfriend*, Gilda thought. *I guess I asked too many questions. Clearly I was just supposed to listen and giggle and not offer my own opinions.*

"Listen," said Julian, "my piano teacher is probably looking for me, and he'll give me a hiding if I don't get to the practice rooms at some point today. Pointless as that may be when Waldgrave is one of the judges, of course."

"Oh, sure." Gilda felt a twinge of regret that Julian appeared to be in a sudden hurry to extricate himself from spending more time with her. "I need to go do some research anyway."

"What kind of research?"

"Oh, just some homework for school. Nothing that would

interest you." At the moment, she no longer wanted to tell him about her work as a psychic investigator.

After Julian left, Gilda sat on a bench at the edge of Dead Man's Walk. She considered heading to the Music Faculty Building to find Wendy, but she didn't want Julian to suspect that she was following him.

A feeling of homesickness came over her, and she felt compelled to write a letter. She knew her mother and her older brother, Stephen, would be expecting a postcard, but she felt the need to write a note to her dad instead.

Dear Dad:

I think I actually had a DATE today! I mean, there WAS a boy there, and we did eat lunch together at a real café, so I've decided to think of it as my first date. His name is Julian.

I know: you're thinking, "I hate the name Julian." But Dad, he's totally cute and funny, and he has this adorable way of talking. I just know the two of you would hit it off.

I might have asked him too many prying questions, though, because he seemed in kind of a hurry to get away at the end—kind of miffed. I don't see why. Ghosts are my area of expertise, right? I guess he has no idea that I'm a psychic investigator, so maybe he just thought I was being annoying.

Well, I AM a psychic investigator, so he's just going to have to get used to it, right? If he becomes my boyfriend, this will probably be something we'll joke about in the future when we look back on our first date—the way you and Mom used to tease each other about how your car got a flat tire the first time you went to the movies together, and how she showed up wearing the highest platform shoes you had ever seen....

"Oh, I remember you asked me a hundred annoying questions," Julian will say. "A real pest, you were!"

Okay—I know. I'm getting carried away!

I miss you, Dad!

Gilda saw that rain clouds were again gathering overhead. Thinking of Julian's story about the Wandering Children, she decided to head toward Blackwell's Bookshop to do some research on English ghosts.

17

The Haunted Melody

The sign outside Wendy's practice room door announced: THIS IS ONE OF TWO SOUNDPROOF PRACTICE ROOMS AT THE MUSIC FACULTY BUILDING. TWO-HOUR TIME LIMIT PLEASE! Inside, the tiny practice room reeked of microwave popcorn, cigarette smoke, and the cedarlike scent of rosin used for stringed instruments.

As she set up the tape-recording equipment she had borrowed from the Music Building, Wendy perceived a distinct patch of cold air near the piano. It reminded her of a feeling she had experienced once while treading water in a northern lake in Michigan—the sensation of moving over a spring of freezing-cold water that bubbled up from the ground. *Gilda would probably say that's a sign of "spirit activity,"* she thought, blowing on her fingers to warm them up.

After adjusting the bench and running some scales and arpeggios, Wendy turned on the tape recorder and took a deep breath before beginning the Mozart Fantasy in D Minor. *I know this piece backward and forward*, she told herself. *Why did I get lost?*

She played through the music from beginning to end, then began once more. As she played, she began to question her interpretation of the music.

"Try to tell a story with the music," Professor Maddox had urged.

"Play the piece the way Mozart would want it played," Professor Waldgrave had argued.

But what is the story? Wendy wondered. *And how should I know how Mozart would play it?*

Wendy stopped playing for a moment and stared into a shaft of sunlight that streamed through a tiny, dirty window, illuminating flecks of lint floating languidly in the air. An answer came to her: *Mozart is telling you about something he dreads. He's telling you he* knows *he's going to die.*

Wendy had no idea *how* this answer popped into her mind, but she began to play the piece again, and this time, she heard the somber tolling of a bell and the echo of a funeral march from within the piano music. She understood now that the bright, major sections of this piece were just *memories* of happy times—ghosts of laughter and dancing that would soon vanish. She remembered that Mozart had died young, struck down by illness. Had he experienced a premonition of his own death? As she played, she had a heightened awareness of the fragility of her own life—a sense of the many fleeting memories that had already disappeared.

When she reached the end of the music, Wendy sat very still, listening to the overtones that hovered in the air for a moment, like a rainbow of sound. *That's it,* she thought. *That's what the judges wanted.*

Goose bumps ran down her arms and legs as she felt the soft touch of a hand on the back of her neck. It was as if someone else in the room was offering a tiny gesture of approval.

Wendy quickly turned to look behind her, but she was alone in the room. *Did that really just happen, or am I going crazy?*

She suddenly remembered reading about a boy who developed schizophrenia—a disease that made him hear voices and see things that weren't really there. *But I can't be schizophrenic,* Wendy told herself. *I'm Wendy Choy—a smart, rational person who's in control of her life.*

As if mocking her, the melody in A minor entered her mind again, interrupting her thoughts with maddening persistence.

"Okay," Wendy said aloud to whomever might be listening. "You win."

Wendy slowly placed her right hand on the keyboard and began to sound out the notes of the melody that haunted her. She was beginning to feel convinced that *somebody* desperately wanted her to play this music.

18

Professor Sabertash and the Tarot

Gilda walked down Broad Street and into Blackwell's Bookshop, where she immediately began perusing texts devoted to ghosts and English hauntings. As she scanned the shelves, Gilda noticed a book that caught her interest entitled *The Oxford Guide to the Tarot* by Alphonse Sabertash. She opened the book and began to read:

> Tarot cards find their beginnings as a mere card game during the Renaissance in Italy. It was only later—during the eighteenth century in particular—that the tarot became known as a powerful, and potentially even dangerous, tool for divination or "fortune-telling."
>
> While the supposed "mystical origins" of tarot cards may be overblown, the magical properties of the tarot are nevertheless very real. This is because the ability of tarot cards to tap into the most intuitive and even psychic potentials of the human mind is a function of the cards' deep-rooted symbolism.
>
> Images on the cards reveal ideas from ancient religions, mythology, fairy tales, and numerology. Even in modern

society, where the original sources of this symbolism have been forgotten or ignored by a culture of amnesia, the symbols retain a vital power to tap into the unconscious regions of the mind.

Gilda flipped through several more chapters until she found an image of the card Wendy had received—the Nine of Swords. She saw that it was from a deck of cards created by the artist Elizabeth Gill.

The Nine of Swords is commonly viewed as "the nightmare card." The card indicates anguish, despair, anxiety, and worry. It may be a signal of cruelty that people inflict on one another, an emotionally intense conflict, or simply of the battle to gain control of one's own mind—the ghosts and demons that may be conjured by fear of the future or a "dark night of the soul."

Intrigued, Gilda flipped to the end of the book in search of some information about the book's author.

Professor Alphonse Sabertash is Professor of History at Merton College in Oxford University. His recent and very diverse published works include *Village of the Damned: Occult Doings in Sixteenth-Century Perigord; The Ghost of Self-Loathing: The Folklore of College-Age Adolescents;* and *Naked with Lampshade Hat: A Social History of Oxford Dons Through the Ages.*

Professor Sabertash lives right here in Oxford! Gilda thought with excitement. *I bet he'd have some insights about the tarot card Wendy received.*

Without wasting a moment, Gilda turned to a clean sheet of paper in her notebook and began to write very quickly:

Dear Professor Sabertash:

I am a scholar from America (oh, that wayward and perpetually adolescent colony!) and an admiring student of your many astute works. My own works-in-progress include the paranormal mystery: Ghost in Miniskirt: The Hard-Boiled Adventures of Psychic Detective Penelope Stunn.

Like you, I have considerable experience with that wily deck of cards we like to call "the tarot." In fact, I have recently stumbled upon a situation here in Oxford that may intrigue you.

I am currently attending the Young International Virtuosos Competition as Page-Turner and Manager for the concert pianist Gwendolyn Choy, and will also be conducting my own researches in Oxford for the next few days.

I am residing in Wyntle House, and would be charmed to make your acquaintance and discuss the mysteries of the tarot over tea with you as soon as possible.

Yours sincerely,
Dame Gilda Joyce,
Psychic Investigator

Gilda decided she would stop by Merton College and drop off her letter on her way to the Music Building to find Wendy.

She carefully folded her note and addressed it to Professor
Sabertash's attention:

TO THE PORTER OF MERTON COLLEGE:
  PLEASE DELIVER THIS URGENT MESSAGE TO THE
ATTENTION OF PROFESSOR ALPHONSE SABERTASH
AT YOUR EARLIEST PORTLY CONVENIENCE.
              YOURS TRULY,
              DAME GILDA JOYCE

19

The Voice

Wendy turned off the tape recorder as Gilda burst into the practice room and tossed her hat on top of the piano. "So!" Gilda brushed a lock of limp, rain-bedraggled hair from her eyes. "What's different about me?"

Wendy scrutinized Gilda. Her cheeks looked happily flushed. Her hair hung in messy, windblown waves, and mud coated the toes of her shoes. It was obvious Gilda had been outside having some sort of interesting experience or adventure—an experience completely opposite of Wendy's own afternoon in the practice room. "Your eyes look kind of glassy," said Wendy with a note of irritation in her voice. "Maybe you're fighting a cold or something."

"I'm in love!" Gilda twirled around in a little pirouette. Somehow, between reading the book about tarot cards and walking down Dead Man's Walk to St. Aldate's Street, she had convinced herself to forget about the little argument she had with Julian.

Wendy stared. "Not with that weird English boy."

"What do you mean, 'weird'? You said Julian was cute."

"No, I didn't."

"You *pinched* me."

"He was okay."

"You *definitely* thought he was cute."

"Okay—so he's cute."

"And you should hear him play the piano! I've never heard anyone play the piano like that; it was like being at a concert..."

Something in Wendy's face seemed to close, and Gilda realized too late that she had stuck her foot in her mouth. "I mean, he doesn't play as well as *you*, but he's pretty good."

"If he plays better than me, he plays better than me," Wendy snapped. "I gave him an easy act to follow, that's for sure."

"If it makes you feel any better, Waldgrave was even tougher on him than he was on you."

Wendy shrugged. "I'm just glad that one of us is having a good time in England."

"Wendy, I would have done something fun with *you*, but you said you wanted to practice."

"I know." Wendy sighed and rummaged through her bag in search of a book of music.

"You know," said Gilda, now staring at the back of Wendy's head, "if *you* were the one who had just told *me* that you were in love, I'd be excited for you. I'd want to hear every detail."

"Oh, really? When I had a boyfriend at music camp, I recall a letter from you telling me to 'spend more time practicing my instrument.'"

"Oh." Gilda had forgotten about this. "Well, that was because you described him as 'a chubby boy who plays trumpet.' I was just looking out for you."

"Whatever."

"Plus, you made it sound as if the two of you were French-kissing in public all over the place. I didn't want you to get a bad reputation."

Wendy pushed the REWIND button on the tape recorder. "Okay." Wendy sighed. "Tell me about Julian. Did you actually *talk* to him?"

"What do you mean? Of course I talked to him!"

"I'm just asking because of the whole Craig Overcash saga back at home. In your mind, you were practically married to him, but I don't think the two of you ever talked for more than thirty seconds."

"I did a tarot card reading for Craig that took exactly six minutes and thirty-two seconds."

"He obviously was your boyfriend."

"Why are you being so snotty?"

Wendy rubbed her temples. "Sorry. I guess this has been a bad day."

"You need a vacation—maybe a trip to a foreign country or something."

"You're a funny person, Gilda."

"Thank you."

"Actually, I really need to use all my reserved time in this practice room. This is the best piano in the building, and I just tape-recorded a bunch of music I want to play back."

"Great!" Gilda sat down in a plastic chair in the corner. "Let's hear it."

Wendy pressed the PLAY button, and the practice room filled with the Mozart D Minor Fantasy. Gilda and Wendy listened to the entire piece in silence. The music sounded different from Wendy's performance earlier in the day, almost as if someone else were playing.

"Wow," said Gilda. "It sounds different, doesn't it?"

Wendy nodded. "I don't know if Mrs. Mendelovich is going to like this interpretation, but I think it sounds better this way."

"It sounds *great*," said Gilda sincerely. "It's like you're telling a story—just like Professor Maddox said you should."

"*Okay,*" said Wendy's small voice from the tape recorder. "*You win.*"

Wendy's face reddened and she quickly turned off the tape recorder.

"Wait a minute! Who were you talking to?"

"Nobody. I was just talking to myself."

Gilda grinned. "So let's hear what you were saying!" When she was younger, in the days before she started keeping a diary, Gilda had often been caught having lively conversations with herself. It was very embarrassing to look up and find her parents giggling as they eavesdropped on her. Now it was her turn to tease Wendy.

"I wasn't saying anything," Wendy insisted.

"Then why the big hurry to turn off the tape recorder?"

"No reason."

Gilda reached past Wendy and turned the tape recorder on. Wendy immediately turned it off.

"I bet you said something about me!"

"You're so self-centered."

A small scuffle ensued, and Gilda managed to sit down on

the piano bench, elbowing Wendy out of the way. Wendy retaliated by pushing Gilda off the piano bench and onto the floor. Gilda pulled herself back up, sat heavily on Wendy's lap, grabbed the tape recorder, and waved it just out of Wendy's reach. "I'm turning this on, Wendy, whether you like it or not!"

"You're squishing me! Get off!"

"Not until we listen to this, Wendy." Gilda turned on the tape recorder.

There was a moment of fuzzy silence followed by the sounds of an unfamiliar melody.

Gilda couldn't help feeling disappointed. "I was hoping you were just about to launch into an embarrassingly personal monologue."

"If I was going to do that, I wouldn't be dumb enough to leave the tape recorder on."

Gilda and Wendy both fell silent, listening to the music.

"That's really pretty," said Gilda quietly. "Kind of haunting. But it's not one of your competition pieces, is it?"

Wendy shook her head. She twirled a lock of hair and tapped her foot nervously.

"Who's the composer?"

"I don't know."

"You don't know?"

"I have *no idea* who the composer is." Wendy met Gilda's eyes with an unusual fierceness, and Gilda immediately understood something.

"This is the music you heard last night in the house, isn't it?"

Wendy encircled her own neck with the palms of her hands, as if trying to protect herself from a vampire bite. "I think it is."

Gilda stood up and began to pace back and forth like a tiger in a small cage. "This is *very interesting*."

"Gilda—" Wendy looked close to tears. "I can't stop thinking about this music. Every time I try to practice my own pieces for the competition, that melody creeps into my mind instead."

Gilda's mind churned with questions. Was the music caused by a genuine haunting? If so, what was the spirit trying to tell Wendy? And what was the connection between the tarot card under Wendy's door and the eerie piano music?

Wendy twirled a lock of hair nervously. "Do you think it's possible I'm losing my mind?"

Gilda held up three fingers. "How many fingers am I holding up?"

"Gilda, I don't have a head injury, so that test doesn't really prove anything."

"What country are we in right now?"

"Guatemala. Gilda, I'm serious."

"Listen, Wendy, I saw a ghost last night, too, so either A) we're both crazy, or B) we've encountered a real haunting."

"What if both are true?"

Gilda decided to ignore this question. "This music you keep hearing... I have a feeling it contains some kind of message."

"Like what?"

Gilda rummaged through her bag and found her pen and notebook. "Why don't you play the melody again, and I'll write down the names of the notes?"

"Worth a try, I guess." Wendy placed her right hand on the keyboard and began to call out the notes as she played, "A, B, C, D, C, B, C..."

"Wait—slow down."

"...B, A, G, G, F, F, G, A..."

After Gilda took notes for several more phrases, the two girls sat on the piano bench, feeling baffled as they stared at the scribbled letters.

"If we look at these letters as an anagram," Gilda suggested, "I can see the word *bag*." Gilda wrote the word *bag* in the margin of her notebook. "I also see the word *cab*."

"I've never heard of a ghost communicating with an anagram."

"If a ghost can play an invisible piano, why shouldn't it create an anagram? Anyway, I thought you were supposed to be good at cracking codes. The world's greatest cryptographers are good at math."

"It takes longer than three minutes to crack a code, Gilda. Besides, we don't even know if we're looking at a code here. What if it's just a *melody*?"

Gilda thought for a moment. "Okay, maybe you're right. Let's listen to the tape again to see if we notice any other clues."

Wendy hit PLAY and the girls closed their eyes to listen carefully. The music had a simple, mournful quality, like a folk song sung by a single voice. As Wendy played, she had gradually added some dissonant harmony in the left hand.

Just then, a strange sound interrupted the tape—an electronic-sounding *voice* that didn't sound anything like Wendy.

"What was *that*?"

"I have no idea. Maybe some kind of interference?"

Gilda pushed REWIND and restarted the tape. Both girls leaned forward, listening.

As the melody began again, Gilda heard the distinct sound of a very high-pitched, reedy voice *speaking* on the tape.

Wendy shivered. "That's so creepy."

"Wendy, is there any way that could be *you* making that sound?"

"It doesn't sound like me. Besides, I don't talk while I'm playing—at least, not that I'm aware of."

Gilda rewound the tape once more and turned up the volume. The voice had a slightly mechanical, inhuman quality, but something also suggested the sound of a child speaking, as if the tape had picked up a young person playing and talking in another room.

Gilda and Wendy stared at the tape recorder warily, as if they had just realized that the machine was possessed by a sinister force.

"I've read about using tape recorders in psychic investigations," Gilda whispered, "but I've never actually tried it before. In my *Psychic's Handbook*, Balthazar Frobenius says you're supposed to use an external microphone just like the one you're using. He also says that if you actually hear a ghost's voice on tape it probably won't sound human."

"But why didn't I notice the voice while I was playing?"

"Because it's like the ghost has to use the tape recorder as a kind of mechanical voice box in order to be heard. You can't hear the ghost until you play back the tape."

"If that's a ghost talking, I can't understand a word it's saying."

Gilda had another idea: she slowed down the speed of the

tape before playing it back. Now the piano music sounded low and warped.

Wendy wrinkled her nose. "Yuck—I hate hearing the music that way."

"Just wait."

Out of the murky piano music, a voice spoke very faintly. It sounded deeper now—more human.

"Fry wide," the voice said, followed by something completely indistinguishable.

"Fry wide?" Wendy asked. "What does *that* mean?"

"Tea cull," said the voice, followed by "fry wide" once more.

Gilda hurriedly scribbled "fry wide" and "tee cull" in her notebook, having no idea whether these sounds were actual words. One thing was for sure: they were listening to a real voice.

"For all we know, it could be speaking in another language," Wendy pointed out.

They listened to the tape for a few more minutes, but the voice said nothing more.

"So what do we do now?"

The girls looked at each other, not wanting to admit that they both felt out of their depth. As far as they knew, it was the most direct encounter with the supernatural that either of them had ever experienced.

20

A Visit from a Stranger

While the guests of Wyntle House were away at the piano competition, Mrs. Luard made the mistake of perching precariously on a three-legged stool while peering up into her kitchen cabinets to search for a tin of chocolate-chip biscuits. She had hidden the biscuits on a high shelf to keep them from her son, Danny. Ever since the local GP had warned Mrs. Luard that her sixteen-year-old son had the circulatory system of a forty-year-old, she had been trying to help Danny by hiding the fat-filled snacks they had formerly shared.

"Drat him!" Mrs. Luard realized that the biscuits were gone; not only had Danny already discovered them, he had also hidden his own stash of jelly-roll snacks and potato crisps from *her*.

Mrs. Luard reached even higher to grab the crisps that Danny had placed in a far corner of the cabinet when she suddenly lost her balance, causing the stool to topple over. A searing pain shot through her leg as she fell heavily to the ground.

Yapping with agitation, her little dog, Bunny, trotted into the room to investigate the crashing noise.

"Danny!" Mrs. Luard gasped. "Danny! My leg's broken because of you and your crisps!"

Bunny licked Mrs. Luard's leg helpfully.

"What you want, Mum?" Danny called from the next room.

"Danny!"

"I'm watching telly."

"Get in here, *now*!"

Danny lumbered slowly to the door. He stared blankly at the heap of his mother on the floor. "Your leg looks wonky."

"It's bloody broken!"

"What were you doing, then?"

"Never mind what I was doing. What did you do with them biscuits I had up in the cabinet?" Mrs. Luard was not about to let the shooting pain in her calf make her forget the true cause of her injury.

"Nothing."

"You found them, and you ate them." Mrs. Luard winced.

"No, I didn't."

"You did."

"We should get you to a doctor," said Danny. "And I didn't."

When Gilda returned to Wyntle House later that afternoon, she decided on impulse to knock on Mrs. Luard's door in hopes of questioning her about the strange occurrences in Wyntle House.

"Come in!" yelled Mrs. Luard without getting up. As always, Bunny jumped up and down in a frenzy of shrill barking.

Gilda found Mrs. Luard and Danny sitting on the couch with

a large bag of crisps between them. Mrs. Luard's leg was set in a plaster cast and propped up on a pillow.

"As you can see, I've broken my leg," said Mrs. Luard, "so you'll have to forgive me for not getting up, luv. Please come in. Have you met my son, Danny?"

"Nice to meet you."

Danny mumbled a response and shot Gilda a sullen glance before returning to his television show, which appeared to be some kind of mystery featuring a grumpy middle-aged detective.

"How did you break your leg?"

"I had a battle with a footstool this morning. The footstool won."

Gilda noticed Mrs. Luard's crutches leaning against the couch and an assortment of pills and liquid medications on a side table. In one corner of the room, there was an ominous contraption that resembled an oxygen tank, and the remnants of carryout containers cluttered a small coffee table. The room was dark and Gilda perceived the faint odor of feet. She watched as Danny stuffed a handful of crisps into his mouth.

"Danny helps me run the place, don't you, Danny?"

Danny nodded without looking at Gilda.

"He's a dab hand with the repairs and upkeep."

"That's good to know," said Gilda. "I think the shower upstairs is broken." She couldn't help thinking that Danny didn't seem to be much of a "dab hand" with anything that didn't involve potato chips.

"Have to turn on the switch," said Danny, still not looking at Gilda, as if actually looking at her while talking would be an admission of some defeat. "Americans always get that wrong. I had three people knocking on my door this morning with that same question."

Gilda couldn't remember seeing any "switch," but she decided not to press Danny further since the process of speaking seemed to irritate him. Besides, she sensed that he and his mother wanted to watch their television show, and she needed to ask a few probing questions while she had a chance.

"Something we can help you with, luv?"

"I just had a question about the house."

"It's a push button what flushes the toilet," said Danny.

"It's not a question about the *toilet*," said Gilda. "I wondered if you've ever noticed anything unusual about this house—any evidence of a haunting?"

"You're asking if we have a ghost?" Mrs. Luard peered at her with slightly unfocused eyes that seemed dilated from medication.

"My friend Wendy and I heard some strange noises, and I actually saw something in my room—something that looked like the ghost of a boy."

Mrs. Luard looked at her son. "Have you seen any ghost-boys in Wyntle House, Danny?" She seemed amused.

Danny shook his head wryly.

"No ghosts here, luv," said Mrs. Luard.

"We don't do refunds for hauntings, neither," Danny added.

"I wasn't going to ask for a refund."

"You want Danny to go check out your room for you, then? Make sure everything's okay?"

Gilda could tell that the last thing Danny wanted was to leave his television show to trudge up four flights of steps. That was fine with her: the last thing she needed was Danny glumly checking under her bed for ghosts.

"Thanks anyway," said Gilda. "Hauntings are an area of interest for me, so I thought I'd ask you about it before conducting my own investigation."

"Hauntings are an area of interest, eh?"

"I'm a psychic investigator." Gilda usually pursued her work in secret, but every now and then she felt compelled to blurt out the truth about herself—sometimes in blunt reaction to a dismissive remark. It was as if she needed to remind herself that her interests weren't pointless and silly.

Mrs. Luard peered at Gilda with clearer eyes, as if realizing for the first time that Gilda viewed ghosts as an enhancement to her stay at Wyntle House rather than a cause for customer complaint. "Well, there may be a ghost or two in this old house," she said. "And there are lots of ghosts in Oxford, aren't there, Danny?"

"Sure," said Danny, reaching for more crisps.

"You've had enough crisps now, Danny," said Mrs. Luard. "Isn't there a beheaded ghost that kicks his head around the grounds of one of the colleges? St. John's, I think it was."

"Could be." Danny crunched his crisps as he spoke, as if making it clear that the topic of ghosts filled him with exquisite boredom. "There's a bunch of headless spirits roaming 'round, I 'spect."

"And I'm sure you've heard about the ghost of Rosamund the Fair, who haunts Godstow Nunnery," Mrs. Luard added.

Gilda was intrigued; she hadn't heard of Rosamund the Fair.

"Everybody's heard of her," said Danny. "And you call yourself a psychic investigator?"

"If you can call yourself a dab hand," Gilda blurted, "I can call myself a psychic investigator."

"I never did call myself a dab hand; that's what Mum calls me!"

"Hush, Danny. We have to be polite to our guests." Mrs. Luard regarded Gilda blearily. "Rosamund was the secret girlfriend of one of them kings of long ago—King Henry the second, I believe. The king kept her locked away in a secret garden, hidden deep in a maze so full of twists and turns, nobody could find her. In fact, in order to find his own way to Rosamund, the king had to tie one end of a very long piece of string to her finger and the other end of the string to a knight who stood outside the maze guarding her.

"Well, as luck would have it, the king's wife found out about Rosamund. She killed the knight, followed the string to Rosamund, and forced her to drink a glass of deadly poison. And ever since, Rosamund haunts the ruins of the nunnery here in Oxford."

"I thought she haunted the Trout Pub," said Danny.

"Maybe she haunts both."

Gilda couldn't help wondering if everyone in Oxford had a ghost story to tell. *Maybe ghosts are so abundant here, you can't help but encounter them*, she thought.

"Well, thanks," said Gilda. "That was an interesting story."

"Hope Danny and I didn't scare you, luv."

"I don't scare that easily," said Gilda, turning to leave.

"Someone left you a message today," Danny blurted, delivering this non sequitur with what struck Gilda as a slightly sinister smile.

"Who?"

Danny shrugged. "Odd-looking bloke. A stranger." He continued watching television without explaining himself further.

"Well—what was the *message* from this mysterious stranger?" Gilda found it difficult to refrain from rushing across the room and giving the chubby boy a good hard shake.

Danny shrugged. "I left it outside your door."

What 'odd-looking bloke' could have left her a message? Something about the slight smirk on Danny's face made Gilda feel suspicious.

"Fine," said Gilda. "I'll go see what it says."

Propped against the door to Gilda's room was a folded piece of stationery. She opened the tissue-thin paper with a feeling of anticipation. *Maybe it's from Julian*, she thought hopefully.

As she began to read the fountain-pen handwriting, she was stunned. The note was from Professor Sabertash.

Dear Dame Gilda:

Many thanks for your most intriguing missive. So many of the situations that interest me took place long ago, so it would be a treat to learn about something going on in present-day Oxford.

Your letter suggested some urgency. Perhaps we could discuss this further over a glass of sherry in my rooms at 6 P.M. tonight? Ask at the Porter's Lodge for directions to my lair.

Professor Alphonse Sabertash

TO: Gilda Joyce

FROM: Gilda Joyce

RE: INVESTIGATION PROGRESS REPORT

A surprising success!:

I just received an invitation from
Professor Sabertash--an Oxford don and an
expert in the tarot!

I'll wear my most sophisticated outfit and
do a brilliant acting job, and with any
luck, he won't realize he's just invited a
ninth-grader to visit him at the college.
This will definitely take all my undercover
skills!

WYNTLE HOUSE UPDATE:

Mrs. Luard and her son admitted that
there "might be a couple ghosts in Wyntle
House," but they wouldn't reveal any interesting stories about the apparition I saw
in my room. I am suspicious of that boy
Danny; he seems weirdly unfriendly, considering the fact that it's supposed to be
his job to help run a guesthouse. Besides,
he's always smirking about something. On
the other hand, he might just be bored
with explaining the shower and toilet to
visiting Americans.

(Oops--I'd better hurry! I don't have
much time, and I still have to type up
today's travel diary entry and select my
most sophisticated clothes and makeup to
visit Professor Sabertash!)

TO: Mrs. Rawson—English Instructor, USA
FROM: Gilda Joyce
RE: TRAVEL DIARY ENTRY—British
    "Words of the Day"

Hi, Mrs. Rawson. It just tickles me how
the English and the Americans are forever
divided by the same language! Here are a
few tips I've picked up, just in case you
ever venture across the ocean to this
island nation and find yourself wanting a
snack: in England, potato chips are
"crisps," cookies are "biscuits," and des-
sert is "pudding" or "a pud." If anyone
offers you "bangers and mash" or "spotted
dick," don't try to send them to the prin-
cipal's office or run away screaming! Just
smile, grab a fork, and dig into some sausage and mashed potatoes followed by a
cake with raisins and custard on top. Yum!

21

Professor Sabertash

Gilda arrived at Professor Sabertash's rooms in Merton College just as an undergraduate was leaving her tutorial in tears.

"How could anyone be so brutal?" the girl sniffed, digging into a large shoulder bag for a tissue. Smudges of mascara and eyeliner rimmed her red eyes. Her puffy tulip skirt and flat, pointy shoes reminded Gilda of an elf's costume. "I worked and worked on that essay, and that Sabertash—he wasn't satisfied until every single one of my points was completely and utterly destroyed!"

"That's terrible." Gilda wasn't sure what to say. She had half a mind to turn and run back down the stairs. If Professor Sabertash routinely drove his college students to tears, how on earth would he receive a fourteen-year-old posing as a serious scholar?

But it was too late to turn back: as the tearful girl fled, Professor Sabertash thrust open the door and beamed at Gilda quizzically through thick, cloudy glasses. "Dame Gilda, I presume?"

"Pleased to make your acquaintance, Professor Sabertash." Gilda nervously extended her gloved hand. Tufts of unruly hair sprouted from the professor's nose, ears, and eyebrows. A bit of elastic from his underwear peeked out over his pants and shirt, and a few splotches of mustard from a high table lunch decorated his lapel.

"You'll have to excuse me," said Professor Sabertash, shaking her hand and squinting into her face. "I'm nearly blind as a mole!"

Gilda couldn't believe her luck. As far as she could tell, Professor Sabertash was too near-sighted to see that she was considerably younger than her letter had implied.

"Please, do come in! I do hope my last tutorial of the day didn't pester you with her tears."

"In my view, it isn't a proper lesson if someone isn't sobbing." Gilda did her best to play the role of a self-assured dame of the British Empire as she followed Professor Sabertash into a large, square room complete with a fireplace, several plush couches and armchairs, and a table stocked with china teacups, wineglasses, and bottles of sherry and port. The entire circumference of the room was lined floor-to-ceiling with overstuffed bookshelves.

"I'm opening a bottle of sherry in honor of your visit," said Professor Sabertash. "I hope you'll join me?" Professor Sabertash held a small wineglass in the air.

"Of course." Gilda hoped that "sherry" referred to either a very girlish drink with whipped cream or something akin to a Slurpee. "I'll have a tiny umbrella and a cherry in mine," she added.

Professor Sabertash laughed uproariously as he held a wineglass toward Gilda.

"On second thought, I think I'll pass," said Gilda. "I like to keep my wits about me when I'm involved in an investigation."

"As you wish, Dame Gilda." Professor Sabertash swirled his glass and gestured for Gilda to take a seat in one of the armchairs. "Now before we begin discussing your intriguing findings, I must confess, Dame Gilda, that I am curious. You say you are American, on a visit here to supervise a young concert pianist, yet you speak with a most unusual regional English accent. Furthermore, Queen Elizabeth has made you a dame for your scholarly contributions to the field of paranormal studies, and as we know being granted what is essentially a knighthood is a most rare achievement for an American woman. Indeed, I suspect you have had a most interesting life."

"I have had an interesting life, indeed," said Gilda, realizing that impulsively giving herself the title "dame" in her letter to the professor now required an elaborate fabrication if she was to maintain her inflated identity. "My life has been so utterly overwhelmed with sordid intrigue and complications, I couldn't begin to explain it all to you, Professor Sabertash."

"Oh, but that makes me all the more curious, Dame Gilda!" Professor Sabertash raised a finger in the air. "First, I am guessing you were born here in England but are a dual citizen of the U.S. and U.K., no?"

"Yes, that's correct," Gilda fibbed, thinking it was easier to simply let Professor Sabertash stitch together a plausible life story than to make one up herself.

"And I can hear a hint of the American Midwest in your speech, no?"

"Right again. Much of my recent work has taken place in the city of Detroit—or *Daytwah* as the French say."

"Yes, yes. I have a good ear, you see, the better to make up for my failing eyesight. When the senses are blunted in one aspect they become stronger in another, don't you think?"

"Absolutely."

"But this—this Midwestern *twang* in your voice is intertwined with an accent that is from a part of England that, I must confess, *eludes* me. Tell me—*where* did you grow up in England?"

"Oh, it was a place you've never heard of, and hopefully will never visit," said Gilda. "A quite dreary village called—called Piddle Itchington."

"That must be in the north."

"It's actually in the east," said Gilda, feeling by now that she had absolutely no idea what she was talking about. "But I'd prefer not to go into that part of my life, if you don't mind."

"I understand. You came here to talk about more important matters. Matters of research into the tarot!"

"I was hoping you could shed some light on a little mystery I've stumbled into here in Oxford."

Professor Sabertash leaned forward eagerly. "I am at your service, Dame Gilda."

Gilda took a deep breath and told Professor Sabertash about the strange events that followed her arrival in Oxford: the vision of a boy's face in her room, the voice on Wendy's tape recorder, the music Wendy heard in the night, the disturbing tarot card that turned up in Wendy's room without explanation.

"Wonderful! I just knew you would bring some interesting tidbits to whet my appetite, Dame Gilda. Now, may I take a peek at the tarot card that appeared so mysteriously under young Gwendolyn's door?"

Gilda showed him the Nine of Swords, and Professor Sabertash peered at it through a magnifying glass.

"Ah yes. This card is from the Gill deck of tarot cards—a deck that uses symbolism from Kabbalistic numerology. As you see, the back of the card has an image of the tree of life—a tree made up of ten spheres. This tree represents a map of the universe and the human psyche. From a scholarly perspective, I myself do not prefer this deck of cards, as I feel there is no true connection between the Kabbalah and the tarot. . . ."

Gilda hated to admit it, but she was already feeling slightly baffled. "But Professor Sabertash—what do you think receiving this version of the Nine of Swords *means*?"

"As I'm sure you know, Dame Gilda, the number nine in this deck may represent the realm of the subconscious mind, things that are hidden and not completely obvious. It is supposed to suggest deeply buried anxieties, secret agendas—things of that nature. We see in the picture that this person stands alone upon an empty plane and that nine swords are thrust into the ground around him or her. This could symbolize pain, or some injury to the self. *If* there is a message in this card, I would describe it as: look for what is hidden. And perhaps—look for what is hidden in *yourself.*"

Gilda thought about how, ever since they had arrived in England, Wendy had seemed different—as if constantly disturbed and preoccupied by something Gilda couldn't perceive or understand. But what secret could Wendy be hiding? And what did this have to do with a haunting?

"Professor Sabertash, this might sound odd, but I'm wondering if a ghost might have left this tarot card as a kind of message for Wendy. There's been evidence of a haunting in Wyntle House."

"Certainly that is possible." Professor Sabertash drained his glass of sherry. "You also mentioned that your young friend has been hearing music in the night. Some might view this as evidence that she's discovering some clairaudient abilities. Maybe these experiences are related in some way."

For a moment, Gilda almost felt jealous that Wendy might be developing such a valuable psychic skill. "You think Wendy can *hear* spirits?"

"As I said, some would suggest this explanation, particularly for a sensitive pianist who most likely has very acute hearing."

I bet Wendy wouldn't even want to be clairaudient, Gilda thought. While Wendy shared Gilda's psychic interests, she always preferred to operate in the realm of logical reasoning.

"Now, having said this, I must acknowledge, Dame Gilda, that particularly where young people are involved, my natural skepticism becomes yet more skeptical, if you follow me."

"I don't follow you, Professor Sabertash."

Professor Sabertash stood up and accidentally knocked over several glasses as he attempted to pour himself another helping of sherry. "Oh, bother!" He stooped to pick up the glasses. "While I am always open-minded and open to the *possibility* of a true haunting—and indeed, have encountered a sparse handful of cases that have no other known explanation—we both know the fundamental difference between you and me in our researches, Dame Gilda."

"What's that, Professor Sabertash?"

"In most cases, I don't actually *believe* in this sort of thing, of course."

"You *don't?*" Gilda couldn't help feeling shocked. She had assumed that anybody who would take the time to write books about the tarot and other occult subjects must believe they had some validity.

Professor Sabertash sat down, crossed his legs, and twiddled his foot as if using it to direct a miniature orchestra. "I merely find it interesting that *others* believed these things years ago and still continue to believe these things today. I like to understand *why* people believe things. Most often, it has to do with the manifestation of human fear."

Gilda couldn't help feeling disappointed. She had hoped Professor Sabertash might do a tarot card reading for her or demonstrate some new technique for conducting séances. Instead, he was sipping sherry and telling her that he was skeptical about the whole concept of ghosts.

"Now, I must say—it was an entirely different story for a quite brilliant graduate school colleague of mine whose studies led him to a great conviction that ghosts are absolutely real, that spirits roam the earth, and that the mind has vast, untapped potential to know things that can't be observed. He was an American, but it was at Oxford that he realized he was a true psychic—and a quite convincing one, too, despite the scoffing of his college tutors. Following a series of formal spring balls where he dressed in some absolutely garish costumes, he disappeared entirely—simply left town and never returned to finish his degree. The last I heard, he was on a journey throughout the world in search of paranormal activity. I recall that he had begun to call himself something quite outlandish... Balthazar Frobenius, I believe it was..."

Professor Sabertash looked startled because Gilda suddenly jumped to her feet, as if ready to salute someone. "Balthazar Frobenius is my hero!"

"So you've met him."

"Well, no. But I'd love to meet him someday. I carry his *Master Psychic's Handbook* with me everywhere! Do you know where I could find him these days?"

"I'm afraid not," said Professor Sabertash. "He keeps a very low profile and certainly has never returned to Oxford to visit his old haunts, so to speak—at least not to my knowledge."

"Oh." Gilda sat down. "I wish I could ask him some questions."

"He would be touched to have such an accomplished follower of his works," said Sabertash. "Now, Dame Gilda, I hate to cut our delightful conversation short, but if you'll excuse me, I must head to high table for the dinner hour."

"Oh—okay. I should be going, too." Gilda paused at the doorway. Their interview seemed incomplete; she had been hoping to find answers that still eluded her.

"Something else I can assist you with, Dame Gilda?"

"Professor Sabertash, I'm sure *something* very strange is going on at this piano competition, but it's hard to know how to go about investigating it."

Professor Sabertash made a tent with his hands, pressing his two index fingers against his mouth. "Keep your mind attuned to the signs that speak to you, Dame Gilda, and they will lead you to the source of the mystery."

"I'll do my best," said Gilda, nodding.

Professor Sabertash chuckled. "That was actually something Balthazar Frobenius used to say. My response to him was, 'Keep looking for ghosts, and you will surely find them.'"

22

The Clue in the Bookshelf

When Gilda returned to Wyntle House, something on the small bookshelf next to her bed caught her attention. The spine of one of the clothbound books protruded noticeably from the bookshelf, as if someone had pulled it out as a reading suggestion for her. *As if someone WANTED me to look at it*, Gilda thought. She noticed a distinct ⬛️ in her left ear as she pulled the book from the shelf and read the title, *Alice in Wonderland*. As a child, Gilda had been intrigued by the idea of a girl who falls down a rabbit hole and finds herself tr.⬛️d in a nonsensical underground world where animals and even playing cards talk—a place where snacking on little cakes could make a person as tall as a tree or as small as a caterpillar. The fact that none of her friends had actually *read* the story (they had only seen the Disney movie) made its strangeness all the more appealing.

Gilda flipped through the pages of *Alice in Wonderland* and felt a surge of interest when she reached the chapter about the ⬛️ad Tea Party. An illustration depicted a rather insane-looking man and a long-eared rabbit called the March Hare having a tea party at a table piled high with dirty dishes. A dormouse was telling a story about three little sisters who lived at the bottom of a well.

"What did they live on?" said Alice, who always took a great interest in questions of eating and drinking.

"They lived on treacle," said the Dormouse, after thinking a minute or two.

"They couldn't have done that, you know," Alice gently remarked; "they'd have been ill."

"So they were," said the Dormouse; "VERY ill."

Gilda considered the word *treacle*, feeling, for some reason, that something about the word was significant. Wasn't treacle supposed to be sticky and sweet, like molasses? She pictured three sisters living in the bottom of a well eating nothing but treacle, and decided this was actually a bizarre, scary idea.

On impulse, Gilda sat down at her typewriter and punched in the phrase she and Wendy had heard on the tape recorder:

```
"tea cull"
```

Maybe it was a long shot . . . but was it possible the voice was actually saying "treacle"? Gilda leaned back and stared at the letters she had typed. "But why in the world would a ghost want to tell us about *treacle*?" she asked herself.

She remembered Professor Sabertash's comment: "Keep your mind attuned to the signs that speak to you." She decided there must be some significance to the fact that the book had been left protruding from the shelf—that she had been drawn to reading the Mad Tea Party chapter in particular. *Maybe it's not just treacle that's significant but something about the story of* Alice in Wonderland, *Gilda thought.*

The wind outside rose, rattling the shutters on the window. Gilda climbed into her narrow, sagging bed and curled up to read *Alice in Wonderland* under the covers.

In room number nine, Wendy lay in bed, trying to fall asleep—trying not to listen to Gary splashing childishly in the bathtub with his toy submarine, trying not to think about her flawed performance in the first round of the competition, and trying not to think about Mrs. Mendelovich, who had seemed to ignore her during dinner that evening. She, Ming Fong, Gary, and Mrs. Mendelovich had sat together at a table, but when Mrs. Mendelovich put her arms around Gary and Ming Fong, she seemed to avoid Wendy's eyes. Throughout the evening, Wendy felt as if her disappointing performance in the first round of the competition was an invisible but disturbing ghost in the room. Throughout the evening, she sensed Ming Fong's silent scrutiny.

Stop thinking, Wendy ordered herself. *You have a sight-reading competition tomorrow, and you need your sleep.*

But when Wendy closed her eyes, she found something waiting for her, blocking her sleep. Beginning softly at first, then growing louder, the ghost music wafted up the stairs, through the thin walls of Wyntle House, and into her bedroom.

23

The Five of Swords

Julian took Gilda's hands and gazed into her eyes. "Stay with me," he said. "Stay with me here in England. Don't go back to that gormless country where nobody could ever understand or appreciate you. Stay here."

I can't believe I'm here, Gilda thought. *Here I am, sitting in a boat and punting down the River Thames with Julian!*

Julian suddenly seized her hands, pulled her to her feet, and kissed her fiercely on the lips, causing the two of them to lose their balance and topple into the icy water. They gasped for air, splashed each other, and then drew close in another eager embrace.

"Don't you know that water's narsty?!" a plump, scruffy-looking boy yelled to them from the shore. "You lot will get rat syphilis in that river!"

Gilda felt a wave of revulsion when she realized that Mrs. Luard's son, Danny, had been watching them the entire time.

The hysterical buzzing of an alarm clock jolted Gilda awake. She slammed her fist down, attempting to turn it off, but only succeeded in knocking it to the floor, where the clock buzzed even louder.

"Shut up! Shut up!" Gilda finally managed to silence the alarm. She shivered under the covers, not wanting to face the cold, damp chill of the morning air. Then she remembered that today was the sight-reading competition—the day when she would actually share the spotlight onstage with Wendy.

The idea of being scrutinized by the audience in the Holywell Music Room—and possibly by Julian—motivated Gilda to spring out of bed and splash water on her face. After all, she would need enough time to select the perfect outfit. She also had to make sure that Wendy didn't oversleep again.

Hearing someone in the hallway, Gilda peeked through the doorway and was relieved to see Wendy exiting the bathroom with wet hair and strawberry shampoo in hand.

Gilda gave Wendy a thumbs-up sign. "You got up in time for your ritual!"

"Shh! I don't want everybody knowing about that."

"We're gonna blow everybody out of the water today, Wendy."

"Just get dressed, okay?"

Gilda returned to her room and decided to wear her "tainted royalty" outfit—a Queen Elizabeth–inspired monochromatic dress and jacket that she dressed up with white gloves, a long strand of fake pearls, a felt hat, fishnet stockings, and stiletto heels. She decided she would also wear her giant fake-diamond cocktail ring over the gloves to add some flair to her page-turning.

Heading toward the communal bathroom, Gilda encountered Ming Fong, who emerged from her room wearing a dress every bit as frilly and Victorian as the one she had worn for her first performance. She wore lacy tights and Mary Jane shoes, and carried her music in a tote bag printed with the business name HAPPY NAILS!

"Gilda!" Ming Fong stage-whispered. "I got one, too!"

"You got one what?"

Ming Fong pulled something from her Happy Nails tote bag and waved it in the air. "See?" She handed Gilda a tarot card— the Five of Swords. The card depicted a blood-red sky with one bright sword pointing toward the heavens and four swords pointing downward, toward ominous clouds below. There was a single word printed on the card: LOSS.

The card was nearly as disturbing as the Nine of Swords that Wendy had received, but Gilda couldn't help regarding Ming Fong warily. *Did Ming Fong plant this on herself to make me less suspicious?* Ming Fong certainly didn't seem upset to receive the card; she seemed almost happy to find it.

"Someone wants me to lose," Ming Fong declared brightly.

"That could be true," said Gilda. "But I think the Five of Swords can also mean you're going to lose some illusion about yourself."

"Someone wants me to work less hard," Ming Fong insisted. "Give up and lose competition."

Gilda had to admit this was possible. *Is there someone sneaking around who wants to sabotage both Wendy and Ming Fong? Or is this yet more evidence of a weird haunting—a ghost that tries to communicate using tarot cards?*

"Ming Fong, do you have any idea who might have given this to you?" Gilda thought for a moment. "Do you think it could be Gary?"

Ming Fong wrinkled her nose and shook her head as if this idea didn't appeal to her at all. "No, no. Cards left by somebody very *jealous*," she said brightly. "Maybe Wendy?"

"Look, Ming Fong, Wendy didn't do this. For one thing, she isn't jealous of you, and for another thing, she doesn't waste her time trying to play mind games with other musicians in the competition."

Ming Fong peered at Gilda slyly. "Maybe *you*? You know all about cards."

Gilda was surprised at Ming Fong's ability to turn the tables on her. She had to admit Ming Fong had a good point: her own interest in tarot card readings would make her a very likely suspect. "Good try, but it wasn't me."

"Not me either."

Gilda sighed. "Then would you mind if I took a quick look in your room? I just want to see if whoever left this for you also left any clues behind." Secretly, Gilda wanted to check for evidence that Ming Fong herself was the culprit.

"I must practice now."

"It'll just take a minute."

"You need a shower."

"That can wait, too." Before Ming Fong could protest further, Gilda breezed into a tiny room that looked almost identical to her own: the main difference was that Ming Fong's bed was neatly made, and no clothes, books, shoes, or teacups were strewn about. Gilda peered into a red bucket that contained Ming Fong's toothbrush, toothpaste, and shampoo—a functional bucket completely devoid of frivolous toiletries like hairbrushes, lip gloss, or perfume. Ming Fong's suitcase was propped open next to her bed, and inside Gilda saw another neatly folded frilly dress, probably the one she hoped to wear in the next round of the competition.

"I like your dresses," Gilda lied. "Where do you do your shopping?"

Ming Fong shrugged. "My mom goes shopping."

I bet her mom forces her to wear those dresses, Gilda thought.

Gilda surveyed the room, boldly peeking into drawers and under Ming Fong's bed as Ming Fong tapped her foot and shifted her tote bag from one arm to the other, clearly wishing that Gilda would leave.

Just as Gilda was about to give up, she slyly peeked inside the drawer of Ming Fong's writing table and noticed something interesting—a small, framed photograph of a handsome Asian boy with short, spiky hair. The boy looked much older than Ming Fong—possibly in his late teens or early twenties. Next to the photograph was a red silk flower that matched the flower Ming Fong wore in her hair.

"Who's in the picture?" Gilda tried to sound nonchalant, but she was burning with curiosity. Something seemed very special and significant about both the picture and the flower. Did Ming Fong have a secret boyfriend, or was this just someone for whom she harbored a crush?

Ming Fong's face reddened. "Lang Lang, of course." A note of contempt entered her voice, as if failing to recognize Lang Lang was a sign of complete idiocy. "Best and most youngest pianist in the world."

Now Gilda vaguely remembered hearing Wendy mention something about the concert pianist Lang Lang: *"My father's dream is that I'll become the next Lang Lang,"* or something like that.

"Why do you have his picture?"

"For good luck."

"Does it work?"

Ming Fong nodded. "Always works." Ming Fong shifted her Happy Nails tote bag uncomfortably. Gilda squinted at the bag, suddenly wanting to seize it and rummage through the contents. What if Ming Fong was hiding some important evidence in there with her music?

"I must practice," said Ming Fong. Before Gilda could question her further, she hurried through her bedroom door, then down the hallway. "Bye, Gilda!" she sang. "Good luck!"

Gilda glanced at her watch and realized she had better hurry, too. She had only a few minutes to get ready, and Wendy needed to get to the Holywell Music Room on time.

24

An Icy Message

Gilda burst into Wendy's room and found her best friend perched on her bed, staring at something in the window. She didn't even turn to greet Gilda.

"Hey, Wendy—what are you doing?"

"Just look."

Then Gilda saw what transfixed Wendy—an intricate design of sparkling white frost coated the windowpane.

"Hey, the temperature must have really dropped last night!" Moving closer to the window, Gilda noticed something else— the reason Wendy seemed almost hypnotized. Etched in hoarfrost in a corner of the glass pane was a distinct shape—*the number nine.*

"Do you *see* it?"

Gilda scrutinized the crystalline pattern of the 9, which struck her as a uniquely miraculous—or ominous—fluke of nature.

"What are the chances that the frost would form this specific design on my window?"

"Very unlikely, I think." Gilda sat next to Wendy and stared at the window. The delicate nine certainly didn't appear to be the work of a person tracing a shape with a finger or a stick. *Besides,* Gilda thought, *the frost is outside the window, and this room is at the top floor. Somebody would have to climb up there with a fireman's ladder to write this in the window on purpose.*

"I feel like it's a message someone left on purpose," said Wendy. "And to be honest, it's really freaking me out."

Gilda hated to admit it, but she felt scared, too. There was something far too ominous and inexplicable about the number nine in the window. "Wendy," she said, "remember how I told you I was going to meet that expert on tarot cards and stuff like that?"

"Gilda—I'm the one who covered for you, remember? Mrs. Mendelovich was wondering what you were doing at dinnertime yesterday. Don't tell me this tarot card expert is your new boyfriend."

"Oh, please. His underwear was over his pants and he was practically wearing his lunch. Not to mention the fact that he was about sixty years old."

"Sounds like your type."

"As I was *saying,* this professor told me that the Nine of Swords you received—and the number nine in general—could mean you're supposed to 'look for something that's hidden.'" Gilda paused. "He also said it's possible you're becoming clairaudient. I mean, he wasn't sure, but he said it could be a possibility."

"Clairaudient?"

"It means you might be able to hear ghosts talking to you—or you might hear things that happened in the past."

"I know what clairaudient means, Gilda, and I'm *not* clairaudient—much as you'd like to believe that."

"But the music you keep hearing and everything—"

"I'm a pianist, not a kooky psychic."

"But are you a kooky monster?"

"That was the dumbest joke you've ever made."

"Well, suggesting that all psychics are 'kooky' was one of the dumbest things you've ever said to me."

"I'm sorry, Gilda, but I have to get my act together, and worrying about being clairaudient is not helping me right now. I have a competition this morning, remember?"

"Fine. *You* were the one sitting here staring at the number nine, telling me you feel like you're receiving some kind of message. If you don't want my help, just say so."

Wendy stood up, smoothed her skirt, and grabbed her coat and mittens. She *did* want Gilda's help, but she hated being in the position of needing it. She hated feeling afraid of something she couldn't understand, and at the moment, feeling snappish and irritated with Gilda somehow made her feel stronger. "Gilda, you can help me by walking fast in those high-heeled shoes."

"I can sprint in these shoes if needed."

"Then maybe we'll get to the Holywell Music Room on time for once."

"If you can tear yourself away from this room we might."

"Fine—I'm going."

"Then go."

As the girls left the room, they neglected to notice yet another clue: next to Wendy's bookshelf, a yellowed copy of *Alice in Wonderland* lay open on the ground.

25

The Sight-Reading Competition

Mrs. Mendelovich hurried toward Gilda and Wendy, clicking across the floor in high-heeled shoes. She wore green tights that called attention to a pair of surprisingly athletic legs. As always, Gilda observed that Mrs. Mendelovich had an uncanny way of looking at once ancient and youthful.

"Geeelda! Thank God you are here! They are calling the first performer in just a few minutes!"

"But Wendy and I have plenty of time, don't we?"

"You are official page-turner!"

"I'm *Wendy's* official page-turner."

"Oh, no. Other performers need page-turning, too!"

"*Other* performers?" Gilda instantly felt her stomach tie itself in several knots.

Professor Heslop approached with her clipboard in hand. "Is this our page-turner?"

"Here she is!" Mrs. Mendelovich placed her hands firmly on Gilda's shoulders. "Geelda is best in the business," she added, causing Wendy to have a sudden coughing fit.

"You've got a long job ahead of you today, my dear," said

Professor Heslop with a note of gallows humor. "I wouldn't want to be in your shoes."

Neither would I. Gilda's palms turned sweaty with the full realization that she would be expected to turn pages not just for Wendy, but for *every one of the performers in the competition.* Wendy always gave her a signal when it was time to turn a page, but other people would simply expect her to read the dense music and turn the page at precisely the right moment. How in the world was she going to pull this off?

Then Gilda had a happier thought: she would be onstage with Julian while he was performing! The idea filled her with giddy excitement and temporary amnesia about the appalling situation in which she found herself.

"Omigod," Wendy whispered as soon as Mrs. Mendelovich and Professor Heslop had moved along to greet other students. "This is awful."

"I know. On the positive side, I bet I can throw the other performers a few curveballs."

"Curveballs?"

"If other people screw up because of my page-turning, it'll make you look good."

"Gilda, if you're *that* bad, they'll pull you off the stage before it's my turn."

"But I'm not *that* bad at page-turning."

"To be fair, you had improved the last time we practiced."

Suddenly, Gilda's mind was a thousand miles away from the mundane subject of page-turning. If she had been a cat, she would have puffed herself up to three times her normal size and hissed, because she had just spied something that made her feel like clawing someone.

On a velvet bench in the reception area, Jenny Pickles and Julian sat next to each other. The two appeared to be deeply absorbed in conversation: Julian turned his body completely toward Jenny and gestured with broad enthusiasm. Jenny simply sat with her legs crossed, swinging a foot adorned with a delicately pointy shoe.

He's telling her a story, Gilda thought. She felt something very unpleasant—a hot, liquid drop of jealousy that burned the lining of her stomach. She noticed with annoyance that Jenny looked cute. There was no denying it: her vibrant red hair looked fantastic after using hot rollers. What in the world were the two of them talking about?

"Looks like that Jenny Pickles chick is trying to steal your boyfriend," Wendy observed.

"There's no law against people talking to each other, Wendy." Gilda did her best to squelch the cauldron of envy that fumed and bubbled inside her.

"Gilda, you're totally jealous."

"I'm *not* jealous."

"I don't blame you. How does she get her hair to look like that?"

"Hot rollers."

"I knew there was something about that girl I didn't like."

"They're just *talking*, okay?"

"Looks like flirting to me."

"It's not like Julian is officially my boyfriend, Wendy. We just had lunch one time."

"You said you were in love."

"Are you trying to help me or hurt me right now?"

"I'm just *saying*, it looks like something's going on over there. So why don't you just stroll over and break things up?"

"How?"

"I don't know. Maybe you could join in the conversation?"

"Maybe I'll do just that."

"Go fight for your man! I really want to see what happens when you walk over there."

"I bet you do."

But Gilda discovered that she couldn't move. There was no denying the fact that Jenny and Julian looked *interested* in each other. A warm circle seemed to envelop them—a force field that made the idea of interrupting them with small talk akin to throwing cold water on sunbathers napping by a swimming pool. Gilda watched as Jenny and Julian laughed uproariously at *something*.

I bet he's telling her that dumb story about Waldgrave and his cat, Gilda thought.

"I suggest you go break up the lovefest over there," said Wendy.

"Don't rush me. I'm thinking of something to say."

"How about, 'Hey! How's it going?'"

"Too mundane."

"While you think of something brilliant to say, I'm going to find a practice room."

"Okay." Gilda sighed. "See you onstage."

Gilda edged her way toward Julian and Jenny and found a spot where she could stand partly concealed by a plant. She watched Jenny take delicate sips from a water bottle as Julian talked. She watched with horror as Jenny offered Julian a sip of water and he accepted. *The two of them were swapping spit!*

Gilda scanned the room to see if she could flirt with someone else in an attempt to make Julian jealous, but the only people in sight were Professor Heslop and a plump, bearded man who handed out brochures at the entrance to the performance hall.

A heavyset woman with leathery, freckled skin and red hair sidled up to Gilda to watch the flirting couple. With a wave of annoyance, Gilda knew right away that this had to be Jenny's mother.

"Leave it to my girl to find a beau in any country!" Ms. Pickles drawled. "That Jenny picks up boys like a dog picks up fleas."

"Maybe you should take her to the vet," Gilda blurted.

"Pardon?" Jenny's mother regarded Gilda through narrowed eyes.

"Oh—I meant the *boy* she's chatting with looks like he might have fleas." Gilda hoped Ms. Pickles was the type who would prefer to see her daughter receive the attentions of one of the damp-haired, bespectacled boys in the competition.

"Julian is a little different, I guess. But my lord, how he plays the pianah! I don't know when I've heard someone so talented—except my Jenny, of course." Ms. Pickles squinted fiercely at Julian, as if she might be able to actually *see* the substance of his talent if she focused intensely enough. "His piano teacher thinks that if he just buckled down a little, he could actually win this whole competition."

"He's very talented," said Gilda, wanting to squelch Ms. Pickles's enthusiasm. "But you should hear him *talk*."

"Don't you love hearing that English accent?"

"I mean, he's got a real potty mouth. I bet the two of them are cursing up a storm over there as we speak." Gilda glanced at Julian, who still appeared to be telling an anecdote that required exuberant gestures.

"Now that can't be true! Last night he was such a gentleman. Oh, how he kept us laughing!"

Gilda felt as if she had been socked in the stomach. *Last night?!*

"Jenny and I went to the Eagle and Child Pub to get a bite to eat and soak up the atmosphere after she finished her practice session. We were just sitting there chewing the fat when, who do we see but Julian and his piano teacher, Mr. Goodwin, who is such a *lovely* man, bless his heart. And Julian recognized Jenny right away from the competition, so the next thing we knew, we were all sitting together, and Julian is telling us stories about the quaint little town he's from called Creeping—such an interesting name...."

"Crawling," said Gilda grimly.

"Oh, yes. Crawling. And he told us such impressive stories about his father's chain of hotels all across the country—"

"He said his father owns *hotels*?"

"Oh my goodness, yes. And Julian, bless his heart, he entertains the family's guests—sometimes even royalty—by giving recitals. He said he keeps everyone up all night singing."

Gilda felt outraged and confused. Hadn't Julian said that his father installed toilets for a living? Which of these stories was made-up—and why?

"He told *me* his father installs toilets." Gilda decided, a bit cattily, that Jenny's mother might as well know this fact.

"Oh no, sugar. People like him *pay others* to do that. Anyway, he offered to show Jenny around the city today after the competition. He knows about the interesting places the American tourists always miss."

Gilda felt her face growing hot. "Ms. Pickles," she said, doing her best to emphasize the ridiculousness of the word *Pickles*.

"Please call me Martha."

"Martha *Pickles*, I think you should know that Julian has a rather unsavory reputation. You might think twice about letting your daughter go wandering around town with him." Gilda realized she knew nothing whatsoever about Julian's reputation, but at the moment, she felt too jealous to care.

"I think English boys are such gentlemen compared with American boys," Ms. Pickles insisted. "They speak so politely, and Julian comes from such an accomplished family. I would love for Jenny to marry into a really upscale English family like that someday."

Gilda stifled an urge to gag openly at Ms. Pickles's reference to marriage. By now, she felt nearly as irritated with herself as she felt toward Julian and Jenny. More than anything, she hated the fact that she *cared* that Julian was talking to Jenny. She felt as if she had left some part of herself across the room where they were sitting, and that she would do almost anything to get it back.

Ms. Pickles frowned as Julian leaned toward Jenny to examine a pendant that hung around the neck of her daughter's rather low-cut dress. "I suppose I *could* tag along to chaperone their little date...." Ms. Pickles mused. "But Jenny won't like it."

"It's for the best."

"Geelda! What are you doing?" Gilda was startled to turn around and find Mrs. Mendelovich's kohl-rimmed, flashing eyes gazing into her own. "You are supposed to be on stage!" Mrs. Mendelovich grabbed her arm and yanked her toward the performance hall with surprising strength.

Gilda had no choice but to meekly follow Wendy's teacher into the performance hall.

26

The Page-Turner

Alone on the stage floor of the Holywell Music Room, Gilda felt slightly ridiculous sitting next to the grand piano in her "tainted royalty" outfit. She was aware of the many eyes gazing down upon her from the upper rows of the performance hall.

I am an experienced page-turner, Gilda told herself, hoping that asserting this untruth might somehow make it a true fact. *I've done this a million times, and I'm the best in the business.*

Professors Maddox and Waldgrave were greeted with a smattering of applause as they entered the performance hall. Carrying his cat under his arm, Professor Waldgrave strode across the room wearing a shapeless, oversize sweater that hung well past his hips—a sweater that resembled a bizarre minidress or a shortened version of a monk's hooded cloak. His face looked weary. Professor Maddox also looked tired: her eyes were noticeably puffy despite evidence of an attempt to brighten her dark undereye circles with concealer and blue eyeliner.

Maybe the two of them got into a big lover's quarrel last night, Gilda mused. She gave them a little hello wave just to be friendly. Professor Maddox waved back politely, but Professor Waldgrave looked momentarily alarmed, as if Gilda had suddenly given him the finger.

"Good morning!" Professor Heslop strode into the room, projecting her voice into the upper rows. "I want to welcome everyone to the sight-reading portion of the Young International Virtuosos Competition. In a moment, I will unseal the sight-reading music for the first performer. None of the competitors has seen this music before. How do I know this? Because this rather difficult piece was only very recently composed by a graduate composition student here at Oxford University."

Professor Heslop ripped open the envelope to reveal the sight-reading music. She placed it on the piano's music stand. Gilda gasped: the pages of the dense score were literally black with tiny notes.

"Announcing sight-reading performer number one," said Professor Heslop.

A tall, thin boy whose long, frizzy hair seemed to float around his head walked onstage, eyed Gilda suspiciously, and sat down at the piano bench. He looked at the music and swore under his breath in German. Sighing, he took a very long time adjusting the piano seat.

"Anytime now, performer number one!" shouted Professor Waldgrave.

Performer number one abruptly launched into the music, and Gilda struggled to follow him in the score. It was hard enough to make sense of the dissonant, contemporary music, and the task was made even more difficult because the boy's hair blocked much of Gilda's view. As he played he muttered to himself.

Gilda felt a knot of dread forming. What was this boy going to do if she turned his page at the wrong spot? *It must be nearly time to turn the page,* Gilda thought, realizing that she had absolutely no clue where performer number one was in the music. She stood up and moved closer, hoping that he would give her some sign when it was time to turn.

Just then, a rotund man sitting in the front row broke into a coughing fit and a woman in a back row joined in with a series of loud sneezes.

To Gilda's surprise, the boy abruptly stopped playing and gazed out into the audience. "Why don't we all have a big, hacking cough right now and get it out of our system, shall we?" He spoke with a German accent.

Gilda slapped her hand over her mouth to suppress a fit of giggles and a group of college students laughed heartily at this outburst.

Professor Waldgrave looked furious. "That's enough from you, performer number one."

"But Professor," the boy protested, "the audience was being inconsiderate."

"A *professional* would keep playing even if every person in the audience leaned over and vomited simultaneously."

"You can't be serious."

"I'm completely serious, despite the fact that I share your sensitivity to sound. Do you have perfect pitch?"

"No."

"Here we go," muttered Professor Maddox, who sat with

her chin resting in her palm. "The old 'victim of perfect pitch' story."

"*I* have perfect pitch," Professor Waldgrave continued, ignoring Professor Maddox, "and when I was a boy, my parents owned a record player that played every piece of music in a slightly warped way—so that it sounded as if it was written in a lower key. After listening to that absolutely *diseased* record player for years, many of the major piano works sounded so *wrong* to me that I couldn't bear to hear them."

"That's horrible," said the German boy.

"That wasn't the worst of it. I also was so sensitive to every extraneous sound that I could hardly perform. Once—during a recital—the ticking of a clock began to drive me mad—a loud, persistent *tick-tock, tick-tock* that seemed to grow louder and louder, until I couldn't bear it any longer. I stood up from the piano, walked through the audience, climbed up on a chair, and dismantled the clock while everyone watched."

"You didn't!"

"I *did*. People thought I was mad; I was the only one in the room who had even noticed the clock."

"You were very sensitive," said the German boy.

"I was very *insensitive*. Because if I could hear a clock, I wasn't listening to the music, was I? And that's your problem, performer number one. You need to become a better listener. You need to become someone who actually *listens to himself* play."

Performer number one glumly tucked his hair behind his ears in response.

"And cut down on the German swearing while you're at it."

"Shall we continue with the piano competition, then?" said

Professor Maddox. "These lengthy reminiscences are causing us to fall behind schedule."

"Next performer please!"

Gilda breathed a sigh of relief. The first performer had exited the stage and she hadn't had to turn a single page. With any luck, the next few competitors would also lose their tempers and get disqualified. Gilda's feeling of hope was immediately dashed, however, because Jenny Pickles had just walked onstage.

Gilda offered Jenny a sullen, tight-lipped greeting, avoiding her eyes. She imagined herself whispering *"Stay away from Julian"* in Jenny's ear as she played. But as Jenny performed, Gilda found it difficult to maintain the intensity of her resentment. For one thing, Jenny helpfully whispered "Now!" every time she needed her page turned, and she never grimaced or muttered "Too late!" under her breath as Wendy often did during practice sessions. Because of this, Gilda managed to turn pages without embarrassing herself—a goal that suddenly seemed more desirable than sabotaging Jenny's performance.

Jenny was followed by musicians including a girl who kept asking if she could start over (she wasn't allowed to), a boy who hummed to himself as his fingers moved across the keyboard, a girl who shed tears as she exited the stage, and a boy who meticulously wiped the keyboard with a rag, as if afraid of catching some disease from the sweaty fingers of other musicians. Everyone missed notes, but Gilda was beginning to recognize the patterns of this bizarre composition—the glissando that signaled the first page turn, the series of octaves that meant it was time to turn the last page. Now she knew how to stand up at the right moment, place her gloved hand over the top of the page, and wait for the pianist to give her a subtle signal—usually a little nod of the head.

As Professor Heslop announced performer number eight, Ming Fong walked toward the piano wearing her lacy dress and the bright red flower in her hair. She regarded Gilda coolly, but Gilda noticed a twinge of alarm in her eyes. "No page-turning, please," she said in a low voice.

An hour ago, Gilda would have been thrilled to hear this, but now she felt more confident in her skills. "I'm supposed to turn your pages," Gilda whispered. She flashed Ming Fong what she hoped was a menacing smile. "It's my job."

"No, thank you."

"Listen, Ming Fong. I'm the official page-turner for the competition, and your pages are bloody well going to be turned!"

"Is there a problem up there?" Professor Waldgrave eyed the two of them with impatience.

"She doesn't want me to turn her pages."

"Then don't turn them."

Ming Fong turned her attention primly to her music, and Gilda leaned back in her chair. She couldn't help feeling a little annoyed when Ming Fong delivered what sounded like the most close-to-perfect performance she had heard yet. *I hope Wendy can't hear her playing from backstage*, Gilda thought. Once again, she tried to send Wendy a psychic message: *Forget everything around you and just remember: you're good at this.*

Wendy walked onstage looking pale. She walked slowly, dragging her feet with a shuffling gait, as if she didn't want to arrive at her destination too quickly.

I need to talk to Wendy about her walk, Gilda thought. *She doesn't look confident.*

"You can do it," Gilda whispered as Wendy took a seat at the piano and adjusted the bench. "Everybody else has screwed this up completely."

Wendy's eyebrows flew up when she saw the score, but a moment later, she managed to play through the entire piece from beginning to end with surprising ease.

Wendy is a great sight-reader, Gilda thought. *In fact, she might be even better than Ming Fong.* Again, Gilda noticed that both judges regarded Wendy with interest, as if they wanted to remember her. By now Professor Waldgrave's cat had curled up contentedly for a nap. *I hope it's purring*, Gilda thought.

"You totally nailed it!" Gilda whispered as Wendy reached the end of the piece. She flashed Professor Waldgrave a brilliant smile and did her best to send him a psychic message: *Give Wendy a high score!*

"Here comes your boyfriend," Wendy replied in a low voice as she stood up to take a bow.

Waiting with Professor Heslop at the backstage door, Julian's face brightened with surprise when he glimpsed Gilda sitting in the page-turner's chair next to the piano. But was there also something nervous and evasive about his smile? Gilda felt irritated that her stomach still felt fluttery when he looked at her. *You're mad at him*, Gilda reminded herself.

Julian strolled onstage confidently and adjusted the height of the piano bench. "You going to turn my pages?" He spoke in a loud whisper, which somehow made the phrase "turn my pages" sound flirtatious.

Something warm stirred in Gilda's stomach—something that felt like hope. She tried to squelch the feeling. "It's my job," she replied with a casual shrug.

"My lucky day."

Gilda let out a giggle that sounded more like a snort, and immediately wished she had remained silent.

Julian squinted at the piano music. "Looks bloody difficult," he said to the judges.

"It *is* bloody difficult," Professor Waldgrave replied.

The audience laughed.

"Please begin, performer number ten," said Professor Waldgrave, clearly agitated by the swell of chuckling throughout the performance hall.

Gilda glanced up into the benches and saw that the audience had increased, as if people had made a special effort to see Julian's performance in particular.

Julian was in his element. *Everyone likes him, and he likes everyone*, Gilda thought. For some reason, the thought made her feel vaguely sad, as if she had lost something.

Julian launched into the music, playing with greater speed than anyone before him. Parts of the composition sounded completely different than anything Gilda had heard that morning, and as she watched his well-developed hands move over the keyboard, she had a dual urge to kiss the back of Julian's neck and give him a stinging flick with her fingernail. A moment later, Gilda found herself merely listening to his performance instead of following the music notation.

"OH, PAGE-TURNER!"

With horror, Gilda realized that Julian was looking

directly at her as his hands continued to move across the keyboard.

She had completely missed the page turn. Gilda jumped to her feet and lurched toward the music. She turned the page with a great flourish, but her giant cocktail ring caught on the music book and the entire book of music toppled to the floor.

First, the audience gasped. Then giggles erupted through the hall as Julian launched into a corny boogie-woogie version of the dissonant, modern music he had been playing a moment before.

Red-faced, Gilda picked up the music, located the correct page, and placed it back on the music stand in front of Julian, who shouted a sardonic "Thank you!" then quickly found his way back into the score.

Gilda did her best to look mildly amused, as if she and Julian had purposefully planned this little slapstick comedy together, but she felt mortified. She glanced at the judges: Professor Maddox gazed at Julian with something close to adoration while Professor Waldgrave sat with his eyes closed and fingertips perched on his temples. It was hard to tell whether he was listening to the music with a special intensity or struggling to suppress a burgeoning headache.

Enthusiastic applause greeted the end of Julian's performance, but Gilda noticed that Waldgrave's cat slunk under the judges' table.

"Sorry about that," Gilda whispered as Julian stood up to take a bow. Miffed as she felt, she hadn't actually set out to completely botch Julian's performance.

"I was making up half of that rot by the time we got to the page turn anyway."

"Have fun on your date with Jenny Pickles, then," Gilda blurted. She immediately regretted the jealous comment.

"Sorry?"

"Off the stage, please!" shouted Professor Waldgrave.

"Just leaving."

"The little red-haired girl," said Gilda, feeling strangely out of control. "I bet you didn't know her last name was Pickles!"

"Page-turner, do you have a problem?"

"No, sir."

"Your job is to turn pages, not to chat up the competitors."

Giggles surfaced from a few scruffy-looking college students in the audience, and Gilda glared in their direction as Julian retreated backstage, presumably to go on his sightseeing date with Jenny.

Now that the novelty and sheer terror of sitting onstage and turning pages had worn off, Gilda sensed a tedium setting in. She faced several more hours of sitting in the same chair, turning pages for the same piece of music, and imagining what might be going on between Jenny and Julian.

27

The Stranger

Wendy walked down St. Aldate's Street hugging her arms to her chest. The sparkling hoarfrost had melted, but the afternoon was still cold as she walked under a pallid sun. Wendy was used to cold weather in Michigan, but there was something about the *dampness* of England—the drafts of cold air that slipped under her clothes and seeped under her skin, down into her bones; the sheets of low clouds that looked as if they might fall to the ground at any moment. It was somehow harder to bear than the subzero chills she often withstood back at home.

On the bright side, Wendy was relieved that she had redeemed herself in the sight-reading competition that morning, and doubly relieved that Gilda had somehow managed to turn pages despite her lack of experience, not to mention the cumbersome white gloves and giant cocktail ring. For once, the haunting melody in A minor had not slipped into her mind at the worst possible moment, and she had been able to concentrate as she performed.

Still, Wendy felt a taut, grainy sort of weariness; she hadn't had a single night of good sleep since she had first arrived in

England, and it didn't help that she kept waking up to strains of piano music that evaporated as soon as she climbed out of bed to peer into the hallway or look out the window.

Her head ached as she recalled the bizarre event of the morning—the number nine mysteriously etched in the frost on her windowpane. Wendy had stared at that nine for a very long time, feeling an inert sort of panic, almost as if something had paralyzed her. Then—just before Gilda entered the room—she had sensed *something* trying to speak.

Leave me alone, she had replied. *Go away.*

Wendy stopped abruptly in the middle of the sidewalk, realizing that she was walking in the wrong direction—toward Wyntle House and the Jericho neighborhood instead of the Music Building. *What is my deal?* Wendy thought. *It's not like I don't know how to get to the Music Building.*

Maybe you don't want to get there, something in her head replied. She remembered the eerie sound of the voice she had picked up on the tape recorder and felt a coldness in her chest—a feeling of dread. *Maybe I'm afraid to go to the practice rooms*, she thought.

But there was no choice; she *had* to go. Mrs. Mendelovich wanted to review Wendy's entire performance program just in case Wendy made it to the next round of the competition. *You have to go to your lesson, and you can't be late*, Wendy told herself sternly. She took a deep breath, turned around, and hurried back toward the Music Building, bracing herself against the cold.

When Wendy arrived at the Music Faculty Building, she found Mrs. Mendelovich chatting enthusiastically with a gray-haired

Oxford don who seemed to be edging toward the exit as he listened to Mrs. Mendelovich speak. "I have three students in the competition!" Mrs. Mendelovich declared. "All have good chance of winning."

"You must be very proud," said the professor politely, sounding unconvinced.

"And here is Windy now!"

The professor took the opportunity to scoot out the door hastily as Mrs. Mendelovich greeted Wendy the way she always did before a lesson—with a broad smile and outstretched arms ready to seize Wendy in a hug. *She's proud of me again*, Wendy thought. Still, there was something stiff and false about her teacher's smile; something in their relationship had changed.

"Windy! Good to see you! Brava for your playing today!"

"Thanks." For some reason, Wendy always spoke in monosyllables or small, quiet sentences when she was around her teacher. Despite her tiny physique, Mrs. Mendelovich had a charismatic presence that filled the entire room, and Wendy sometimes felt as if her teacher's big personality were drowning out her own.

"I convinced them to give us the recital room!" Mrs. Mendelovich led Wendy to a room stuffed with music stands, rows of folding chairs, and some percussion instruments. "They do master classes in here with some very great musicians, and this is the best piano in whole building."

"Now!" Mrs. Mendelovich sat down in the front row and crossed her slim, stocking-clad legs. "I am the audience. I want for you to walk onstage and play through whole pearformance—beginning to end."

Adrenaline surged through Wendy's body. She sensed a test: *if you can do it now, you can do it later. Show me that you can still play this music perfectly.*

"But Mrs. Mendelovich," Wendy ventured, "do you really think there's much chance I'll make it into the finals? I mean, my first performance wasn't my best."

"*Always* pleepare as if you weell play in finals. *See* yourself playing in the Sheldonian Theater for big audience on that final night."

Wendy hadn't even peeked inside the Sheldonian Theater yet, so the only thing she could picture were the sculpted stone heads that surrounded its exterior. She imagined the heads staring down at her as she played the piano.

"And Wendy—one more thing."

"Yes?"

"Stay in the moment. As Professor Waldgrave says—'*Leesten* to yourself.' If your mind is only in this moment, you never get lost. In a pearformance, there is no past or future—just one moment. Now. The plresent."

Wendy nodded, but she felt the need to explain something about her problem to her teacher. "Mrs. Mendelovich—what if something keeps interrupting your thoughts so you can't stay in the moment? Maybe something from the past that doesn't belong there?"

Mrs. Mendelovich stood up and scanned Wendy's face quizzically with her kohl-rimmed eyes, as if she might be able to *see* the stray thought written on Wendy's skin. "Tell it to go away," said Mrs. Mendelovich. "Say, 'Leave me alone. I'm busy now.'"

"But I've already—"

"Okay? Yes. Okay!" Mrs. Mendelovich clapped her hands impatiently. "Let's begin!"

Wendy sat down at the piano dutifully.

"No, no! I want to see you *walk* onstage."

Wendy walked to the side of the room. She closed her eyes and tried to send a message to the ghost—or whatever it was that was haunting her. *Whoever you are, please let me just play my music, okay? I'll play through the A minor thing later—as many times as you want. Just please let me get through this music right now.*

She took a deep breath and walked toward the piano.

"Shoulders back!" yelled Mrs. Mendelovich. "Posture! Approach the piano with mastery! No, no, no, no, no. Tlry again!"

Mrs. Mendelovich made Wendy walk toward the piano three more times before she was satisfied enough to let her actually play.

Several minutes later, Wendy concluded her performance and looked up at her teacher. She felt relieved: she hadn't gotten lost. The phantom melody had not interrupted her thoughts, and she actually felt confident that she had played well.

So why was Mrs. Mendelovich staring at her with an expression of quiet alarm?

"You sound *different*," said Mrs. Mendelovich, a note of accusation in her voice. She seemed to be considering the possibility that Wendy might be an alien in human disguise.

"Different?"

Mrs. Mendelovich hesitated. "I think eet was good," she said crisply. "But all the work we did—the shading, the dynamics, even your technique—was all so different. If I heard you from outside this room, I would think someone else's student is playing."

"Maybe—it might be better this way?" All Wendy knew was that it had *felt* better.

"Take the Bach. You almost sound as if you are playing Chopin—all those liberties in your timing and too much pedal!"

Mrs. Mendelovich viewed her students as receptacles for the greater artistic insights of their more experienced teachers. She shaped the color of their music, dictating each pianissimo and forte as if guiding a young visual artist through a paint-by-number set. The fact that one of her prize students now seemed to willfully forget every lesson she had learned was bewildering.

Wendy's transformation was also unnerving—even frightening—because the truth was that the music had sounded very accomplished. It was simply not Mrs. Mendelovich's interpretation, nor did it sound as if it were Wendy's. Mrs. Mendelovich felt chilled—as if an invisible imposter had slipped into the room.

"Wendy, have you been seeking lessons with another teacher?"

The question baffled Wendy. "Of course not."

"You're sure? Lots of teachers here for the competition."

"My parents can't afford another teacher."

Mrs. Mendelovich nodded. "If we still had several months to work, we would take these pieces apart measure by measure and start from the beginning. But it might confuse you if we did that now." She fell silent for a moment. "I think we should stop."

There was a finality to the word *stop* that alarmed Wendy. Was her teacher giving up on her completely?

Once again, she knew she had disappointed Mrs. Mendelovich, but this time, Wendy had no idea how it had happened or *why* her playing sounded so different. *Maybe something is terribly wrong with me*, Wendy thought. She felt the need to at least try to explain herself. "Mrs. Mendelovich," Wendy ventured, "maybe I have culture shock."

"Why would you have culture shock?"

"Well, I'm in a foreign country where I've never been before, and I've just been feeling kind of odd." Wendy remembered her mother describing an experience of culture shock after first arriving in America—how she hadn't wanted to talk to anyone, how she had cried for home, how her stomach had ached and strangest of all, her hair had mysteriously turned wavy.

"As musicians, we are world travelers," said Mrs. Mendelovich. "Music is international language, and when you're among fellow musicians—no culture shock."

If only that were true, Wendy thought. It seemed there was nothing more to say. The piano lesson was apparently over, and Wendy felt even more alone than before.

28

The Alice Trail

<u>TRAVEL DIARY ENTRY:</u> PAGE-TURNING FIASCO!!

<u>Item to Add to List of Most Embarrassing Moments of My Entire Life:</u> Knocking Julian's music on the ground at an International Piano Competition followed by self-revealing, jealous comment about Jenny Pickles. <u>DELETE THIS MOMENT FROM LONG-TERM MEMORY BANK!!</u>
   I wonder what Julian and Jenny are doing now. I bet they went to the Covered Market, to the very same places Julian and I went together. I could spy on them, but then I'd look like a stalker if they see me. I've already embarrassed myself enough for one day.

<u>TO DO:</u>
Turn focus back to psychic investigation! Maybe Wendy and I can pick up more clues on her tape recorder....

Scribbling in her journal as she made her way up St. Aldate's Street, Gilda glanced up and found herself in front of a little store called Alice's Shop. She remembered reading about this shop in an Oxford guidebook, and was eager to explore it after discovering the copy of *Alice in Wonderland* in her room.

Inside the tiny, dim shop, a clerk with dyed fuchsia hair sat at a cash register eating a sandwich. Gilda browsed through editions of *Alice in Wonderland* and an assortment of refrigerator magnets, tea cozies, tea towels, thimbles, postcards, lollipops, and Christmas ornaments shaped like Cheshire cats and white rabbits. Remembering that she needed to find some souvenirs for her mother and Stephen, she selected a grumpy-looking Queen of Hearts refrigerator magnet for her mother and a Tweedledum paperweight for her brother.

"I like your hat."

Gilda glanced up and realized the pink-haired clerk was watching her. "Oh, thanks." She had forgotten that she was still dressed in her "tainted royalty" outfit.

"You're an *Alice* fan?" the clerk asked.

"I guess."

"Well done! I've noticed we don't get as many kids reading *Alice* these days. Some of them think it's too odd."

"It's just weird enough for me."

"American, are you?" She didn't wait for Gilda to reply. "If you have enough time during your visit, you'll want to follow the Alice Trail to discover some of the book's secrets. Here— this pamphlet has a map you can follow."

Gilda flipped through the pamphlet, skimming a description of how *Alice in Wonderland* was based on the bizarre dream of a real little girl named Alice Liddell, whose family had lived in Oxford. She read about the summer afternoon when Alice Liddell and the book's author, Lewis Carroll, took a boat ride down the Thames, and how the Oxford landmarks they visited were woven into the whimsical, dreamlike story.

"Only three quid for the book," said the clerk, suddenly sounding impatient, as if she expected Gilda to actually buy the booklet instead of merely reading it in the shop.

Gilda searched through her bag and located a ten-pound note to pay for the little book, the refrigerator magnet, and the paperweight, half-wondering if she really wanted any of these things.

"Now, you might be interested to know that some people— and not just kids, mind you—think that somewhere along the Alice Trail there's a *real* entrance to Wonderland." The woman nonchalantly punched numbers into the cash register as she spoke.

"You're kidding, right?" Gilda assumed the clerk must be joking, but it was impossible to be sure from her humorless facial expression.

"Well, there is something interesting about the way so many writers who lived in Oxford describe magical worlds and parallel universes that have secret entranceways," said the pink-haired woman, handing Gilda her receipt. "Take the Narnia books, for example. One can't help thinking there might be *something* about Oxford that's special."

Gilda had to admit she had an intriguing point. Still, it was pretty wacky to hear an adult talking about "magical worlds" as if they might actually exist in real life. Maybe this woman had become delusional after spending too much time alone in Alice's Shop.

"I just work here part-time," the woman explained, as if

answering Gilda's thoughts. "I'm doing graduate work in math at Christ Church College—the same place where Lewis Carroll was a mathematician. I'm studying a theory that parallel universes may really exist," she added.

Gilda now wondered if the clerk was completely loony. "I didn't know math could be so unusual," she said politely. Math at school always seemed to involve tedious questions about stuffing apples in lunch bags and how many kids could fit into different carpool vans.

"Oh, it's *very* strange. For example, at this very moment, you're standing right here in Alice's Shop. But in theory, you might *also* exist in a parallel world where all the choices you've made and all the random events that have ever happened to you in life had outcomes completely the opposite of those they had in *this* world."

Gilda considered this idea. *Maybe, in a parallel universe, my father isn't dead*, she thought. *But if I'm here now, how could I exist in another world at the same time?*

"The problem with the theory," said the clerk, "is that it's impossible to test it if the parallel worlds can't interact with each other."

Gilda suddenly thought of the voice on the tape recorder and the music Wendy kept hearing. "What about ghosts?" Gilda asked.

"Ghosts?"

"I was just wondering: if you see or hear a ghost, is it possible that you're actually perceiving a message from someone who's dead in this world but still alive in a parallel universe or something?"

"I don't know about *that*." The clerk hopped back on her stool and picked up her sandwich.

Gilda decided this must be her signal to leave. "Well, thanks anyway—for the book and everything."

"People used to believe something like that in medieval times," the clerk said as if she hadn't noticed that Gilda was just about to leave the store. "In those days, there were worlds of spirits and fairies that lived side by side with the human world."

Something about this conversation in the dim, confined atmosphere of Alice's Shop was beginning to make Gilda feel as if she had already slipped into another world. She waited to see if the clerk would say more, but instead the woman took a large bite of the sandwich and opened her book. "Anyway, hope you find what you're looking for on the Alice Trail."

As Gilda left the store, she noticed that the eccentric clerk was reading a copy of *Alice in Wonderland*.

That's weird, Gilda thought. *She's probably read it about a million times already.*

As Gilda walked up St. Aldate's, she skimmed the little book she had just purchased. She read how Alice Liddell, her sisters, and Lewis Carroll had followed the river through a place called Port Meadow. Then—something caught Gilda's attention— something that made her stop in the middle of the sidewalk so abruptly that an elderly woman bumped into her from behind and then turned to glare at her.

"Sorry," Gilda muttered, still not looking up, because she had just discovered what might be an important clue: according to the booklet, there actually was a real *treacle well* in Oxford.

> *If you follow a path through Port Meadow, you will eventually find your way to a quaint churchyard—St. Margaret's Church near the small village of Binsey. This simple, one-room church dates from the 12th century and is untouched by modern times.*
>
> *Just behind the church, you will discover the well that inspired the "treacle well" in Lewis Carroll's* Alice in Wonderland. *The treacle well at St. Margaret's Church does not contain molasses and sugar! The well sprung from the ground in response to a prayer of St. Frideswide, the patron saint of Oxford. Ever since, the well is believed to have magical properties—to be a "treacle well" in the ancient sense of the word "treacle" as a source of healing.*

Was it possible that the odd phrase "fry wide" she and Wendy had heard on the tape was actually a reference to Saint Frideswide and the treacle well in Oxford? Gilda had no idea why a ghost might want her to know about this ancient well, but she decided she had to make her way down the Alice Trail to investigate it.

29

Julian and Jenny

So, Julian...honey"—Ms. Pickles huffed and puffed as she followed Julian up a series of narrow wooden staircases leading to the cupola at the top of the Sheldonian Theater—"tell me again, *where* are your father's hotels?" It was about the twentieth prying question Ms. Pickles had asked since she, Jenny, and Julian had begun their sightseeing stroll around Oxford.

It was one thing, Julian thought, to make up a lively little story over dinner (while your piano teacher was in the Men's room) just to add a little spice to the evening. It was another thing entirely when you had to keep talking about it for hours.

"Oh, most are in Scotland and Wales, in point of fact," he said, praying that Jenny and her mother weren't planning a trip to Scotland or Wales anytime soon.

"And what are they called?"

"Oh, various names. There's Mabinogi Castle, there's, um, Gwilymnogi Lodge and Tywynogi Manor House...hard to keep them all straight, you know."

"And do you and your family visit up there often?"

"Oh, not so often."

It was true that Jenny was friendly and smiled a lot and had great hair—*the kind of girl you'd want to be seen with back at home*, Julian thought. It was also true that being away from home for a few days had provided him with a rare opportunity to meet more than one girl who actually liked him. *I guess it's true what they say about American girls*, he thought. *It doesn't matter whether you're funny-looking or whether you speak the Queen's English, Cockney, or some version of Scouse: they fall for an English accent.*

Pleased as he was with Jenny's attention, Julian couldn't help thinking that her mother was a bit of a bore. The problem was, the two of them seemed to come as a pair. *That's why it's best to have more than one girl*, he reminded himself. *You never know when someone's going to go off you or you're going to go off her, so you always need a backup.*

They reached the top of the Sheldonian Theater, where they gazed across the entire city. Julian reminded himself to *act* as if he had seen it all before, even though it was the first time he had ever seen this view of the Oxford statues perched on college rooftops and the tips of pointy spires as far as the eye could see.

"Wow!" Jenny and her mother gazed across the city. "Isn't it amazing? We're standing here in a building that's more than three hundred years old, looking out over *Oxford University*!"

"And just think, Jenny. You could be performing in the final rounds of the competition in this very building in a matter of hours," Jenny's mother added.

Julian wished that Jenny's mother wasn't around because it would have been the perfect opportunity to put his arm around Jenny. Maybe he wouldn't have done it even if she *hadn't* been around, but he liked to think that when an opportunity presented itself with a cute girl, as it rarely did, he would be man enough to take it.

"When I win the competition," he said, "I'll take us all on a trip up to one of my dad's hotels." He immediately wondered why he had been foolish enough to bring up the subject of his father's nonexistent hotels when it had finally dropped from conversation.

Both Jenny and her mother regarded him with cold, blank faces. It took a moment for him to understand that this was because of his suggestion that he might actually win the competition. It had been a joke, but they clearly didn't think it was the least bit funny.

Julian hadn't even considered the possibility that Jenny might expect to win the competition herself. First of all, he hadn't heard her play yet. Secondly, Jenny didn't really talk about music the way the more "serious" kids did, so how would he know she wanted to win? Thirdly, why would a cute girl with such bouncy red hair bother to spend so much time playing classical piano music?

"Or—when *you* win," he said, quickly correcting himself and feeling annoyed as he did so, "you can take us all there with the prize money."

Jenny and her mother smiled with relief.

"With your family's success and position, I'm sure *you* wouldn't need the prize money to take a trip," said Ms. Pickles, adding to Julian's growing urge to extricate himself from the whole situation. He glanced at his watch. "I almost forgot," he said, "my teacher will be expecting me, so I have to shove off soon."

"I probably should go practice, too," said Jenny, glancing at Julian with disappointment.

"I think I'll head back to Wyntle House and grab a couple winks," said Ms. Pickles, suppressing a yawn. "This jet lag is getting to me."

At the mention of Wyntle House, Julian's ears perked up. Didn't Gilda say she was also staying at Wyntle House? He had a sudden urge to see if she was there. She was more fun to talk to than Jenny and her mother. Besides, the day was winterish and gray, and the idea of being cooped up alone in the practice room seemed too depressing to face.

After parting ways with Jenny and her mother, Julian made his way down Walton Street toward Wyntle House. Bracing himself against the cold wind, he stuffed his hands into the pockets of his leather jacket and felt something in his pocket—a small piece of paper. Curious, he pulled it out and discovered a card with a strangely disturbing image—a tall stone tower beginning to crumble as lightning struck it from above. Tumbling from the upper turrets of the tower, a man and a woman dressed in medieval clothing fell headfirst toward the ground.

It was a tarot card titled The Tower.

30

Port Meadow

TRAVEL DIARY: PILGRIMAGE TO THE ALICE TRAIL IN
SEARCH OF THE MYSTERIOUS "TREACLE WELL"!

PHASE ONE OF THE JOURNEY:
As the inspired traveler passes through Jericho on the way to
find Port Meadow and the Alice Trail, she wisely decides to
stop at Wyntle House to change from her stiletto heels into
hiking boots. There, an unfortunate exchange occurs with the
surly houseboy Danny, who exits the second-floor bathroom
carrying a plunger:

DANNY: Do you know who left the crapper in this state?
GILDA: I've been gone all day; I have no idea.
DANNY: (holding the plunger a little too close to Gilda's
           face) Someone bollixed up this crapper.
GILDA: I'm kind of in a hurry.
DANNY: Off to do some ghost-hunting?
GILDA: (trying to edge past Danny) Maybe. I'm just
           going out.
DANNY: Looking for Rosamund the Fair?

GILDA: No.

DANNY: They say she comes out when it rains.

NOTE:

I got the feeling Danny was trying (unsuccessfully) to scare me, but he retreated back into the bathroom with his plunger before I could think up a good comeback.

PHASE TWO OF THE JOURNEY:

Sights observed in the neighborhood of Jericho:

1. The Oxford University Press! (Note to self: stop in to introduce my literary works to the editors when time allows.)
2. The Phoenix Picturehouse (a movie theater currently featuring several art films and a "prize-winning documentary on hedgehogs")
3. Jaunty row houses and little boutiques
4. Elderly man glumly repairing giant tricycle in the middle of the sidewalk
5. Little girl wearing a sequined skirt and riding a scooter

PERSONAL NOTE:

Something about the late-afternoon air here makes me feel nostalgic, although I'm not sure why. Maybe it's the feeling of quiet or the muted sunlight that reminds me of an old movie from the 1960s. Sometimes I get the feeling that everyone who lives in Oxford has agreed to allow time to move a little more slowly than it does everywhere else, as if they don't have to rush into the future with the rest of the world. It's hard to explain what I mean, but during the past few days, I keep getting the feeling that I'm walking just at the edge of another time.

PHASE THREE OF THE JOURNEY:

Following her Alice Trail map, the lonely traveler crosses a bridge over train tracks and passes through the entrance to Port Meadow. There, she spies some teenagers huddling together in the cold. They pass a single cigarette back and forth as if it's a little fire that will keep them warm.

"I know she fancies him," one of the girls says.

"She's a right slapper," her friend replies.

WORD OF THE DAY: SLAPPER!

Definition: A very flirty and potentially "loose" girl.

Use in a sentence:

"Mrs. Rawson, you are certainly no slapper!"

PHASE FOUR OF THE JOURNEY:

Once in the meadow, the wind slaps and stings the weary traveler's cheeks with renewed fury, as if reprimanding her for venturing toward an unknown destination.

The traveler arrives at the river and passes houseboats painted in clownish colors and displaying names like <u>Ghost Buster</u> and <u>Little Pooh</u>. She follows a worn, muddy path along the river, past willow trees that tickle the water with drooping branches and squat trees that look like little trolls with wild hair.

By now, the traveler can't help wondering if she's taken a wrong turn. What if the entire Alice Trail map is a hoax—a silly joke to send naïve American tourists wandering off into the countryside?

Refusing to lose hope, the traveler bravely turns onto a country road that stretches before her with flat fields on either side. The day grows dim and forlorn as darkened clouds drift across the sun. The wind roars ominously through the branches of leafless trees along the edges of the fields.

Now feeling nervous, and realizing she is miles away from everything familiar, the traveler momentarily considers giving up. She feels a twinge of fear as wind whistles through the trees that line the empty road. She glances over her shoulder, half-expecting to discover a willow tree tiptoeing down the path behind her. She walks faster, unable to shake the feeling that some shadowy presence is in close pursuit, unable to shake the memory of an eerie poem once recited by a former love:

> Ellum do grieve,
> Oak, he do hate;
> Willow do walk when ye travels late.

Just then, the traveler glances at her map, and her spirits suddenly lift; she sees that she is very close to the supposed location of the treacle well!!

Gilda entered a small church graveyard shaded by yew trees

and filled with mossy, tilting grave markers sunken halfway into the earth. Many of the tombstones were so old, she could no longer read the dates or inscriptions. The silvery trees surrounding the churchyard gleamed in the weak, golden light, and Gilda's heart beat faster as she realized she must be very close to the location of the treacle well. According to her Alice Trail map, it was supposed to be behind the tiny stone church.

She felt the familiar tickle in her left ear as she approached the church, walking past a row of Celtic-shaped stone crosses that marked a family grave.

Behind the church, shallow steps led down to the opening of the treacle well. Gilda stood at the top of the steps, sensing coldness emanating from the black water below. At first, she was surprised at how unremarkable and easy to miss this "sacred landmark" was. She had expected to find something akin to the illustrations she remembered from nursery rhymes and fairy tales of her childhood: wells encircled by high stone walls and equipped with buckets hanging from pulleys. This well was far more subtle and easy to miss—but also somehow more mysterious. It was a circular hole in the ground that lacked even a simple plaque or inscription to explain its significance. Someone had left a bouquet of wilted roses at the edge of the water. As she peered into the murky depths of the well, Gilda reflected that something about the water actually *looked* treacly—as if it might be mixed with molasses and maple syrup.

For a moment, she imagined herself jumping into the well and discovering a secret entranceway to some magical world. After all, there was something about that circular hole in the ground that reminded her of Alice falling down the rabbit hole.

For some reason, she also thought of her father. *If he were still alive I'd probably try to bring him some of this water in a bottle, just in case it really is a "healing" well*, Gilda thought.

Gilda walked slowly down the steps that led to the well, feeling as if she were stepping down into a grave. She remembered the strange story from *Alice in Wonderland*: *"Three little girls lived at the bottom of a well..."*

Gilda's reverie was interrupted by the cracking of a twig behind her and a hand touching the back of her neck. Startled, she fell forward, down toward the dark water.

31

A Clue in the Graveyard

Crikey! Are you okay?"

Gilda caught herself just at the edge of the cold water, but she scraped her knuckles and thoroughly drenched one of her knees in the process. When she looked up she was shocked to see Julian peering down at her. *What happened to Jenny? How did Julian find me here—all the way across Port Meadow?*

"I'm sorry!" he said, a nervous laugh in his voice. "I didn't mean to scare you."

"I wasn't scared."

Trying to compose herself, Gilda stood up and slowly walked up the steps from the well. As always, her heart beat a little faster around Julian. Along with her surprise at seeing him, she was also suddenly conscious of the random eccentricity of her clothing—the cloddish hiking boots she had paired with fish-net stockings, and the scarf she had wrapped over her pillbox hat and tied under her chin.

"What were you doing down there?" Julian observed her with an impish twinkle in his eye.

"I was just going to ask you the same question. What are *you* doing *here?*"

"Oh, I can see I'm not wanted." Julian hung his head and pretended to shuffle away. "I'll just be on my way, then."

"I thought you were supposed to be on a date with Jenny Pickles."

"I put her back in her jar."

"Her jar? Oh, I get it. Pickle jar. Ha-ha."

"That Jenny is a cute girl," Julian continued, "but her mum asks too many questions."

"Jenny isn't *that* cute," Gilda heard herself say, immediately wishing she had censored herself. She couldn't help feeling mild satisfaction at the news that Jenny's mother had actually tagged along on the outing.

"You're jealous?"

"Of course not."

"Then why slag her off?"

Gilda removed the scarf she had tied around her neck. She had an urge to tie it around her knee, which ached from being drenched in freezing water. "I didn't say anything *mean* about Jenny. I just meant she's okay-looking if you're into the 1950s-beauty-parlor look."

"Works for me."

"Fine, Julian. Then why are you *here*?"

Julian's face broke into a dimpled grin. "Maybe I like fishnet tights with hiking boots, too."

"Who wouldn't?"

"Look, I just didn't much feel like practicing on such a gorgeous, gloomy afternoon, so I thought I'd see what was happening in the graveyard, that's all."

"Did you follow me here, or what?"

"That boy Danny told me you might be around here."

"Danny?"

"The plump one at Wyntle House. Seems he has his eye on you."

"Oh. *That* Danny. He better not have his eye on me."

"He told me you were out ghost-hunting. He said, 'She's looking for the ghost of Rosamund the Fair, what wafts 'round the ruins of the nunnery beyond the meadow. I'm the one who gave her the idea.' Strange little bloke."

"That Danny has no idea what I'm up to."

"What *are* you up to?"

Something about Julian's bemused, curious gaze made Gilda waver, wanting to tell him the truth about her investigation. *He told me he saw a ghost once*, she thought. *What if he could help me?*

"Julian," she said, meeting his blue eyes and trying to convey an attitude of gravity. "There's something I didn't tell you about myself."

Julian placed his hands on Gilda's shoulders. "Don't tell me: you're engaged to a top member of the Russian mafia, and for my own safety, you can no longer associate with me."

"Obviously true," Gilda joked, feeling acutely aware of the touch of Julian's hands on her shoulders. She paused. "I'm actually a psychic investigator."

"And I'm the ghost of Princess Diana."

"I'm serious."

"I left my tiara in the grave though, and—"

"Julian, there's evidence of a haunting surrounding this piano competition, and I'm trying to get to the bottom of it."

As the two of them walked slowly through the graveyard,

Gilda described some of the strange events that had happened during the past few days.

"It does sound a bit creepy," said Julian. "And I'll grant you this; there are eerie things happening 'round here."

"Like what?"

Julian pulled the tarot card from his pocket. "What do you make of *this*?"

Gilda studied the dramatic image of lightning striking a tower. She immediately recognized the style of the Gill tarot deck: it had to be from the same deck as the cards Wendy and Ming Fong received. "Where did you find this, Julian?"

"I found it in my pocket when I was walking here. I assumed *you* gave it to me."

"Why would I leave you this tarot card?"

"I reckoned it was a sort of flirty joke—something to give me a bit of a scare."

"I know how to do tarot card readings, but I'm not the one who gave this to you."

"So, who did?"

Gilda stared at the card, thinking. "Well, Jenny is the last person you saw before you found this, right?"

"Yeah, but she doesn't seem like the tarot card type. I saw Danny, too. . . . Truth is, I left my jacket in the coatroom during my sight-reading performance, so almost anyone could have slipped me this card." Julian considered the image of two people falling from a burning building. "Not a very encouraging fortune, is it?"

"That's why my guess is that it's from someone who wants

to psych out their competition . . . unless something more supernatural is at work."

"A ghost who wants to play cards?"

"Maybe a ghost who needs to disrupt things in some way—
possibly a spirit who's drawn to this piano competition for
some reason. Oh—ick!"

Gilda stumbled. Her boot had stuck in a soft patch of mud.
Her shoelace had come untied, causing her to pitch forward. Her
shoeless stocking foot landed in the cold, squishy ground.

"Oh, crumbs! Here, grab my hand." Julian grabbed Gilda's
arm helpfully, but was unable to conceal the note of mirth in
his voice.

As Gilda balanced on one foot and leaned forward to retrieve her shoe, she felt such a strong and sudden tickle in her
left ear, she almost fell once again. She quickly shoved her wet
foot back into her boot and knelt down to examine a diminutive tombstone marking the grave exactly where her boot had
planted itself deep in the mud.

The tombstone was smaller and newer than many of the flat,
greenish slabs that jutted from the ground throughout the
churchyard. The inscription read:

CHARLES DRUMMOND
So young, so bright, so brief

"Hey, that bloke was about our age when he died." Julian
noticed the boy had died only four years ago.

A cloud overhead darkened the late-afternoon sunlight as
they both stared at the grave.

"I wonder *how* he died," Gilda mused.

"I know a way we could find out."

"A séance?"

"Something like that...There's an old tradition in my village—a way to communicate with a person who's died and to raise their spirit from beyond."

"Is this another one of your ghost stories?"

"No. All the kids know about it, but most of them are too scared to do it."

"How about you?"

"I tried it once, ages ago."

"And?"

"I admit nothing happened then, but you never know. Maybe it's different with a real psychic investigator."

As Julian spoke, Gilda felt a chill, as if a draft of cold air had just wafted up from the grave itself. "Okay. How does it work?" For some reason, she found herself whispering.

"Well, you get a group of kids together and everyone holds hands and circles counterclockwise 'round the grave nine times. And each time you go 'round, you chant the dead person's name."

Gilda reflected that this seemed exactly like the kind of wonderfully spooky but fundamentally *bad* idea that some kid might have in a horror movie—a movie in which everyone ends up getting killed.

"Can't hurt to try it." Gilda tried to sound more nonchalant than she felt.

The two stood on opposite sides of the small tombstone, and Julian took Gilda's hands. Gilda sensed a warm, electric energy flowing between them. She was also intensely aware that rows of corpses and skeletons surrounded them, just beneath the ground. They began to circle around the boy's tombstone.

"Charles Drummond," they said at the first circle, gazing into each other's eyes and giggling at the sense that what they were doing was at once very silly and somehow potentially very dangerous.

"Charles Drummond," they repeated at the second circle.

Their circles grew faster, and Gilda began to feel dizzy. Julian's pitcher-eared face became distorted; the tombstones glimpsed in her peripheral vision looked lopsided; the earth and the sky seemed to be switching places. As they completed the ninth turn, Gilda felt so light-headed, she thought she might fall down on the ground, but instead, Julian pulled her toward him, and then something very strange was happening because his mouth was touching hers.

I'm kissing a boy, Gilda told herself. *Omigod, I'm actually kissing a boy! My first kiss! In an English graveyard!*

Technically, it wasn't Gilda's *very* first kiss; earlier in the year, she had been in a school play in which her character had been required to kiss a boy named Felix, but neither Gilda nor Felix had *wanted* to kiss each other in the scene. They had pressed their mouths together as briefly and reluctantly as possible, and Felix had even asked the director if the scene could be cut "just so nobody gets the idea we're a couple."

Kissing Julian was different: there was nothing reluctant about it. In fact, he seemed to be trying to tear his lips from her face with a fierce suction. *Maybe we're not doing it right*, Gilda thought. She was aware of her shinbone pressing into the cold stone of the tombstone between them, and the drops of icy rain that had begun to fall. *It's not quite what I imagined*, Gilda had to admit. She had assumed that when you finally kissed a boy you actually *liked*, the experience would be akin to being launched into outer space or the first downward plunge on a roller coaster. Didn't the old movies and television programs show fireworks going off when people kissed? The truth boiled down to the reality of someone's mouth touching yours— someone else's lips, tongue, and saliva. *Maybe I'm analyzing it too much*, Gilda thought.

Almost without warning, the skies opened and the cold drizzle crescendoed into a heavy downpour.

Julian grabbed Gilda's hand and the two of them hurried toward the church. Relieved to discover that the heavy wooden doors were open, they walked into an eerie quiet.

32

The White Rose

Gilda and Julian entered a tiny, stark sanctuary filled with rows of wooden pews and oil lamps that hung from the ceiling. The only light came from a couple of small stained-glass windows.

Some pamphlets left near the door explained the significance of the treacle well and the "twelfth-century church built on ancient pagan worship grounds."

Julian took Gilda's hand and began to pull her close again, but this time, Gilda resisted. "Not in a *church*." She realized this sounded like the kind of prim statement her mother might make, but something about the silent spookiness of the twelfth-century church made her feel as if the two of them were being *watched*. Besides, something else bothered her—something about Julian.

"Tell me the truth, Julian," she blurted impulsively. "Does your dad install toilets, or does he own hotels?"

Julian was startled by the unexpected question. He glanced at the door as if looking for a quick escape. "What, you and Jenny been gossiping about me?"

"Of course not. I actually heard your story about owning hotels from Jenny's mother."

"Oh. Well, what did you tell *her?*"

"What do you think? I told her your father installs toilets."

"That explains why she pestered me with about a million questions, then." Julian sat down in one of the pews, looking dejected. "If you must know, neither one is true. My father is an estate agent. He sells houses."

"So why lie about selling houses?"

Julian shrugged. "Don't you ever wish things were more interesting than they are?"

"Every now and then." *More like all the time*, Gilda thought. She knew she and Julian had something in common because she often caught herself blurting half-truths in an attempt to liven up conversation or get out of a scrape. Hadn't she just presented herself as "Dame Gilda" to Professor Sabertash? Still, this tendency only made Gilda feel doubly annoyed whenever she discovered she was on the *receiving* end of a fib. "What *other* things did you make up?" Gilda persisted.

"None."

"What about your story about seeing a ghost?"

"That *happened*, actually. The irony is that nobody believes the strangest *true* story I tell."

"I guess I can relate to that," said Gilda. She had noticed that her mother and some of her teachers seemed to prefer half-truths to the bizarre, but completely *true* experiences she encountered as a psychic investigator.

"Anyway," Julian continued, "who knows why I made up that rot about my poor dad."

Gilda sat down next to Julian in the pew. "Why *did* you?"

"Maybe because he doesn't want me to be here, doing this competition in the first place. Maybe he's right. I probably *shouldn't* be here." Julian clutched the fingers of his left hand and began pulling his fingers back one by one, as if trying to stretch out his joints.

Gilda observed the ropy veins in Julian's hands. She felt surprised to hear self-doubt from someone who normally seemed so assured. "I think you should follow your dreams no matter what, Julian."

"Spoken like a true American—optimistic and naïve."

"What's the point of being pessimistic, thinking that nothing you hope for could ever really happen?"

"I'm not being pessimistic; I'm being *realistic*. I see how people's lives turn out. It's *never* exactly what they imagine or hope for."

Gilda thought of the adults she knew. How many of them had actually ended up where they had once imagined they would be? Her mom had apparently always wanted to be a nurse, but she also complained that the job of working in a hospital was much more draining than she had expected. And what about her father? He had died before achieving his dream of becoming a writer. "I guess some people are just unlucky," Gilda ventured. "But I get the feeling most people never really *go* for it enough."

"And what is it, exactly, that *you're* going for?"

Gilda detected a sardonic note in Julian's voice—almost a tone of hostility. "I already told you," she said. "I'm a psychic investigator."

"Right. So when you're all grown up you'll go to work at the psychic investigator office and pay your bills with all the dosh you make from catching ghosts?"

"It's not about money." Gilda had never actually thought of her investigative work in such practical terms. "It's more like something I do because I'm driven to do it," she explained. "I almost can't *help* it."

Julian nodded, watching her closely—almost hungrily.

"Besides, being a psychic investigator isn't my only career. I'll probably also write a couple best-selling novels and direct some Broadway hits to help support my investigative work and designer shopping sprees."

"So—at the age of fourteen, you're a novelist, a theater director, *and* a psychic investigator."

"Exactly." Gilda enjoyed hearing the summary of her careers.

"And a page-turner."

"Oh, right."

"Would you also say you're a bit of a faffer?"

Gilda couldn't remember the specific meaning of the term *faffer*, but it had a flaccid, windy sound that she didn't like. Julian wore a patronizing expression she remembered seeing on her brother's face when he was teasing her in some way she couldn't quite figure out. "I'm not a faffer," she said.

"But you faff about," said Julian, grinning.

"I do *not* 'faff about.'"

"Are you sure?" Julian gazed at her with a combination of mischievous affection and something akin to malice. It clearly bothered him that Gilda pursued her far-fetched goals with such complete confidence.

"If a faffer is a multitalented person, then yes—I am one."

"It's more like a person who dabbles—someone who does a little of this, a little of that, but doesn't really accomplish any one thing."

"Who says I don't accomplish anything?"

"Don't get your knickers in a twist. I'm a bit of a faffer myself; my teacher always says so."

"For your information, Julian, I was making great progress on an investigation until you showed up in this graveyard."

"Don't get all in a pother. Back home, everyone gets teased all the time, so I guess it's just habit for me."

"I've never been in a pother in my life!" Gilda stood up and headed for the door. "I should get back to my work instead of faffing about in this church with you." Gilda thrust open the heavy church door. Looking out into a steady drizzle of rain, she glimpsed something in the graveyard that made her forget her argument with Julian. In fact, for a moment, she almost forgot to breathe.

A tall figure stood amid the tombstones wearing a hooded cape that dragged upon the ground. Carrying a black umbrella, the figure began to move at a strikingly smooth speed, almost appearing to float just above the wet grass.

Is that the ghost of Rosamund the Fair? Gilda felt momentarily paralyzed. *But what about the black umbrella? Didn't Rosamund live too long ago for umbrellas?*

Gilda came to her senses and ran into the rain, attempting to pursue the cloaked figure, but he or she disappeared into a grove of trees before Gilda could catch up.

As Gilda paused to catch her breath, something equally mysterious caught her attention: a single white rose that lay in the mud upon Charles Drummond's grave.

33

Mrs. Choy and Mrs. Chen

Your mum rang twice, luv," said Mrs. Luard as Wendy walked through the front door of Wyntle House. "She said she wants you to use your calling card to get in touch."

"Okay, thanks for letting me know." Wendy realized there was no way around it; she had to call home at some point.

"You're welcome to use the telephone in here by the telly if you want." Breathing heavily as she maneuvered herself on her crutches, Mrs. Luard directed Wendy to the telephone. "I'll be back in a mo'; I have to let Bunny out in the garden for a wee." Mrs. Luard moved heavily down the hallway with her tiny dog scurrying behind her.

Wendy sat down on Mrs. Luard's worn couch, found her calling card, and stared at it for a minute before finally picking up the phone and dialing.

"Wendy! That you?"

"Hi, Mom."

"Why not call sooner?"

"Just busy practicing."

"Something wrong?"

"No." There was an echo on the line, and Wendy had the disconcerting sense of shouting into a canyon.

"Wendy—Mrs. Chen say there is a hole in you music."

"What?"

"A hole! She say, you brain forget you music!"

Wendy felt intensely annoyed. Ming Fong must have blabbed something about that glitch in the first round of the competition to her mother, who had predictably blabbed the news to Mrs. Choy.

"Mom, it's called a 'memory slip,' and it can happen to anyone."

"Not practice long enough? Out eating scones and greasy Italian curry with Gilda!"

"I haven't had a single scone—or Indian curry—since I've been here, Mom! I've been practicing my butt off, and it has nothing to do with Gilda."

"I'm being trailed by a ghost," Wendy imagined herself saying. What would her mother do if she heard the truth? *She'd probably withdraw money from her savings account, jump on the next plane to England, and bring me some ancient Chinese herbs and rearrange my furniture.* The idea of dealing with her mother along with a ghost and the piano competition would be far too much to handle, so Wendy decided to keep the true nature of her problem to herself.

Mrs. Choy fell silent for a moment. "Can you still win competition?"

"Mom, this is an international competition. That means there are plenty of people here who have won contests at home just like me. It's very competitive."

"Great honor for you family if you win."

"Yes, I know."

"You father and I work ver' hard, you know? Expensive lessons, trip to England . . . Would be nice to hear you at least *wish* to win."

Her mother began talking about Ming Fong and Mrs. Chen, but Wendy was only half-listening. There was music in her head, and it was growing louder. For once, she didn't mind hearing the intrusive melody. At the moment, the competition seemed small and insignificant because *someone* had other, bigger plans for her.

34

The Breakthrough

Gilda took in her surroundings—the exposed wooden beams of the low ceilings, the noisy tables crowded together, the crackling fireplace—and couldn't help but think that her mother would be outraged if she knew that at that very moment, her daughter was in a smoke-filled Oxfordshire pub, sitting at a table with a boy whom she had just kissed in a damp graveyard.

"I'll have a lager," Julian told the barman who had approached their table with menus.

"You here with your mum or dad to give you permission?"

"Why would a man of my advanced age be out with his mum and dad?"

"No lager for you, mate."

"Worth a try."

"I'll bring you a glass of warm milk with your fish and chips," the barman joked.

Julian leaned forward to be heard above the jovial din in the pub. "So didn't I tell you that graveyard ritual would work?"

"*Something* definitely happened," Gilda agreed. She was still baffled by the cloaked figure she had seen. She also had the frustrating awareness that the mystery she had stumbled upon was more complicated than she had imagined; the more pieces of the puzzle she encountered, the less she understood how they all fit together.

"I guess I'd make a pretty good psychic investigator myself," said Julian.

"There's more to it than doing rituals in a graveyard, Julian. I mean, I've been working to develop these skills for a few *years*."

"I always thought being psychic was something you're born with."

"Sure it is. But you still have to practice and study..." Gilda was distracted by a familiar voice that cut through the boisterous banter of the pub—an officious, posh-sounding voice suited to sailing across concert halls and lecture halls. Gilda glanced around the room and was shocked when she discovered the source of the voice. "Don't look now, Julian," she said, speaking in a low voice, "but the competition judges are here."

"You can't be serious."

Gilda pointed to a dim corner of the pub where Professor Waldgrave sat at a table with Professor Maddox. "What do you think the two of them are doing here together? They hate each other!"

"Maybe they kissed and made up."

Gilda glanced back at the two music professors and noticed that Professor Maddox wore a distraught expression. Her hair looked wilder than ever, as if walking in the rain had caused her spiral curls to stand straight on end. Gilda impulsively pulled her dark cat's-eye sunglasses from her bag and put them on.

She felt that she simply had to know what they were talking about. "I'm going to sneak over there to spy on them," she announced.

"Those sunglasses don't quite make you blend in with the crowd," Julian observed.

"Maybe not, but I bet they won't recognize me." Gilda removed her hat and opened a compact mirror to apply a blood-red shade of lipstick. "In my investigations, I've learned that most people actually have very short, superficial memories. If they *do* remember you, it's only because of a couple of details— maybe your hair color or a quirk about your clothing or the way you speak or walk. Half the time, all you need as a disguise is a pair of sunglasses."

"Go on, then; I'll watch the show from here."

Gilda used a menu to conceal her face as she sauntered slowly toward the judges' table. Peeking over the menu, she saw Professor Maddox leave the table for the ladies' room. In her absence, Professor Waldgrave reached across the table to feed his cat a morsel of fish from her plate.

Gilda found a spot at the end of the bar and climbed onto a bar stool. She did her best to act as if she was the sort of local person who simply happened to stop into her local watering hole for a drink while her dogs waited outside yelping in the rain. She perused her menu and was pleased to see that both "bangers and mash" and "spotted dick" were available.

A barmaid approached to take Gilda's order. "I'll have an Old Tubthumper, please," said Gilda, copying an order she had heard someone else make and forcing herself to avoid looking in Julian's direction for fear of bursting into giggles. "The warmer and darker, the better," she added. One of her guidebooks had mentioned that "unlike Americans, the English prefer their beer warm and dark."

"Half pint or pint?"

"Pint."

To Gilda's surprise, the barmaid actually slapped down a beer that looked as thick and dark as molasses into a glass, large enough for the heftiest pub-goers in the room. Now Gilda couldn't help glancing in Julian's direction, and could barely stifle her laughter when she saw his jaw drop with disbelief and outrage. For Julian's benefit, she pretended to take a sip and decided that the drink smelled like warm fungus or something that might be used to lubricate a machine.

"What's the matter?" Professor Waldgrave asked.

Gilda's ears perked up at the sound of Professor Maddox returning to her table.

"Rhiannon, Sophia ate only a few bites of your fish. I thought you didn't want it."

"It isn't the fish." Professor Maddox's voice sounded hoarse.

Is Professor Maddox crying? Gilda wished she could turn around to observe the two professors more directly.

"Rhiannon, we have our differences of opinion, but we'll sort it out. That's why they asked both of us to judge—because we come from such opposite orientations. Besides, Winterbottom will be here to help judge the final round."

Who in the world is "Winterbottom"? Gilda wondered.

"Despite our differences, I think the group we've pulled

together for the finals is a fine selection of performers," Wald-grave continued. "There will no doubt be some raised eye-brows when Professor Heslop announces the list tonight, but so be it."

They've picked the finalists! It was all Gilda could do to keep from swiveling around in her seat and demanding to know whether Wendy and Julian had made it. *Mention some names!* she thought. *Mention some names!*

"I'm not thinking about the judging either," said Professor Maddox.

"What, then?"

"Being at this competition again..." Professor Maddox sud-denly spoke in a softer voice, and Gilda had to strain to hear her. "Well, I keep thinking about *him*. Don't you?"

THINKING ABOUT WHOM?! Gilda wished people wouldn't use so many vague pronouns, and she wondered why there was such a very long silence following Professor Maddox's com-ment. Why wasn't Waldgrave saying anything in reply?

Still wearing her sunglasses, Gilda stealthily turned to peek behind her. Professor Maddox sat with her hands flat on the table, on either side of a virtually untouched plate of fish. Her eyes looked red, as if she had just recovered from a crying spell. Waldgrave's mouth was a thin line; his face stony and drained of color. He rubbed his bald head with one hand, as if trying to remove a smudge he had discovered up there.

"Rhiannon," Professor Waldgrave finally said, "Charles Drummond has been gone for five years now."

CHARLES DRUMMOND! Hearing this name, Gilda felt so excited and agitated, she accidentally knocked over her entire pint of dark beer, which sloshed across the bar and onto the floor. Luckily, the barmaid was too busy ringing up orders at the other end of the counter to notice.

"I know it's been five years," said Professor Maddox. "But I've had this odd feeling ever since I arrived in Oxford this week. We can't deny the fact that if you hadn't——"

"If I hadn't *what*? Why don't you go ahead and *say* it, Rhiannon?"

Gilda grabbed some napkins and tried to soak up the brown puddle of beer that now spread in front of her on the counter while doing her best not to miss a moment of the drama unfolding behind her. *Go ahead and say WHAT?* she wondered.

"If I hadn't *killed* him," said Professor Waldgrave, in a slightly lower voice. "That's what you were going to say, wasn't it?"

Gilda sat motionless with a wad of beer-soaked napkins in one hand, trying to will every cell in her body to become a listening device.

"No. That's *not* what I was going to say."

"It's what you were thinking."

"Nigel, you're projecting your own guilt onto me."

"I could say the same to you!" Professor Waldgrave's voice grew louder. "You're projecting *your* guilt onto *me*."

Gilda glanced behind her and glimpsed Professor Waldgrave pointing at Professor Maddox with an accusing index finger, as if it were a handgun.

"Don't point at me that way, please."

"You're not so innocent, you know. You had your role to play, and you know that if you hadn't gotten involved, it never would have turned out this way. Never!"

"Not being able to accept responsibility is a sign of immaturity, Nigel."

"And I think we're *both* very immature, sad people."

Professor Maddox stood up at the table and Gilda quickly turned around in her seat. She found the barmaid mopping the puddle of beer on the other side of the counter and eyeing Gilda's empty pint glass irritably.

Rhiannon Maddox breezed out of the pub. Gilda wasn't the only person who watched her leave: many eyes were drawn to the strikingly dramatic hooded black cape she wore—a cape so long, its muddy edges dragged across the pub floor.

Psychic Investigation Breakthrough Report!

TO: GILDA JOYCE
FROM: GILDA JOYCE
RE: POSSIBLE IDENTITY OF PIANO COMPETITION
GHOST UNCOVERED!

A BREAKTHROUGH DISCOVERY:

Two judges of this piano competition had <u>something</u> to do with the death of a boy named Charles Drummond who died four years ago.

Did Professor Waldgrave actually murder him?? The two professors seemed to accuse each other. Now I'm almost certain it was actually Professor Maddox who left that white rose on Charles's grave. She seems to feel very guilty and sad, whereas Waldgrave sounds completely defensive—but also guilty.

HYPOTHESIS:

My guess is that Charles Drummond was a musician. What if the two professors got jealous of his great talent and killed him?

If these competition judges are capable of murder, are any of the talented performers here safe? What if the ghost is trying to <u>warn</u> us about something?

TO DO:

1. Find out more about Charles Drummond and how he died.

2. Keep a close watch on Professor Waldgrave and Professor Maddox! What possible motive could they have for causing a boy's death?

3. Investigate mysterious clues—still baffled by the significance of the number nine and the tarot cards that keep turning up!

35

The Finalists

Gilda and Julian drew resentful stares as they walked into the Dennis Arnold Hall, several minutes late for the announcement of the competition finalists. It didn't help that their hair was wet from the rain and that Gilda's knees were stained with mud.

Mrs. Mendelovich shot Gilda a withering glance but quickly turned around in her seat, too excited to hear the list of finalists to bother reprimanding a tardy page-turner. Julian's teacher beckoned to him with a stone-faced *"you'd-better-get-over-here-right-now!"* look, pointing at the empty chair next to him.

"See how his ears turn red when he's angry?" Julian whispered. "I'd better go sit next to him."

Gilda slipped into a chair at the back of the room as Professor Heslop stepped up to the microphone.

"First, I would like to commend every musician here," said Professor Heslop. "Most of you gave your very best performance in the first two rounds, and it was a difficult decision, indeed. The judges tell me their criterion was simply picking the ten individuals they would like to hear from again—students whose artistry *intrigued* them the most. The ten names I will announce will compete in the final round of the competition at the Sheldonian Theater. If I call your name, please walk to the front of the room and draw a performance number. I will now begin announcing the finalists."

The room fell silent with anticipation.

"Ming Fong Chen!"

Ming Fong let out a squeal of delight and bounced to the front of the room as if she were a participant in a televised game show. After she turned around to face the stony stares and false smiles of her rivals, however, she walked more slowly as she returned to her seat.

Professor Heslop called out a series of names Gilda didn't recognize. Each announcement triggered flurries of hugs and whispered congratulations along with the silent stomach-tightening of those whose names had not yet been called. Across the room, Julian chewed his thumbnail and tapped his foot on the ground.

Professor Heslop frowned and hesitated before calling out the name. "Jenny Pickles!"

Jenny smiled brightly and sashayed to the front of the room with a kind of fashion-runway smoothness. Ms. Pickles sat up very straight, her eyes glued to her daughter as she applauded and smiled fiercely.

"Julian Graham!"

Weary relief relaxed Julian's face at the sound of his name.

He tries to act like he doesn't care about this competition, Gilda thought, *but he obviously would have been devastated if he didn't make it.*

Only one more finalist remained.

"And last but not least," said Professor Heslop, "we have Wendy Choy."

"YES!" Gilda didn't care that her outburst caused half the room to turn and stare. Wendy looked stunned, as if she hadn't quite recognized the sound of her own name. Mrs. Mendelovich had to nudge her to hurry up and claim the last number in the hat.

Gilda grinned broadly at Wendy from across the room, but Wendy didn't smile back. Why did Wendy's face have that familiar tormented look as she walked back to her seat?

Wendy received Mrs. Mendelovich's forgiving bear hug and muttered perfunctory congratulations to Ming Fong, who eyed her warily. Gary stuffed his hands in his pockets and did his best to regard Wendy and Ming Fong with calm benevolence; he had not made it into the finals.

Wendy knew she should feel euphoric. Instead, she simply couldn't believe that she had actually been selected for the finals. She thought how very strange it was that she had beaten the odds—but not necessarily in a way that felt the least bit *lucky*.

Once again, she had drawn the number nine.

36

Substitute Ghosts

I have a very strong feeling about this Charles Drummond, Wendy. I think he might be the key to this mystery."

"And you actually think the competition judges might have *killed* him?" Wendy sat on her bed, twirling her hair and clutching a pillow as if it were a teddy bear.

"I'm not sure what happened—but I definitely smell foul play."

"It's just so hard to imagine. I mean, Waldgrave is mean and everything, but I wouldn't think of him as a *murderer*."

Gilda noticed Wendy's pallor. "You're doing the hair-twirling thing again, Wendy."

"I know."

"Are you okay?"

"I guess." Wendy nibbled on a lock of her hair.

"Wendy—"

"I know, I know. 'Watch out for giant hair balls.'"

"Believe me, you really don't want them."

"I'm glad we both agree that hair balls are my biggest problem right now."

Gilda was crouching down on her knees to peer under Wendy's bed.

"Gilda—what are you *doing?*"

"Just checking. We don't want to miss any new clues—like another tarot card or something."

"I don't even want to know what's under there."

"It's pretty gross under here, actually. I don't think this place has ever been cleaned."

Wendy examined the tips of her hair for split ends. "Anyway, I was just remembering a weird story my mom told me once."

"What story?"

"She said that in China, there were ghosts who would find someone to take their place."

Gilda stood up abruptly. "What do you mean?" She brushed the lint from her knees and sat on Wendy's bed.

"Like, a person who died an 'unclean' death because he or she was murdered or committed suicide or something like that would automatically become a ghost. But this person wouldn't *want* to be a ghost; she'd be looking for some living human being to take her place in the ghost world—a *substitute.*"

"Like a substitute teacher?"

"Yes, Gilda. Exactly like a substitute teacher."

"Sorry."

"I thought you were serious about this."

"I'm totally serious."

"You don't seem serious. In fact, you seem a little abnormal—kind of giddy."

"I'm *listening.* Tell me the story."

"As I was saying, the ghost might pick anyone at all to take his or her place—*any* random person who happens to be in the wrong place at the wrong time. And here's the spookiest part: after finding someone to influence, the ghost leads that person into a situation where he or she will die in *exactly the same way* the ghost died."

The dim, yellow lamplight in the room flickered, and Gilda couldn't help sharing Wendy's unease. "Your mom tells the creepiest stories," Gilda whispered, meaning this as a high compliment. At the moment, the idea seemed to have a very unpleasant plausibility. "So, you think you might be haunted by a 'substitute ghost'?"

"Well, if this Charles Drummond got killed . . . and if he's the one who's haunting this competition—I don't know. What if the same thing could happen to me?"

"No way. You aren't going to die, Wendy."

"But ever since we arrived here, I've had this feeling that something has been *following* me."

"Wendy, if it makes you feel any better, I've never read about 'substitute ghosts' in my *Psychic's Handbook*. Maybe they exist only in China."

"Yeah, probably just another one of those crazy *Chinese* things." With sudden impatient energy, Wendy jumped up from the bed, picked up her toothbrush, and turned on the water in her tiny sink.

"Just don't freak yourself out, okay? There's no way I'm going to let any ghost use you as a substitute."

"I've never felt safer." Wendy brushed her teeth vigorously, as if attempting to channel her anxiety into good dental hygiene. She spat into the sink. "Anyway, if anything like that *did* happen to me, I guess you'd be next in line."

"What?! You'd kill me if you turned into a 'substitute ghost'?"

"Well, I'd be looking for someone to take my place, and there you'd be, pestering me with your Ouija board—a perfect target."

"Why not Jenny Pickles or Ming Fong?"

"You'd be more convenient."

Gilda knew the timing wasn't right, but she couldn't help it: she had been itching to tell Wendy *all* the details of her experience with Julian, and she simply couldn't wait any longer. "So, Wendy . . . this is a little off the subject, but do you notice anything *different* about me?"

"Well, aside from your sudden attention deficit disorder and the mud stains on your knees, that shade of lipstick is pretty dark." Flossing her teeth, Wendy viewed Gilda's reflection in the mirror.

"You haven't noticed anything *else*?"

Gilda looked bedraggled from walking in the wind and rain, but she also bore the flushed, happy appearance of someone who'd been outdoors having a stimulating adventure. Wendy again felt a twinge of annoyance; she knew Gilda had been out doing *something* with Julian. In contrast, her own reflection looked anemic and housebound.

Gilda pointed at her mouth. "It's not the *lipstick* that's different. Can't you tell that these lips have finally been *kissed* by a cute boy? My first kiss—on English soil!"

Wendy turned to face Gilda. "You *kissed* him?"

"Well, he kissed *me*."

"And you kissed him back?"

"No, I slapped his face and ran away giggling."

"Why?"

"I'm *kidding*, Wendy. Of course I kissed him back!"

"But you always told me that your *first* kiss was with Felix in the school play."

"That was acting. This was the *real* thing."

Wendy dropped her used dental floss into the wastebasket with a gesture of disdain. "Well, was he a good kisser?"

"The best. His mouth was like a tiny plunger over my lips."

Wendy folded her arms and frowned at Gilda.

"That's how it's supposed to feel, right?"

"That sounds kind of unpleasant, to be honest."

"You don't seem very excited."

"I'm excited, okay? The main thing is; I'm glad *someone* is having fun here in England. Other people are dealing with the pressure of an international competition and a psychopathic ghost, but that doesn't mean that my best friend shouldn't be out snobbing with English boys."

"Snogging."

"Whatever."

"Wendy, I wasn't just rolling around in a graveyard with Julian. The whole reason I was there in the first place was because I was working on this investigation to help you."

"You and Julian were 'rolling around in a graveyard'?"

"Not exactly. We were actually standing up, and there was this tombstone between us."

"That better not have been Charles Drummond's tombstone."

"What if it was?"

"You kissed a boy over the grave of the ghost who wants to murder me?!"

"Wendy, we don't have any evidence that the ghost wants to *murder* you. Besides, you make it sound so cheap and sordid."

"It does sound a little tasteless."

"Well, it wasn't. It was really romantic, with the rain falling and old mossy tombstones around us everywhere."

"The worms, the corpses..."

"It was very Gothic." Gilda watched as Wendy twisted her long hair into a tight, angry ponytail. "Hey, maybe I could ask Julian if he has a friend you could meet. Then we could go on a double date! I also think Julian could really help us with this investigation. I mean, this ritual I was telling you about seemed to really work—"

"I'm not *jealous*, Gilda. The last thing I have time for right now is a boyfriend."

"I didn't say you were jealous."

Wendy sighed. In truth, she was a little jealous: she was weary of the competition pressure, and she couldn't help envying Gilda's freedom to do something as zany and adventurous as kissing an English boy in a graveyard. "I guess I just don't feel like talking now. I'd probably better get some sleep," she said. "I have a ton of practicing in front of me tomorrow if I'm going to be in shape for the final round."

"Okay." Gilda stood up but hesitated before leaving. "Are you sure you're okay, Wendy?"

"I'll be better if I can just get some rest tonight for a change."

"Just knock on my door if you want to talk."

"I'm fine."

But Wendy wasn't okay. After Gilda left, she walked across the room to find her pajamas, and for an instant, she glimpsed someone *else's* reflection in the mirror.

37

The Accident

In the middle of the night, Wendy awoke with a feeling that there was something important she needed to do—as if she had left something vital somewhere. She stood up, pulled on her boots, grabbed her coat, then quietly left her room without having the faintest idea where she was heading.

As she tiptoed down the stairs, Wendy had the sense that she was a mere observer of her own actions. Her body had suddenly become a vehicle that some unknown driver controlled, and she herself had become a passenger along for the ride. The stranger had a plan—something he or she wanted very badly, and Wendy did not feel that she could protest.

This is a weird dream, Wendy thought to herself, *because it feels so real.*

She made her way down the flights of steps, then out the front door and into the cold night.

At the same moment, Gilda awoke from a light, fitful sleep to the sound of soft footsteps padding quickly down the old staircase. She opened her door to peek into the hallway and was alarmed to see Wendy's door left ajar.

Gilda hurriedly stuck her feet into slippers and jogged down the long flights of stairs just in time to glimpse Wendy swiftly disappearing through the front door of the house.

Shivering in her pajamas without a coat, Gilda stepped into the cold night air. She heard the *clop, clop, clop* of Wendy's footsteps echoing down the dark street as steadily as a loud metronome.

"Wendy!" Gilda's voice was lonely in the empty street.

Slender in the long, unbuttoned coat that billowed loosely behind her, Wendy moved with unwavering purpose, as if propelled by a little engine set on autopilot. This wasn't Wendy's usual slouching shuffle. For a moment, Gilda had a palpable feeling of unreality, as if she had suddenly awakened to find herself following a stranger she had mistaken for Wendy—as if she herself were dreaming.

"Hey! Wendy!" Gilda yelled. "WEN-DEE! WHERE ARE YOU GOING?"

It was as if Wendy were completely deaf. Was she sleepwalking? Gilda followed her along the curving row of Victorian houses that gazed down at the two girls with darkened, hollow eyes.

Wendy began to walk even faster through Jericho, nearing the entrance to Port Meadow. The sound of a fast-approaching car broke the silence, and Gilda suddenly started sprinting. She knew she must catch up to Wendy before it was too late.

As a car sped toward the two girls, Wendy calmly stepped into the street, directly in its path.

38

Dr. Cudlip and the Baffling Case

The car squealed to a halt just as Gilda grabbed Wendy's coat and pulled her back onto the sidewalk without a split second to spare. The two toppled onto the pavement.

"Bloody students!" the driver yelled. "Get off the road, you daft cows!"

"Daft cow yourself!" Gilda retorted, gasping for breath and wishing she could think up a more original comeback.

"Go home and stop loiterin' about on the streets!"

"We will after you go take some driving lessons!"

The driver abruptly revved her car's engine and sped away, muttering something about "irresponsible American kids."

The impact of hitting the sidewalk and the angry exchange between Gilda and the driver seemed to shake Wendy from her trance.

"Gilda," she said, "I think there's something terribly wrong with me."

The next morning, Gilda and Wendy sat in a dreary National Health Service waiting room. The surroundings vaguely reminded Gilda of the experience of waiting with her brother to get his driver's license at the Department of Motor Vehicles. A weary-looking woman sat across from the two girls with a baby who cried weakly; a toddler solemnly observed Gilda and Wendy while picking his nose. Most interestingly, two elderly women who appeared to be identical twins sat dressed in matching white overcoats and furry white hats, their hands folded and their crinkled mouths set in thin lines of pink lipstick. *I wonder if they both have the same illness,* Gilda thought. The room was devoid of magazines, but posters on the wall reminded patients that AIDS IS STILL REAL! and PRENATAL HEALTH BEGINS WITH YOU!

"Wendy," Gilda whispered, "are you sure you want to see a doctor?"

"Gilda, I stepped in front of a car last night without even knowing what I was doing. What if I do that again—or something worse?"

"I know. I'm worried, too. I just don't know if a regular doctor will be able to help you with problems caused by a ghost."

"But what if it *isn't* a ghost? What if I have a medical condition, like . . . a brain tumor or something awful like that?"

Gilda felt an unpleasant cold sensation in her stomach. "Even if you did have something like that—and I'm sure you *don't*—you wouldn't walk out of here knowing it today. Believe me, you'd only leave a little more worried than you are now." Gilda remembered how her father had been sent from specialist to specialist, each of whom ordered multiple tests— a wearying dance between hope and despair—until finally, a diagnosis was given, and everyone settled into the bleak certainty of bad news.

No, Gilda thought, *this cannot happen to Wendy.* At the moment, even a "substitute ghost" seemed preferable.

"You're saying I shouldn't even go to the doctor?"

"No, you should. I guess I just don't like doctors' offices much."

Wendy's face softened as she remembered why Gilda hated waiting around in hospitals. "Sorry—I forgot. And I know what you mean."

Finally, someone called Wendy's name. The two girls followed a weary-looking nurse into an examination room.

"I haven't been feeling like myself," Wendy explained to the nurse, who regarded her with a level stare. *Why are you wasting our time?* her gaze seemed to suggest. *We don't feel like ourselves either.*

"She might have a brain tumor," Gilda blurted. "She needs to see a doctor urgently." Based on memories of her father's ordeal, Gilda believed that it was necessary to convey hyperbolic urgency if one wanted to be taken at all seriously by the medical profession.

The nurse raised an eyebrow. "You've been having headaches? Dizziness?"

"Some."

"Tell her how you've been hearing things, Wendy."

Wendy shot Gilda an irritated glance. "I—I've been hearing things that aren't there."

The nurse frowned and scribbled a note on her clipboard.

"She almost got hit by a car last night," Gilda added. "She's a potential danger to herself and others."

"I'm not a danger to *others*, Gilda."

"The doctor will see you in a few minutes," said the nurse, deciding to let the doctor get to the bottom of this case.

While she and Wendy waited for the doctor, Gilda passed the time by testing tongue depressors to determine whether they were different from the ones in America. She was sticking a tongue depressor in Wendy's mouth when a young, curly-haired doctor entered the room.

"Best not to play with the medical supplies, if you please," said the doctor, snatching the tongue depressors from Gilda's hand and dropping them in the trash.

"I'm Doctor Cudlip. You must be Wendy Choy, then." Dr. Cudlip quickly shook Wendy's hand. He eyed the notes the nurse had left and glanced at his watch.

Gilda wondered what the nurse had written on the chart. She always found it frustrating that you never got to *see* the notes doctors and nurses left for each other. What if the nurse had written something like, *Annoying kids—move them out quickly!* or *Probable insanity; institutionalize pronto!*?

"Here from the States, are you?"

Gilda and Wendy nodded. "I'm here for a piano competition," Wendy explained.

At this, Dr. Cudlip's face brightened and he looked at Wendy directly for the first time. In an instant, she became a person of interest for him. "You're competing in the Young Virtuosos Competition?"

"Yes."

"Brilliant!" Dr. Cudlip sat down on a stool as if he suddenly found himself with time to kill. "I studied piano myself, but I never quite stayed with it long enough to qualify for one of the big competitions. Now I wish I could still play more than anything; you're very lucky to have that talent."

Wendy was familiar with people like Dr. Cudlip—professionals who had studied the piano as children but quit due to lack of interest or talent—doctors, lawyers, and dentists who had abandoned music for something more lucrative and practical, but who still harbored nostalgia for their dreams of concert-stage glory. As adults, they either wished that someone had *forced* them to continue or wholly rejected all artistic pursuits as ridiculous and impractical.

"I'm Gilda Joyce, Wendy's page-turner and official manager." Gilda extended her hand.

"Pleased to meet you, Gilda," Dr. Cudlip replied, with considerably less interest than he had shown toward Wendy. He reviewed his chart and observed Wendy quizzically. "You've been having some headaches?"

Wendy did her best to describe her sleeplessness, the music that continually interrupted her concentration, the experience of awakening in the middle of the night and feeling compelled to search for some object she had lost.

Dr. Cudlip stood up and placed his stethoscope on Wendy's back to listen to her heartbeat.

"And when did all of this start?"

"Mostly since I've been here in Oxford."

"Is jet lag a problem?"

"I guess so."

"Any history of sleepwalking?"

"No."

"Even when you were a young child?"

"Not that I know of."

"On any medication?"

"No."

Dr. Cudlip removed the stethoscope, sat back down on the stool, and stared at Wendy. "What happened to you last night could be a form of sleepwalking. However, that most often happens to patients who have some childhood history. Of course, sleep deprivation and stress can also make sleepwalking more likely, so we shouldn't rule it out *completely*."

Wendy nodded. She didn't like the idea of being a sleep-walker, but it was certainly preferable to a brain tumor, or something worse.

"Now, there's also an interesting condition called *sleep paralysis*, and with that condition, people see and hear all kinds of bizarre things—space alien abductions, monsters—you name it. Because their eyes are open, they think it all must be *real*—that they can't possibly be dreaming. In fact, their *brains* are still asleep."

"Maybe that's what I have," said Wendy, almost eagerly. "Maybe all these strange things are just my brain being partly asleep?"

"Perhaps, but with sleep paralysis, people generally can't *move*. They say that some alien force is pinning them down in their beds, literally paralyzing them. *You* said you were able to get out of bed and walk down the street."

"So, it can't be sleep paralysis, then," said Gilda.

"Well, I expect it's still some kind of sleep disturbance—perhaps a rather unique one caused by stress. My guess is that it will resolve once Wendy catches up on her rest and the stress of an international competition is over. But if the symptoms continue, Wendy, you should have your parents take you to a specialist back in the States. Oh, and make sure you lock your door or place something in your path that will wake you up just in case the sleepwalking happens again."

The doctor scribbled something on Wendy's chart and stood up, preparing to leave the room.

"Just a moment, Dr. Cudlip," said Gilda, "I think we're missing a possible diagnosis here."

"Gilda," Wendy protested, "please don't."

"And that might be?"

"Spirit possession."

The doctor raised his eyebrows. "I think you'd have to talk to a local vicar about that sort of thing; it's not exactly my field."

"It is *my* field," said Gilda, wishing she also had a clipboard to hold. "I'm a psychic investigator."

"Omigod," Wendy muttered under her breath.

"I must confess, Dr. Cudlip," Gilda continued, "that I haven't come across a case quite this perplexing before."

The doctor regarded Gilda as if he suspected that she should be sitting up on the paper-covered examination table instead of Wendy. The fact that she wore her "London Mod" outfit with spidery false eyelashes and a rather obvious wig of straight black hair didn't help her credibility in his mind. He turned his attention back to his patient. "Wendy, do *you* think you might have a case of 'spirit possession'?"

Wendy clutched the edge of the table with both hands and

bounced her foot nervously. "I don't know," she said in a small voice.

"I agree that stress could cause sleepwalking," Gilda continued, "but it *doesn't* explain the fact that Wendy and I actually recorded the voice of a ghost on a tape recorder. We *both* heard it!"

Dr. Cudlip frowned. "I don't understand."

Gilda did her best to explain how she and Wendy had picked up a mysterious voice on tape after Wendy had recorded the melody that literally haunted her—the melody that often awakened her at night. "I believe Wendy's symptoms are evidence of a genuine haunting, Dr. Cudlip."

Considering this piece of information, Dr. Cudlip looked thoughtful. He leaned against the wall, clutching his clipboard to his chest. "There is one case of spirit possession I remember from the medical journals," he said, almost as if talking to himself.

"There *is?*" Wendy and Gilda leaned forward.

"It was a most unusual account—the case of a young man who believed he had been put under a curse by a jealous friend. This boy came from a very well-to-do and respected family, and he had always been well-behaved—a hard worker and a perfect student. But as a result of this supposed 'curse,' the boy thought he was inhabited by a rather unpleasant spirit who forced him to steal things. Within no time, he became a petty criminal, and he ended up in prison, much to his parents' disgrace. As one might predict, the psychiatrist who examined him assumed that the boy had the early stages of schizophrenia—ongoing episodes of hearing voices that weren't there, feeling that someone else was controlling his behavior, et cetera."

Wendy turned pale at the reference to schizophrenia—a diagnosis she feared.

"But—here's where the really *strange* part comes in. While the boy was in prison, some of the *other inmates* actually heard the faint voice of an old woman and saw a cold mist that drifted toward the boy and then disappeared inside him. A priest who came to visit the young man also concurred that this was indeed a true case of possession rather than mental illness. So the psychiatrists were faced with a bewildering question: was *everyone* crazy? Or was this boy truly a victim of possession by a spirit? Was this one of those rare cases we can't explain with medical science?"

Both Gilda and Wendy were fascinated. "So what happened?"

"I believe they performed an exorcism and also gave the boy psychotropic drugs just to cover all the bases. One or the other did the trick."

Gilda turned to Wendy eagerly, but Wendy quickly shut down this idea. "I'm *not* going to subject myself to an exorcism. And I don't want to take drugs either."

"I was not about to suggest that you do," said the doctor. "This is the twenty-first century, for goodness' sake, and I'm not convinced that you need medication at this stage."

"I think Gilda was about to suggest it."

"I like to be open-minded," said Dr. Cudlip, interrupting the burgeoning argument between Wendy and Gilda, "so I acknowledge it's possible that the two of you are experiencing something that modern-day medicine can't explain. But Wendy, my money's still on stress and sleep deprivation as the most simple explanation." He gave Wendy a little wink as he shook her hand. "Come back if things get worse, but at this point, just try not to worry too much. Try to get some rest. And most importantly, best of luck in the finals of the piano competition!"

39

Beneath the Black Water

Well, what do you suggest now?" Wendy wrapped a long scarf around her head several times, trying to keep warm. She and Gilda stood in the bitter morning sunlight outside the health clinic, unsure of what to do next. Students bundled in overcoats and scarves sped past them on bicycles.

"I think we should go back to that graveyard where Charles Drummond is buried."

Wendy wrinkled her nose. "What would that accomplish?"

"After you came out of that trance last night, you said you had a feeling you had to *get* somewhere—that you had left something important behind, right?"

"But I have no idea what 'it' was, or where I was heading."

"But you were walking toward the meadow—exactly in the direction of Charles Drummond's grave. What if there's a clue in the graveyard that his ghost wants you to discover?"

"What if he just wanted me to get hit by a car?"

Gilda fell silent for a moment. She had to admit she had no idea whether the ghost had helpful or malevolent intentions. She also had no idea why a deceased English boy would be haunting a Chinese-American girl—except that it must have *something* to do with the piano competition.

"Wendy, I don't know if we'll find anything in the graveyard; I just have a gut feeling we should look there. Besides, I really want you to see this place."

Wendy considered the stack of music in her tote bag. She knew she should practice, but she was weary of feeling frightened and out of control. Maybe Gilda was right: maybe there was some reason she had been heading toward the meadow. At any rate, it was clear that neither her parents, Mrs. Mendelovich, nor Dr. Cudlip could help her with this problem. She was going to have to work with Gilda and help herself if she wanted to get to the bottom of the mystery. "Okay. If we're going to do this, let's hurry up. I'm freezing!"

When she and Gilda reached the graveyard, Wendy stood very still, listening to the rush of wind through the trees, thinking how different this graveyard was from the ones she and Gilda had explored back in Michigan. The graveyard at St. Margaret's Church was far away from the rush of traffic. The tombstones were moss-covered and unpolished. No little pots of flowers were left behind by the living—no neat paths for people to stroll along. Eerily beautiful in their mossy decay, all the tombstones and small monuments of the graveyard seemed to be sinking into the earth.

A small, moplike terrier with muddy paws and unkempt curly fur broke the silence as it trotted through the graveyard. Gilda and Wendy watched as it snuffled happily along the edges of the tombstones, as if on the trail of some small animal.

"Hey, puppy!" Gilda knelt down and ruffled the dog around the ears. "Maybe it lives over at that farm next to the church," she suggested.

Gilda was about to lead Wendy to Charles Drummond's tombstone when the small dog suddenly bounded away and darted behind the church. To Gilda's surprise, Wendy followed.

As she followed the dog, Wendy felt as if someone were whispering *warmer! warmer!*—urging her to draw closer to something important.

Behind the church, she found the dog lapping water from a hole in the ground.

Wendy stared at the still, black water. She instantly knew that this must be the "treacle well" that was supposed to have "healing" properties. But Wendy also felt there was something almost sinister about it—something that suggested a gloomy world she wasn't sure she wanted to enter. What was she supposed to do? Reach down into the well? Drink the water? Who knew what was down there?

"What is it?" Gilda whispered, appearing at her side.

"I just have a feeling there's something inside this well."

The dog bounded away, and then returned to drop a long stick at Wendy's feet. It wagged its tail, hoping she would play a game of fetch. Wendy picked up the stick, but instead of throwing it to the dog, she tentatively poked it into the water and quickly pulled it out again, as if afraid of what she might touch.

Gilda decided to follow Wendy's lead. Maybe there was some kind of clue inside the well! She rummaged under the trees until she found a long, slender branch lying on the ground.

Standing next to Wendy, Gilda thrust the stick into the water and discovered that the well was deeper than she had expected. She couldn't reach the bottom, but she did feel something unusual beneath the water—an object protruding from one side of the well. "Can you feel that?"

"What?"

"Over here. It feels like something's wedged into the side of the well." Gilda wriggled the branch, attempting to pry loose whatever was stuck beneath the water.

"Reach in there, Wendy, and see if you can tell what it is."

"Maybe *you* should reach in there."

Both girls gasped, because at just that moment, something floated to the top of the black water.

40

The Message

A glass jar bobbed on the surface of the water. It reminded Gilda of jars she had seen in her grandmother's basement that were used for canning fruit, but this jar looked more antique: the glass was elongated and tinted a cloudy blue. It looked as if something might be sealed inside, but it was difficult to see what it was.

Gilda reached into the water and pulled the jar from the well. "I guess we should try to open it."

The two girls hesitated. They stared at the jar, sensing some great significance about this discovery.

"It *might* just be a jar, you know," said Wendy.

"I know." But Gilda felt certain that it *wasn't* just a jar. She felt as if she and Wendy had just intercepted a message from outer space or from another world—as if opening the jar might release something beyond their control.

Gilda took a deep breath and tried to unscrew the lid, but it wouldn't budge.

"You hold it steady," said Wendy. "I'll twist it." Using all the strength in her pianist's hands, Wendy twisted the lid until her face turned red. Finally, the lid came unstuck with a great release of air pressure.

"Go ahead," Gilda whispered. "Look inside."

"I think there's something in here." Wendy carefully retrieved several tightly folded pieces of paper from the jar. As she unfolded the pages and flattened the creases in the papers, she had a sense of recognition, as if an object for which she had been searching had finally turned up.

The papers were a handwritten manuscript of music—a composition titled Sonata in A Minor.

"Hey, it's music! That has to be significant, right?" Then Gilda saw the change in Wendy's face: Wendy suddenly looked as if she might be close to tears. "It's that music you keep hearing, isn't it?"

Wendy nodded.

"Wendy, do you realize what this means? You heard this music before you had ever seen the score! If that isn't being clairaudient, I don't know what is. And my sleuthing skills led us exactly to the right spot! This is *very* exciting."

Wendy wiped her eyes with the back of her hand.

"What's wrong? You don't think this is exciting?"

"I'm not sure." Wendy felt overwhelmed. What did this music have to do with *her*? Why couldn't she explain or control the forces that had drawn her to it?

"Wait, there's something else in there." Gilda pulled one more folded piece of paper from the jar. This page was different—covered with words instead of notation. Gilda and Wendy sat on the steps leading down the well and began to read:

My Time Capsule
by Charles Drummond

I know everyone at my school will be putting letters from loved ones and pictures of their families and favorite toys and maybe even gadgets like old mobile phones or tickets from a Manchester United game into their time capsules. The idea is: "Twenty years from now we'll all dig up our time capsules—if we can remember where we hid them—and look back on where we were this very day in the history of our lives. We'll appreciate how much we—and the world—have grown and changed and the progress we have made."

Well, what's the point of leaving a jam jar filled with trash and trivia for myself to look at? Instead, I'm leaving just one thing that matters, my music.

If you've found this before I've retrieved it, you can see that I've hidden it in a very special place. Unless this land gets sold to build a Sainsbury's car park or something, I reckon the "treacle well" will always be here, since it's considered a sacred patch of land.

Perhaps, in twenty years' time, I will forget about this time capsule or I'll be living far away, in some foreign country. In that case, maybe you're reading this after I am long dead and time has drifted far into the future—maybe even into the next century.

I doubt I'll ever forget about the music I've left here, though. It's hard to explain, but sometimes I get these funny feelings—almost like a kind of premonition or something.

For some reason, I think there's something very important about my time capsule-some reason I'm drawn to hiding it here in this well.

So if you're someone from the future who's reading this letter, I should tell you that in my day people who searched 'round in wells and other bodies of water were usually looking for some kind of loot, or maybe for a wish to come true. In the old days, some people came to this well looking for a mystical cure for whatever ailed them.

Well, here you go. Here's your fairy-tale magic, mate! I hope you already know the value of what you have just found-an original composition by the composer Charles Drummond-an example of his first, early works, written in his own hand. With any luck, that's like finding a new, unknown painting by Leonardo da Vinci or an unreleased recording by the Beatles.

—Charles Drummond, age 14

"A rather confident lad, isn't he?" Gilda couldn't help feeling that Charles Drummond's cocky tone was considerably less poignant and spooky than the white rose on his grave had led her to expect. "Maybe this explains why his ghost is so pushy."

"Maybe he has a right to be cocky." Wendy looked at Charles's music manuscript more closely. Now that she could see the written score, she noticed dissonant harmonies and a contrasting middle section that she hadn't previously heard in her mind. "This composition looks pretty amazing."

Both Gilda and Wendy felt a prickly awareness that they were reading Charles's letter while standing very close to the spot where his dead body was buried. Something about the letter and the music made them feel that he was alive—standing a few feet behind them and reading over their shoulders. "That music really does look *superb*," said Gilda loudly, for the benefit of any ghost who might be listening.

Wendy began nibbling a lock of hair, then stopped herself. "I just think it's weird that we're finding this because of something he originally hid as a project for *school*."

"I know. Remember when we did that time capsule assignment back in sixth grade? None of us would have ever imagined something like *this*." The time capsule Gilda had created in sixth grade had contained a math homework assignment, a half-used tube of pink lip gloss, a bag of Cheetos, a lunch token, one of her mother's phone bills, a magazine article titled "New Makeup Shades for Fall," a poem she had written about vampires, and a photograph of herself wearing her cat's-eye sunglasses. After she had buried the container, she had been asked to retrieve both the math homework and the phone bill, but she had never again been able to find the exact spot where she had hidden everything.

Gilda made a mental note to create an updated time capsule that contained some drafts of her novels-in-progress and psychic investigation reports, in order to preserve them as historical documents. "One thing's for sure," she said. "Charles Drummond obviously expected to be famous. He also expected to be alive for more than a few months after he wrote this."

"So what do you think happened?"

Gilda jumped to her feet with a businesslike sense of purpose. "That's what I'm going to figure out next. Wendy, I think we need to start asking Waldgrave and Maddox some tough questions—find out whether they know about this music and what really happened to this boy."

"What makes you think they'll answer our questions?"

"You know me. I have a few interrogation techniques up my sleeve."

Wendy stared at the tiny black notes of music, already hearing the way the complete composition would sound. "I have to learn this music," she said. *I have a gut feeling that's what he wants,* Wendy thought. *He's desperate for this composition to be played.*

41

A Tormented Soul

Donning her dark cat's-eye glasses, adjusting her "London Mod" wig, and doing her best to mimic the demeanor of a sleep-deprived university student, Gilda approached the heavy wooden doors leading into New College. She strolled past the porter into a spacious, grassy quadrangle. Enclosed by the high stone walls of the college and perfectly groomed trees and shrubs, the courtyard had the quiet, peaceful feeling of a cloister where the outside world was completely silenced.

Maybe people can think better in here, Gilda thought. *If only it were warmer outside, it would be the perfect place to sit and read a whole stack of good books.*

"Sophia! Sophia! Come down from there immediately!"

Gilda couldn't believe her luck. A short distance across the quadrangle, she spied a thin man who stood with his back to her, gazing up into the branches of a chestnut tree. She recognized Professor Waldgrave's hunched posture and the way he wore his corduroy pants belted a bit too high above the waist. His cat, Sophia, peered down at him from her perch in the tree.

Act like an Oxford student, Gilda told herself, summoning the nerve to approach Waldgrave.

"Good afternoon, Professor."

Professor Waldgrave was visibly startled at Gilda's approach. He stared at Gilda's wig as if considering an animal that had decided to nest on her head.

"I'm Gilda Joyce," said Gilda, extending her hand. "I was the page-turner for the sight-reading competition. Remember?"

"Ah, yes; how could I forget? The flying music score. You certainly helped increase the difficulty level for some of the competitors."

"Happy to be of service." Gilda decided to ignore Professor Waldgrave's thinly veiled insult. "Looks like your cat's stuck in a tree," she added.

"Brilliant observation."

Seems like he's in an even grumpier mood than usual, Gilda thought.

The cat yawned and stared down at the two of them with sleepy eyes. Gilda suspected that Sophia was teasing Professor Waldgrave—enjoying the spectacle of her owner's agitation.

"Please, Sophia!" Professor Waldgrave begged. "I have students waiting!"

"Have you tried tempting her with a snack?" Gilda suggested. *If I can help him retrieve his cat, maybe he'll warm up to me*, she reasoned. "I have half a scone left in my bag."

"She doesn't like scones."

Gilda guessed Sophia must be among the most spoiled, temperamental cats in England. "How about a basket of dead rats from the Covered Market?" she joked.

Professor Waldgrave almost smiled. "*That* might interest her. Do you also have rats in your handbag?"

"No." Gilda desperately wished she could produce some rats.

The cat splayed her hind toes and began to lick between them with exquisite attention to detail as Professor Waldgrave paced back and forth beneath the tree. Gilda noticed that he walked with toes pointed outward, like an uncoordinated ballet dancer.

Gilda decided it was best to approach the topic of Charles Drummond gradually in order to gain Professor Waldgrave's trust. *Maybe he'd prefer to talk about his cat*, she thought.

"Tell me, Professor Waldgrave," she said, "is it true what they say about you and your cat?"

"I have no idea." Professor Waldgrave stopped pacing and began to scrutinize the trunk of the chestnut tree, as if he was considering climbing it. "What, pray tell, do they say?"

"You know. They say that Sophia is the one who makes the judging decisions in the piano competition."

"Who on earth told you that?"

"Just—competitors. People in the competition." Gilda suddenly wondered whether this was another one of Julian's stories.

"Well, you can tell them this: Sophia is a *cat*. Cats don't judge piano competitions."

"Oh, I know that. I guess some people think you have a system, and if Sophia purrs or growls, that influences their score."

Professor Waldgrave snorted.

"I mean, it is odd that your cat attends all the performances, isn't it?"

"It isn't the least bit odd. To be completely honest, Sophia has better taste in music than most humans, and that's a fact. If she's helping me judge the competition, perhaps she should be getting paid for her contributions."

Gilda laughed nervously, but Professor Waldgrave only scowled.

"Well, I thought it sounded pretty silly." Gilda now regretted beginning with this line of questioning. It wasn't at all easy to keep loitering near the chestnut tree when Waldgrave was acting so obviously unfriendly.

"So . . . I imagine you must be pretty busy with the competition judging," Gilda ventured, hoping that a renewed attempt at small talk would lead to more important subjects.

"Quite busy."

"They're a fine bunch of piano players."

"Some show promise."

"That performer number nine—Wendy Choy—is a splendid musician."

"The rules forbid me from commenting on any performance outside the concert hall," Professor Waldgrave snapped.

"Sorry." Gilda decided she didn't have much time left; she had to get to the point soon. "I suppose I was just thinking that being around all this young talent makes me pity the musicians who die young."

Professor Waldgrave stopped in his tracks. "Why? Why would this competition make you think such an absolutely morbid thing?"

"Sometimes the dead have a way of speaking to us, don't you agree?"

Professor Waldgrave's face turned gray. "Yes," he said, staring up at his cat. "I agree. I believe dead composers speak through the performances of their music. However, I must say, Gilda, that I have absolutely no idea what on earth you're talking about."

Gilda decided there was no chance of a gentle transition into the questions she really wanted to ask Waldgrave, so she might as well get straight to the point. "Professor Waldgrave, I have reason to believe that you know something about a boy named Charles Drummond. It's important that I find out what happened to him."

Professor Waldgrave turned to look at Gilda with surprisingly vulnerable eyes. He removed his glasses, wiped them off, and put them back on, as if he hoped this might help him view his problems in a better light. "Miss Joyce, I can't imagine why you would be tasteless enough to mention the name Charles Drummond to me, but you have just helped me remember that I am also not supposed to fraternize with young people involved in the competition; it's against the rules."

"But Professor Waldgrave—"

Professor Waldgrave turned on his heel and walked swiftly across the quad, his cat calling mournfully after him.

42

A Disturbing Discovery

TO: Gilda Joyce
FROM: Gilda Joyce
RE: Psychic Investigation Interrogation Results

Suspicions of Professor Waldgrave confirmed! However,
his <u>specific</u> connection to the death of Charles Drummond
and the music that surfaced in the treacle well remains
a mystery. Same goes for Professor Maddox.

TO DO:
Sneak into the New College Library to conduct further
research!

The New College Library was cozy and dimly lit, crammed floor to ceiling with stacks of books arranged in little alcoves. Students sat at tables or in velvet window seats, poring over books and laptop computers, conversing in loud whispers, or sprawling in unapologetic naps. *I can't wait to be a college student,* Gilda thought. *This is exactly the sort of library I love.*

Gilda spied Professor Heslop trudging along in her flat Mary

Jane shoes, carrying a large stack of books and papers. She disappeared into an alcove labeled COLLEGE HISTORY, and Gilda decided to follow, hoping that Professor Heslop might be able to answer some questions.

"Oh, what a surprise!" Gilda declared, pretending to notice Professor Heslop for the first time. "Fancy seeing you here!"

Professor Heslop frowned, her eyes darting up to Gilda's wig, then down to her mud-stained white go-go boots.

"It's Gilda Joyce, Professor Heslop. The page-turner."

"Oh, sorry. I must say, Gilda, you have quite a travel wardrobe."

"Thank you, Professor Heslop. I'm a great admirer of fine tailoring."

"I don't mean to be rude, Gilda, but may I ask what you're doing here? This library is for students of New College."

"Of course. Well . . . " Gilda tried to think of a quick excuse. "Mrs. Mendelovich sent me here on her behalf—to do some research."

"I see. I suppose we can allow it this time, then. Good day."

"Professor Heslop—"

"Yes?"

"I have a rather unusual question pertaining to the judges—Professor Waldgrave in particular."

"I'm afraid I can't talk about the judging until the competition is over."

"This is about something more personal."

"I must abide by the rules, I'm afraid." Professor Heslop spoke in a clipped voice. "You're welcome to take a look in these files for information about the competition, if that would help. I must be off to a tutorial now."

Gilda stuck her tongue out at Professor Heslop's retreating figure. She sighed and decided she might as well take a look through some of the files.

Not sure where to begin, Gilda absentmindedly opened the file in which Professor Heslop had placed some papers. There, she discovered a folder labeled FIFTH ANNUAL YOUNG INTERNA-TIONAL VIRTUOSOS COMPETITION. Inside, a document labeled FIRST ROUND listed names, performance numbers, and compositions performed. Wendy Choy's name appeared next to number nine, followed by the pieces she had performed—the Bach French Suite in G Major and the Mozart Fantasy in D Minor. A handwritten note next to Wendy's name indicated "qualified for final round."

Gilda thumbed through the folders in the cabinet and found that each one documented previous years and locations of the competition: the Fourth Annual Young International Virtuosos Competition in Stockholm, the Third Annual Young International Virtuosos Competition in Paris, the Second Annual Young International Virtuosos Competition in Prague. Finally, she pulled a folder labeled FIRST ANNUAL YOUNG INTERNATIONAL VIRTUOSOS COMPETITION, OXFORD, U.K.

Inside, the introductory letter from the competition's founder, Professor Eugene Winterbottom, appeared next to a picture of a white-haired man with rabbitlike front teeth. *So that's Winterbottom,* Gilda thought.

When she turned to notes from the preliminary round, Gilda let out a little squeak of astonishment. She squinted at the paper more closely, just to make sure she wasn't seeing things.

Halfway down the page was the name Charles Drummond.

Omigod, Gilda thought, feeling almost dizzy at the discovery. *His performance number is nine. That must be why Wendy keeps drawing it!*

Something else also seemed eerily familiar—the titles of Charles's performance selections—the Mozart and Bach... *Weren't those Wendy's pieces as well?*

A note next to Charles's name said "qualified for finals." But when Gilda turned the page to view the list of final performers, only nine pianists remained: Charles's name had somehow vanished from the list.

Gilda wanted to sit down, but she was too excited to find a chair. She dropped down to the carpeted floor. Sitting cross-legged, she flipped open her reporter's notebook and began to scribble furiously:

> What happened to Charles Drummond between qualifying for the finals of the piano competition and his last performance?
>
> I have an eerie feeling about this. Far too many things about Wendy and Charles Drummond are frighteningly similar.
>
> I hate to even think of it, but what if Wendy's idea about a "substitute ghost" is actually right, and Charles Drummond's ghost is looking for "someone to take his place"?

On the other hand, it seems clear that Maddox and Waldgrave have something to do with all of this, and that suggests a purely criminal element.

What if there's a murderer or serial killer who targets one of the piano students in the competition each time it's held in Oxford?

Gilda remembered glimpsing the rage in Professor Waldgrave's eyes when she had mentioned Charles's name. Was Waldgrave capable of murdering someone?

Gilda felt a new sense of urgency. She wanted to do more research, but she decided she had to hurry to the Music Building to tell Wendy what she had found right away. She had to warn Wendy to be careful.

43

A Drop of Poison

The Music Building hallway reverberated with chaotic sound—a tangle of scales, arpeggios, and pounding passages from Chopin, Liszt, Brahms, and Beethoven. Anticipation, fear, and white-hot concentration pervaded the practice rooms: all ten finalists played with feverish intensity, as if declaring: *This is it. I might actually win this!*

Gilda peeked into a practice room window and spied Ming Fong blasting out a series of running octaves over and over, with robotic precision and focus.

Gilda made her way down the row of practice rooms, glancing into each window in search of Wendy. Just then, she heard a passage of music that sounded distinctly *unserious*—a boisterous, ridiculously embellished version of "Heart and Soul." Gilda remembered learning to play a clunky version of this piece during her short-lived stint as a piano student. She smiled, feeling certain that it must be Julian playing. *It would be just like him to turn the most intense practice session of the competition into a joke*, she thought.

But when she stood on tiptoe and peeked into the practice room window, Gilda's smile faded. Her skin turned hot and cold all at once. She felt as if microscopic spiders were skittering across her nerves.

Inside the practice room, Julian sat at the piano next to Jenny Pickles.

Jenny's face looked flushed. She giggled as Julian reached across her body to drag the back of his hand across the keys in a sweeping glissando that nearly knocked Jenny off the piano bench. Then the music stopped because Julian was leaning closer to Jenny, and she was leaning closer to him. Gilda couldn't believe what she was seeing. *It can't be happening*, she thought. *It just can't be happening.*

But it was happening: right before her eyes, the two of them were actually *kissing*.

Gilda was about to burst into the room, but something stopped her. She turned around and leaned against the practice room door, absorbing her shock and revulsion at the scene she had just witnessed. She reached in her handbag and put on her cat's-eye sunglasses, as if a disguise would protect her from the hot spring of jealousy that bubbled inside.

Feeling that tears might surface at any moment, Gilda whisked out her notebook and marched down the hallway to the ladies' room. Once safely inside, she closed a stall door, sat on a toilet, and began scribbling as fast as she could:

It's come to this!
Here I am—in a foreign country—an ocean away from Ferndale High School and armpit-deep in a psychic mystery. Yet, here I am, writing in my journal in the girls' bathroom and crying about a boy.

I am love's victim, tormented and spurned!
With "mod" hair and vinyl boots,
The lovelorn girl
Wanders through Oxford mists
Trailing her poison tears,
Haunted by the specter
Of a lost and fetid love.

Gilda felt a little better after expressing her feelings in a poem. Her blood still boiled with outrage, but she couldn't help but feel pride in her literary talent. *Maybe this is what it means to "suffer for your art,"* she thought.

I bet Julian comes to these piano competitions with one goal in mind: snogging as many girls as possible. I bet he does it all the time: "Oh, gee! This kiss just happened, and I didn't plan it at all!"

Gilda paused, searching for words that would make herself feel strong again—words that would somehow make her care less.

Come on, Gilda! Get a grip! Who cares if Julian and Jenny want to waste their time touching butts on the piano bench? Who needs the sensation of a tiny toilet plunger over your lips anyway?

You're a psychic investigator with a real career, not some boy-crazy cheerleader! As an investigator, you're supposed to lead a solitary and squalid life. You think nothing of dining alone on hard-boiled eggs and straight whiskey—nothing of facing some of the toughest criminals and most perplexing hauntings in history!

Don't forget, you came to this Music Building with a purpose—to tell Wendy what you discovered about Charles Drummond and to warn her to be careful! Your best friend is about to perform in the final round of an international competition, and she is either being stalked by someone who targets young musicians or possessed by a potentially murderous ghost...or both!

Get back to your work and forget about Julian immediately!!!

Somewhat bolstered by the pep talk she had just given herself, Gilda stood up and checked her reflection in the bathroom mirror. Her false eyelashes were askew, so she peeled them off, slipped her sunglasses back on, and reapplied her white lipstick.

She returned to the hallway lined with practice rooms, determined to find Wendy and to forget about Julian.

Gilda burst into Wendy's practice room, eager to vent her outrage about Julian and announce the discoveries she had made in the library that afternoon. Instead, she fell silent. She felt compelled to sit down and listen.

Wendy leaned forward on the piano bench, squinting at the handwritten, yellowed pages on her music stand as her hands flew across the keyboard. Something about the music she played made Gilda's scalp prickle; she could literally feel her hair standing on end. She knew it had to be the music they had discovered in the well.

Gilda had heard of people who could literally see music—people who had something called kinesthesia, which enabled them to perceive sound waves as colors. As she listened to the Sonata in A Minor written by a boy who died at age fourteen, Gilda could almost imagine what this sensation must be like. *If this music had a color,* she thought, *it would be silver and pearly white, dark blue and black. It would be like a ghost wandering through a moonlit graveyard.*

44

The Ghost in Gloucester Green

So far, Gilda had avoided calling home as a matter of principle. She wanted to be able to tell herself, *I went overseas for the first time in my life and didn't get homesick! I didn't even need to call home once!*

But as she walked toward the Gloucester Green bus station, something about the waning daylight made her feel nostalgic for home. Maybe it was the damp chill that seeped into the air with the settling fog, the echoing *clip-clop* of leather shoes upon the pavement as people hurried home from work, the glimpses through basement windows of lonely students typing papers at their desks. To make matters worse, she kept seeing boys who resembled Julian—tall, thin boys with pale skin and dark hair—boys who hunched their shoulders as they cringed from the cold, wearing jackets that weren't warm enough.

Gilda stepped into a phone booth and placed a collect call to her mother. As she listened to the faraway ringing of her family's telephone back in Michigan, she read the graffiti on the phone booth wall:

Nigel is a daft git
↑ *No, he isn't*

Today could be your last day. Make the most of it.
↑ Okay, I'll go watch telly, then

Blair is a ponce
↑ No he isn't...

Stephen answered the phone. "Hello?"

"Hey, Stephen! It's your long-lost sister!"

"Mom's not here right now, Gilda."

"I miss you, too."

"Sorry—I just assumed you wanted to talk to Mom. Are you in trouble or something?"

"Why would I be in trouble?"

"Because this is the first time you've called. Mom was worried, but then she said, 'No news is good news when it comes to Gilda.'"

"It's good to know my family has such a high opinion of me." Gilda began to regret calling home at all. "Actually, things are fabulous here. I did a fantastic job turning pages and Wendy made it into the final round of the competition."

"Wow. She made it into the finals?"

"We're both practically celebrities around here, Stephen. We're meeting absolutely brilliant people."

"Are you trying to speak in an English accent?"

"This is how I always talk."

"It kind of sounds like you're faking an English accent."

"I also met this absolutely brilliant bloke named Julian." *And he broke my heart*, Gilda thought.

"Uh-oh."

"Why 'uh-oh'?"

"Anyone with the name 'Julian' sounds like a potential problem."

"You're so provincial, Stephen." Secretly, Gilda wanted to agree with him.

"I'll tell Mom you called, okay?"

"Wait, Stephen—"

"Yeah?"

Gilda wanted to confide in someone, and she particularly wanted a boy's perspective. Of course, Stephen wasn't known for his dating expertise. He had suffered a single broken heart in the past, and it had left him almost permanently grouchy. *He's probably the worst person I could talk to*, Gilda thought. On the other hand, Wendy had been preoccupied with preparing for the competition finals, and Gilda simply needed someone to listen. "Stephen," she said, "I need your opinion about something."

"You *do*?"

"Let's just say you were a boy."

"I am a boy."

"I mean, let's just say you were a boy who liked girls."

"What's that supposed to mean?"

"Let's just say you liked a *particular* girl—in fact, you *acted* like you liked her a lot. It was all really romantic and intense."

"What did you *do*?"

"Hardly anything."

"Maybe you should talk to Mom."

"She'll just get all worried and start calling me night and day. Anyway, as I was saying, let's say you like this girl and you let her know it, but the weird thing is that the very next day—you kind of did the *same thing* with this *other* girl."

"Is the other girl cute?"

"What does that have to do with anything?"

"Maybe I like both girls."

"That's all you have to say?"

"Look, for one thing, I'm not exactly sure what we're talking about here, and I don't think I *want* to know. For another thing, I probably wouldn't be *lucky* enough to have two girls get interested in me at the same time."

"You're a huge help."

"You asked me what I thought."

"My mistake."

"Gilda, the only thing I can tell you is that some guys—some people—they don't take everything as seriously as you do."

"I don't take things seriously."

"You take *everything* seriously."

"I do?"

"You have to watch out for being too clingy."

Gilda was indignant at this comment. "What do you mean clingy?! Which one of us is in a foreign country all by herself, and which one is clinging to his mother's bosom?"

"For your information, I've hardly seen Mom all week. Anyway, all I was saying is that you have a way of getting involved and sticking with people, whereas other people might let go more easily."

"Maybe other people are shallow."

"Yeah, they probably are."

"And I don't 'stick' with people, either. I drop people like hot potatoes, right and left."

"You've had the same best friend for years."

"That's a *good* thing."

"Okay. But what about all of this stuff about trying to talk to dead people? Isn't that just a way of not being able to let go of someone who's not here anymore?"

Now Gilda was completely offended. "Listen, Stephen, I'm not chasing dead people around because I'm 'clingy.' They're the ones who talk to *me*!"

"Forget I said anything."

"I will."

"Gilda . . . I just don't want you to get hurt, okay?"

"Oh." This comment surprised Gilda. "Okay." She rarely encountered a protective streak in her older brother. "Don't worry," she said. "I'm as tough as they come."

As she hung up the phone, she had to admit she felt a little better after talking to Stephen. *Maybe by the time I get home and sit down in the kitchen to eat a Pop-Tart and tell Mom and Stephen about my adventures, Julian won't matter to me anymore*, Gilda told herself.

As she made her way back through the square, which was now almost completely empty, Gilda thought about what Stephen had said. *Am I really "clingy"?* she wondered. It was an insulting, diminishing word that in no way reflected how Gilda saw herself—brilliant, sultry, rough-edged—a psychic detective who managed to combine high fashion with the hard-boiled demeanor of a seasoned police officer. Hadn't she proven that she wasn't afraid of ghosts, foreign travel, or performing in front of live audiences? Surely she wasn't the type of fragile girl who could be so easily "hurt" by the silly whims of a boy.

On the other hand, she couldn't help thinking there might be a kernel of truth to Stephen's point. What if there was something about losing her dad that made her want to hang on to certain people—even people who had already disappeared forever?

But why is that such a bad thing? Gilda wondered. *Why does it always seem that people are supposed to care about each other less?*

As Gilda considered these questions, she noticed a boy walking through Gloucester Green—a stranger who seemed somehow familiar. He wore a long, black overcoat and carried what looked like a term paper or manuscript rolled up as if it were a diploma or an antique scroll. He walked through the silent square whistling a somber tune—a melody that also sounded like something she had heard before.

The boy disappeared around the corner onto the High Street, and Gilda decided to follow him.

But when Gilda rounded the corner, the boy had vanished. Standing on the empty street lined with streetlamps and shops that had closed for the evening, Gilda felt a cold, tingling sensation. She remembered reading about "walking ghosts" in her *Psychic's Handbook*—ghosts that materialize to walk a certain path and then vanish just as an onlooker approaches to speak to them.

Gilda remembered the apparition she saw on her first night at Wyntle House. *I feel like I just saw a ghost again*, she thought.

45

The Last Sign

Wendy stayed in her practice room until after nightfall, memorizing the structure of the Sonata in A Minor. The composition was more complex than the simple melody she had heard in her mind, but she loved the way a single familiar voice wandered through the entire piece, sometimes inverted and interwoven with countermelodies as in a fugue.

Something had changed, because Wendy no longer felt scared. Instead, she felt excited, as if she had a special secret—a secret kept between herself and somebody nobody else could see.

I've never really had any interesting secrets of my own, Wendy thought. *My parents always know where I am. I always practice the piano and do my homework. I've always tried to perform my music exactly the way Mrs. Mendelovich wants me to play it. And what do I get in return? I get to feel like I'm a good person—a dutiful daughter who's grateful for everything her parents have sacrificed.*

Wendy still *wanted* to please her parents, but for the first time in her life, she sensed a different calling. When she played the Sonata in A Minor, she felt like a true artist—

someone who was making her own choices, someone who felt compelled to play music for its own sake.

As Wendy played through the composition, an idea was taking shape in her mind—a rebellious, impetuous idea that Mrs. Mendelovich, her parents, and quite possibly the judges would not like.

I've always been afraid of disappointing other people, Wendy thought. *I'm done being afraid.*

It was late, and Wendy knew she would have to head back to Wyntle House in the dark. She turned off the light and shut the door to her practice room just in time to see Ming Fong leaving her practice room at exactly the same moment. Wendy knew the two of them should walk back to Wyntle House together, but she simply didn't want to face Ming Fong's competitive questions and comments: *"Do you feel ready?" "How long did you practice today?" "What did Mrs. Mendelovich say at your last lesson? She told me I have a chance of winning!" "Don't worry; I know you'll be perfect next time, Wendy. Not like your first performance. . . ."* Wendy slipped down the hallway before Ming Fong noticed her, deciding to walk in the opposite direction instead.

Wendy walked past Christ Church College in the moonlight and decided to take a shortcut down Dead Man's Walk. She shivered in the damp fog, walking as quickly as she could. When she reached the Merton College Chapel, she heard the faint, ethereal sound of a boys' choir accompanying an evensong service. Then she heard something that made her heart beat faster—the lonely sound of footsteps walking a short distance behind. *Someone's following me*, she thought.

A familiar icy sensation crept under Wendy's skin and into her bones; it seemed she had wandered into an unpleasantly familiar dream.

You're not afraid anymore, Wendy reminded herself. She took a deep breath and turned to glance behind her. The footsteps immediately stopped.

It was hard to see clearly in the foggy darkness, but Wendy glimpsed what appeared to be the shadowy figure of a young man wearing a dark coat. He slipped through a gate in the college wall.

See? Wendy told herself. *It was just a college student.*

Nevertheless, Wendy walked at an even brisker pace as she made her way back to the guesthouse.

Wendy entered the dim, yellowish light of Wyntle House with a feeling of relief. She heard the television blaring from inside Mrs. Luard's room. As she climbed the creaking staircase leading to the second floor, she heard a mother reprimanding her young son from inside a guest room: "Stop hitting him, Sam!"

"But he loiks it, Mum!" the little boy replied.

On the next floor, she overheard Jenny Pickles arguing with her mother about an evening gown that was "too pink!"

Maybe I have time for a little catnap before dinner, Wendy told herself. But when she opened the door to her room, she discovered something waiting for her. A tarot card lay on the mauve carpeting like an ominous little stain.

The picture on the card showed a faceless figure wearing a dark cloak—a creature with heavy wings and a long, sharp scythe. A thin trail of blood trickled from the edge of its cloak.

At the bottom of the card, the word DEATH was printed in large letters.

46

Art and War

TO: Gilda Joyce
FROM: Gilda Joyce
RE: SUSPECT UPDATE—
INVESTIGATION OF MING FONG CHEN

I think I've only seen Wendy in tears a couple times—once was after she got stung by a wasp, and another time after she got a B minus on an oral report. So when she knocked on my door and showed me the Death card she found without even trying to hide the fact that she had been crying, I knew I had to do <u>something</u> right away.

"Don't worry, Wendy," I said. "I'm turning my <u>full</u> attention to making sure nothing happens to you and to solving this investigation now. I promise you're going to be just fine. You just focus on winning that final round tomorrow night."

Wendy seemed skeptical that I could actually help her, but I managed to calm her down by putting the kettle on, pouring a cup of tea, and turning on the television. Once she was tuned into an Australian soap opera, she began to feel safer.

Meanwhile, I seized an opportunity to sneak into Ming Fong's room. I knew it was wrong to snoop and that I could potentially get into big trouble, but I just had to take the risk. I had to find out once and for all whether Ming Fong had anything to do with this tarot card business!

Naturally, Wendy and I were wondering if the Death card was actually another message from the ghost of Charles Drummond—a more disturbing explanation to say the least. Wendy felt confused. She said that after discovering the music in the well, she had almost come to "trust" his ghost. She said she felt sure that she was meant to perform the music she had discovered.

On the other hand, you never know with ghosts. Neither one of us had ever dealt with a situation quite like this before, and I knew I had to keep investigating every angle of the case.

When I peeked into the hallway and saw that Ming Fong had left her door open while she was in the shower and that familiar Happy Nails! tote bag just beckoning to me, I couldn't help it; I had a strong gut feeling I should take a peek inside.

Objects in Ming Fong's Happy Nails! bag:
Odd, fish-shaped snacks labeled with Chinese characters
Comb
Passport
Vinyl wallet decorated with a plastic pink flower
Stick of Chap Stick (unscented)
Red pencils bundled with a rubber band (she must use
    these to mark up her piano music)
Books of piano music

Initial findings were admittedly disappointing. But then I discovered a secret side pocket in the bag. Inside, there was a tiny, worn paperback book with a <u>very interesting</u> title: it was called <u>The Art of War</u> by Sun Tzu. I looked through the book's introduction and saw that Sun Tzu was a Chinese warrior from ancient times who wrote about warfare and "subduing the enemy."

"Why is an underweight pianist like Ming Fong studying warfare techniques?" I asked myself. Then, as I read through passages in the book about "wearing your opponent down" and "the art of studying moods," I began to feel justified in my suspicions:

"Carefully compare the opposing army with your own, so that you may know where strength is superabundant and where it is deficient."

"If your opponent is taking his ease, give him no rest. If his forces are united, separate them."

"Attack him where he is unprepared; appear where you are not expected."

As I read, I couldn't help thinking how often I had noticed Ming Fong observing Wendy with this weird intensity, almost as if she was looking for areas of weakness to exploit.

"Maybe Ming Fong views this competition as a war," I thought. "And if that's the case, she might be willing to do just about anything to win it."

Well, here's where I became so curious about this <u>Art of War</u> book that I made a huge mistake. I stopped thinking like an investigator, and I didn't even hear Ming Fong padding down the hallway toward her room. When I looked up it was too late: there she was, standing in the doorway with wet hair and a big towel wrapped around her. Ming Fong had caught me red-handed snooping in her room, and it was my own fault. It was VERY AWKWARD, to say the least. I did my best to take control of the situation—to act like a professional investigator instead of a nosy teenage girl.

ME:	Very interesting reading choice, Ming Fong.
MING FONG:	Give it back.
ME:	(waving the book just out of her reach) Just a minute, Ming Fong. We need to talk about this.

Ming Fong tried to grab the book. As I held it just above her head, something interesting happened: a piece of paper fell from the book. We both dove to pick it up, but because she was wearing a towel and trying not to flash me or anyone else in the hallway, I managed to grab the piece of paper first.

I proceeded to read a letter Ming Fong had written, which went something like this:

"Dear Lang Lang:
    I am writing this letter to express my love for you. I am also pianist, about to win Young International Virtuosos

Competition in England. You are my inspiration and I kiss your picture before each time I play. This brings such luck to me and my family!

I know about your life. Your father take you away from home so young to dedicate yourself to piano and how proud you make your family. You inspire me to be perfect too.

If I win the Young Virtuosos Competition, would you like to give a concert with me at Carnegie Hall?

I love you.

Ming Fong"

As I read, Ming Fong's face turned about five shades of red.

ME: "I kiss your picture"?
MING FONG: That letter is a joke. I wasn't going to
                         mail it.
ME: Ming Fong, I don't care if you send Lang
                         Lang twenty lipstick-covered letters and a
                         marriage proposal. What I'm interested
                         in is your little game of psychological
                         warfare.
MING FONG: What game?
ME: This book The Art of War is all about
                         finding people's weaknesses and psyching
                         them out. I mean, all this stuff about
                         "destroying enemies" seems a little harsh
                         when we're supposed to be here as part
                         of an "international community of musi-
                         cians and friends."

MING FONG:	It's just a book.
ME:	I'll get to the point, Ming Fong. This book gives me another reason to believe that you've been leaving tarot cards around to make people nervous.
MING FONG:	I didn't do it.

"But a piano competition EEZ a war," said Mrs. Mendelovich from the doorway.

Both Ming Fong and I were shocked to see Mrs. Mendelovich standing there, watching us. As far as I knew, she hadn't ventured up to our rooms since we had first arrived in Oxford.

Mrs. Mendelovich is tiny, but she always has this huge presence—like a great ballerina onstage. She was dressed for the evening in a black wool coat and red high heels. As always, her eyes were rimmed with smudged eye pencil and her skin looked more shadowed and wrinkled than ever under the yellowish light in Ming Fong's bedroom.

"The musician who weens this piano competition weell approach each day like a warrior—with total focus," Mrs. Mendelovich said. "Theese pierson will be better than human—thinking of only her mission to be pearfect. Takes glreat strength, glreat courage."

ME:	But Mrs. Mendelovich, are you aware that <u>someone</u> around here might be trying to gain an unfair

	advantage by leaving frightening tarot cards for other musicians in the competition?
MRS. MENDELOVICH:	Yes.
ME:	(totally shocked) You ARE?!
MRS. MENDELOVICH:	The Russian boy received one, and also, I think, a Frinch girl. I say to them and to Professor Heslop when they tiell me: "This is a test—a test for the power of the mind. Because there will always be some small pierson who is wishing for you to fail. Do not give this pierson your power," I say to them.
ME:	But did you know that Wendy received tarot cards, too?
MING FONG:	Me also.
ME:	They're also some of the most disturbing images in the deck.
MRS. MENDELOVICH:	No matter. What is a tarot card? Piece of paper with a picture. No power if you don't believe.

Well, Mrs. Mendelovich made it clear that there was no point in talking about it further. I could see her point: whether a tarot card or anything else like a horoscope or even a fortune cookie has the power to upset you is basically determined by whether you're willing to underline believe underline what it says in the first place. On the other hand, it's pretty hard to completely forget about those cards once you do see them, even if you're trying not to give the images any credit. Besides that, you'd think that as a teacher, Mrs. Mendelovich would care a little more if some kid around here is trying to undermine people. Maybe she doesn't want to know. Maybe she's scared it would turn out to be one of her own star students. Then she'd be pretty embarrassed!

Unless some real evidence turns up, I guess I have to take Ming Fong's word for it when she says she has nothing to do with these tarot cards—at least for now. (But I'm still keeping an eye on her.)

I also have to look out for Wendy. At the moment, she seems weirdly calm, considering the fact that she just received the Death card. I, on the other hand, feel nervous. After all, it's the night before the finals, and we know that _something_ happened to Charles Drummond before he got a chance to play his final performance.

47

The Final Round

It was the night of the competition finals, and Gilda had taken it upon herself to act as Wendy's wardrobe consultant and makeup artist as well as her bodyguard. She had come to the tiny backstage dressing room of the Sheldonian Theater prepared with a suitcase containing a choice of two different evening gowns, a makeup kit, a tiara, a wig, a 1960s-style hairpiece, and three different pairs of high-heeled shoes.

Gilda squinted at Wendy, admiring the false eyelashes she had applied and the heavily teased hairdo she had created as Wendy's stylist-for-the-evening. "I think you should wear the yellow dress," she suggested.

"Why? Because it's the most hideous dress on the planet?"

Purchased for five dollars at a neighborhood garage sale, the yellow dress was designed in the style of Princess Diana's wedding gown. It had most likely been worn years ago by a bridesmaid or someone attending a high school prom.

"To an *ordinary* person, it's hideous," Gilda admitted, "but on a great performer, it's high impact—the kind of dress an opera diva would wear as she breezes onstage."

"Maybe if I was a two-hundred-pound opera singer it would look better. On *me*, it looks like a very ugly bridesmaid's dress."

"I wish we had one of those tall, powdered wigs like they wore in the eighteenth century. *That* would really be something with this dress."

"You're insane."

"Wendy, you'd probably win the competition without playing a note if we had one of those wigs. The English act very strict about proper dress for each occasion, but then they secretly love it when someone does something zany. And don't forget how they love tradition. Just look at those ridiculous wigs they wear in courtrooms!"

"I hate to disappoint you, but I'm actually thinking of wearing the red dress my mom gave me. I thought it seemed too 'Chinese,' but red is supposed to bring luck."

"Then you should definitely wear it."

Gilda pulled on her sequined evening gown and peered into the mirror to adjust a rhinestone tiara. "But you have to give me some credit for the hair and makeup," she said. "I mean, we practically look like models."

"It does look cool," Wendy acknowledged, once again feeling grateful that her mother wasn't around to see her wearing so much makeup. "But why are *you* so dressed up?"

"Wendy, as your manager, I have to project a positive impression for the public. Besides, when else do I get to wear this outside my own house?"

"Wendy Choy!" Professor Heslop's voice called impatiently from the performance hall.

"I guess it's my turn to warm up on the piano in the hall."

"I'll come with you." Gilda had decided she wasn't going to let Wendy out of her sight. So far, everything had gone smoothly, but Gilda was still keenly aware that Wendy might be in danger.

As Wendy entered the performance hall, she froze, momentarily overcome with the magnitude of her imminent performance in the Sheldonian Theater. She gazed up at the rows of benches decorated with ornate, sphinxlike creatures, and then at a high balcony supported by marble pillars and coats of arms. Looming over the piano were organ pipes in shades of gold and green. it suddenly struck her that this room of gilded gold and marble would soon be filled with people who had actually purchased *tickets* to hear the music. The fact that she was about to take the risk of performing a piece she had just learned the day before seemed sheer lunacy.

Wendy sat down at the grand piano, placed her hands on the ivory keys, and stared at her slender, feminine fingers. Were her hands really capable of this? Was her brain capable?

"What's wrong?" Gilda observed Wendy's sudden motionlessness with concern.

"I'm okay. . . . Just getting focused." *It doesn't really matter what anyone thinks of me*, Wendy told herself. The simple thought was oddly reassuring. *Just listen for the music and it will be there. After all, you've been thinking about it for days.*

Wendy began to run through scales and arpeggios, and Gilda sat down in the front row of the theater and gazed up at the gilded ceiling that arched above her.

"You look like you're off to a fancy dress party."

Gilda's heart suddenly raced. She was annoyed to feel her

face flush with warmth and a surge of hope as she turned to find Julian standing behind her.

"You're all glittery," he added with a wry grin.

"Same to you." Julian wore a tuxedo with an untied bowtie. Gilda couldn't help noticing that he had a way of making even a formal suit look appealingly disheveled and undone. She also noticed that he looked more pale than usual.

"Haven't seen you about," said Julian.

"I've been busy with my investigation." Gilda did her best to sound nonchalant. "You would have found it quite fascinating if you had been around."

"Making great discoveries, then?"

"Of course. It's truly amazing what one can discover while faffing about."

"Still mad about that, are you?"

"Oh, no. I'm not mad about *that*."

Julian sat down in the seat next to her. "So what did you discover in your sleuthing?"

"Something very intriguing and bizarre about that boy Charles Drummond." As she said the name Charles Drummond, an image of herself kissing Julian over Charles's grave popped into her mind and she felt her cheeks redden.

As if reading her mind, Julian leaned a tiny bit closer to her. "I'm curious," he said. "Tell me more."

He also kissed Jenny Pickles, Gilda reminded herself. *You're mad at him, remember?* "I'm not at liberty to discuss my investigation right now."

Julian shrugged, doing his best to act as if he didn't care one way or another what Gilda might tell him. "Sounds like you've had a better time than I have; my teacher had me practicing nonstop. I don't see the point. You've either got it or you don't."

"Did you get your version of 'Heart and Soul' just right?"

Julian's eyes darted nervously. He exhaled an uncomfortable laugh.

"You look nervous."

"I'm not."

"Are you sure?" Gilda had an urge to make Julian feel uncomfortable.

"Well, to be honest, I never get nervous before a performance, but I feel like something's different this time."

"Feeling *guilty* about something?"

"Like what?"

"Oh—maybe your sordid lovefest with Jenny Pickles in the practice room?"

"What?" Julian pretended to look confused, but Gilda could tell he was acting. "You're bonkers."

"Julian, I saw it with my own eyes."

"We played a duet."

"You kissed."

"You're dotty."

"Julian, at least admit the truth." Gilda sensed that with each sentence she spoke, she was losing ground somehow. She felt as if she were sliding down a rain-drenched hillside, grabbing at tree branches and plants that slipped from her grasp.

"Maybe you were seeing a ghost."

"Don't insult me, Julian."

"Look, Jenny and I were just playing some tunes for a lark.

Maybe there was a little kiss. I can't really remember. It didn't mean anything."

"'Maybe there was a little kiss,' but you can't *remember*? Is that how you feel about what happened with us in the graveyard, too?"

"That was different."

"How?"

"I don't know. Spookier. You're special."

"I'm your 'spooky' date, and Jenny's there for larks?"

"I don't know. Bloody hell, I didn't realize we were married." Julian looked as if he couldn't wait to escape. "I don't much appreciate being spied on."

"I wasn't spying; I was looking for Wendy because I had something important to tell her. It's not my fault you and Jenny were slobbering over each other in public."

He's the most maddening, frustrating, self-centered person I've ever met, Gilda thought. *I hate him!* At the same time, she couldn't help thinking that ever since she had seen Julian kissing Jenny Pickles, he seemed even cuter than before. His slouchy posture, his close-set and very blue eyes, his small mouth with crowded teeth, the spiky, disheveled remnants of a once-neat, school-boyish hairstyle—everything about him was newly appealing as well as infuriating.

"Look, Gilda, I like you." He rubbed his hands together, gazing a few inches over Gilda's head. "It's just—I have a competition to focus on right now."

"Same here."

"Julian!" Professor Heslop's voice interrupted their conversation. "Your turn for ten-minute warm-up!"

"I'd better get to it."

"Break a couple legs."

As Julian headed for the piano, Gilda realized Wendy had already disappeared from the performance hall. Running into the hallway to look for her, Gilda spied Ming Fong wearing her headphones and pacing back and forth with tiny, measured steps, as if she were a toy soldier.

"Hey, Ming Fong, have you seen Wendy?"

Ming Fong didn't respond. Instead, she did something strange: she reached into the pocket of her dress and pulled out a tarot card that she held directly in Gilda's face without making eye contact, as if she were a police officer holding up a hand to stop oncoming traffic.

The image on the card looked anxious and turbulent; it depicted seven swords spinning through the air and piercing a large numeral seven. The word UNCERTAINTY was at the bottom of the card.

"I just found this in my pocket," said Ming Fong. "And I told you I didn't do it."

Before Gilda could respond, she noticed a flurry of activity a short distance down the hallway. The two Italian boys she remembered seeing in their tracksuits at the drawing of numbers appeared to be in a heated argument. One of them was exclaiming about "bad luck!"

They drew a small crowd of competitors—the French girl who always wore her hair in messy braids, the Russian boy with the pants that were too short, two kids from London. Everyone spoke with agitated voices about something.

Gilda drew closer to the group and saw that each of the

competition finalists had received a tarot card. Their voices overlapped as they compared the cards they had just discovered:

"What are these?"

"They're tarot cards—like for telling your future."

"But this looks unlucky."

"Exactly. Looks like someone wants you to think you're going to have rotten luck."

"Where did you find yours?"

"Fell out of my music bag just as I was warming up."

"Mine was in my jacket pocket."

"This is the second one I've gotten."

"'Fess up. Did any of you lot hand these out as a joke?"

"No—someone else. Probably one of the Americans trying to undermine everyone else."

By now, Gilda had moved very close to the group in an attempt to eavesdrop. Suddenly they all stared at her. "Well, *I* didn't do it," she said.

The group looked unconvinced.

"Listen, the Americans who are in the finals also received tarot cards," she added. "In fact, my best friend received the Death card, which is pretty much the scariest one you can get!"

Everyone was distracted by a rumbling sound from outside the theater. The front doors of the building opened, releasing a flood of elderly ladies wearing plastic rain scarves who filed inside. The hallway filled with rubber boots, sleet-encrusted hair, and rueful comments about the weather.

"I can't believe it. Thunder in February!"

"Rain and snow mixed! Sleet!"

"Quite odd indeed!"

The group of finalists disbanded as complaints and exclamations about the weather blended into a dull roar of conversation. Another burst of thunder crescendoed like the roll of timpani drums.

For some reason, Gilda felt increasingly uneasy as the corridors became jammed with people attending the performance. *Where is Wendy?* Gilda hurried up and down the hallway, peeking into the ladies' room, a broom closet, and a rehearsal room, but there was no sign of Wendy. From across the room, she glimpsed Professor Waldgrave with his cat and Professor Maddox with her long black cape. At the moment, both struck her as sinister, witchlike characters. They disappeared into the crowd just as she tried to approach them.

What if every one of these clues is part of some strange game Waldgrave and Maddox like to play with the competitors? Gilda wondered, feeling frazzled by the backstage nerves and creeping paranoia that surrounded her. *What if—every time the competition is held in Oxford—one of the finalists disappears?*

Gilda ran down the hallway. She knew she had to act fast to find Wendy before the performances began.

48

Sequins and Sabotage

Gilda climbed the creaking wooden steps to the balcony level, then headed up another flight of narrow stairs to a large, wooden attic space above the concert hall. From beneath the floor, she heard a rush of applause as one of the performers approached the piano.

"It isn't going to stay up, Mama!"

Gilda caught her breath. Standing in the shadows across the room, Jenny Pickles fiddled with the bodice of an ice-blue strapless gown as her mother squinted at a needle and thread, altering the back of her daughter's dress.

"It'll stay up," snapped Ms. Pickles. "Just stand up straight and quit yer twitchin'."

"Ow!"

"I told you—hold still."

As Gilda drew closer, she saw that Jenny's hair was fuller and stiffer than ever, as if she were about to perform in a country music festival instead of a classical competition.

She and her mother had created a makeshift dressing room with a battery-operated curling iron, a lighted mirror, a makeup kit, and an overstuffed handbag. Several yards of colorful material were strewn across the floor—evening gowns in shades of scarlet, vibrant green, and the hot pink that Jenny had apparently rejected. Jenny's sheet music was strewn across the floor on top of the dresses. Jenny was staring down at the music and moving her fingers through the air, practicing silently as her mother tightened the back of her dress.

As Gilda took in this scene, she reflected that Jenny had the kind of mother she herself had occasionally wished for—a plump mother who took an inordinate interest in her slender, attractive daughter's activities, the kind of mother who had no qualms about applying heavy makeup to the faces of young girls. These mothers never seemed to spend any time on their own appearances, but they were perpetually over-burdened with bags of cosmetics, hair-care products, and glittery costumes for their daughters' talent shows, dance recitals, gymnastics meets, and school plays.

On the other hand, Gilda thought, *if Mom ever started lurking around all my activities, I'd probably end up telling her to get lost.*

As Jenny's mom squinted at the needle in her hand, Jenny suddenly picked up the largest can of hairspray Gilda had ever seen and shook it vigorously. She enveloped herself and her mother in a cloud of aerosol spray that sent her mother into a coughing fit.

"Warn me next time, Jenny!"

"Sorry." The can clattered to the floor as Jenny suddenly noticed Gilda staring at her through a haze of hairspray.

"Omigod, you scared the daylights out of me, Gilda! I thought I was seeing a ghost!"

"Sorry," said Gilda, secretly feeling some satisfaction at having startled Jenny. "I was just looking for Wendy."

"Haven't seen her."

"We're tryin' da stay oud da way," said Ms. Pickles, speaking with a needle clenched in her teeth. "Doo many frazzled nerves downstairs."

"Hey, have you seen Julian down there?" Jenny asked brightly.

Gilda bristled. "The last time I saw him, he was chatting up a bunch of slappers."

"Slappers?"

"Some flirty-looking *girls*."

A look of recognition came over Jenny's face as she met Gilda's eyes—a surprised look that said, *Oh, I see. We're in competition over him.* "That's such a cute tiara," she said.

That's right, Jenny, Gilda thought. *I may not have flaming-red hair, but at least I look fabulous in sequins and a tiara.*

"Oh, Jenny, we should have brought *your* tiara," said Ms. Pickles. "Remember the one you won at the Miss Magnolia Pageant?"

"That would be tacky, Mom," said Jenny, deftly deploying an insult meant for Gilda's ears. "Nobody in Oxford would wear a tiara to perform."

"Then you don't understand Oxford," said Gilda. "They have a soft spot for eccentricity and whimsy here."

"Maybe I'm *glad* I don't understand Oxford then," Jenny countered. "Anyway, leave it to Julian to think about girls at a time like this, right, Mama? Right before he goes onstage to perform?"

"Doesn't sound like he's very focused on winning this competition, that's for sure," said Ms. Pickles cheerfully.

"He *never* misses an opportunity to chat up girls," said Gilda. "He said, 'It's all part of the show,' as far as he's concerned." Gilda couldn't help it; she wanted Jenny to experience the sense of hurt and surprise she herself had felt when she peered into the practice room window the day before.

"Well, we've all met that type before, haven't we, Gilda?"

"Oh, sure." Gilda pretended to be just as experienced with boys as Jenny apparently was. "*Tell* me about it."

Gilda had to admit that Jenny had a special knack for deflecting jealous, competitive comments. *Maybe it's a skill she picked up from all those beauty pageants*, Gilda thought.

"Jenny," said Ms. Pickles, "can you grab that harbrush and the pair of scissors for me, darlin'?"

Jenny reached for the scissors and caused a small avalanche of beauty products to cascade from the folding chair. Her mother's purse spilled open and vomited its entire contents onto the floor. The chaotic pile included a cell phone, numerous lipsticks, a wallet with loose credit cards, packs of gum and mints, a lighter, a key chain, and a miniature photo album labeled BRAG BOOK.

"Oh, Jenny, good night!" Ms. Pickles exclaimed. "That purse had more junk crammed in it than a redneck's front yard, and now look!"

Gilda and Jenny crouched down to help Jenny's mother, who was hurriedly stuffing objects back into her bag.

"Oh, don't bother, hon, I'll get it," said Ms. Pickles, breathlessly, her sun-spotted hands and coral fingernails moving quickly to grab objects and stuff them back in her bag.

Just then, under a wad of tissue, Gilda discovered something so interesting and incriminating, it was all she could do to keep from shouting out loud.

The contents of Ms. Pickles's spilled purse included a deck of cards labeled *The Gill Tarot*.

Ms. Pickles reached for the deck of cards, but Gilda snatched it first.

"Just drop that back in, sugar. Must have been some crazy thing that made its way into my purse at a flea market back home. I don't know the half of what's in here."

Gilda looked at the back of the deck and saw that it was priced at three pounds. "Actually, Ms. Pickles, this deck of cards was purchased here in England."

"That's nice, sugar." Ms. Pickles sounded calm, but her sun-speckled skin looked flushed. She made another sudden lunge to grab the deck of cards from Gilda, but Gilda clung to the cards stubbornly—the way she had seen Wendy's little brother hang on to a favorite toy.

For a moment, the two were locked in an absurd tug-of-war. Gilda met Ms. Pickles's eyes and perceived a gold glint of rage.

"Mother! What are you *doing*?"

"Gilda," said Ms. Pickles, ignoring Jenny's protests, "if you don't mind, please unhand my personal property so I can help my daughter get ready."

Instead, Gilda wrenched the deck of cards from Ms. Pickles's hands. She opened the box and swiftly flipped through the deck to see whether any cards were missing. She felt a triumphant sense of excitement combined with shock at the realization that someone's *mother* was now the prime tarot card suspect. "Aha! Just as I thought!" Gilda waved the tarot cards in front of Ms. Pickles's nose. "The cards missing from this deck are the very ones that have been turning up among the other performers—all of the most *disturbing* cards in the deck, I might add."

"Are you both crazy? What is going on here?"

"Jenny, this girl is talking blarney," said Ms. Pickles. "Let's get you ready."

"But why *do* you have tarot cards in your purse, Mama?"

"Who knows? Probably an old party favor. Lord knows there's a landfill full of trash in that bag."

"Ms. Pickles, was your daughter in on this with you, or was this your own secret little plan to undermine the other performers?"

"Gilda, I hate to be rude, but you're disrupting my daughter's concentration. Jenny, turn around so I can hurry up and finish your dress before your performance time."

Jenny faced her mother with hands on hips. "Mama, tell me what's going on. Is this a repeat of the Miss Blossom Pageant?"

Gilda's ears perked up. "What happened at the Miss Blossom Pageant?"

Ms. Pickles ignored the question. She knelt down to collect the remaining objects strewn about on the floor.

"Mother did something unsportsmanlike at the Miss Blossom Pageant," said Jenny, watching her mother warily. "But she promised it would never happen again."

"I only did that at the Blossom show after that horrible girl stained your evening gown on purpose."

"We don't *know* that she did it *on purpose*."

"Believe me, Jenny, she did it on purpose."

"Still, there was no call for you to ruin her hairstyle that way."

"You think what I did was so bad?" Ms. Pickles snapped. "What about that mom who snuck laxatives into the smoothies?"

"That's not the point, Mama. *This* isn't one of those back-stabbing beauty contests! People around here are thinking about *music*!"

"That does not make them saints, Jenny. Why, I see the dirty looks some of those kids give you because of your talent and your hair."

"I haven't noticed any dirty looks."

Gilda cringed, remembering the comments she and Wendy had made about Jenny's hot rollers.

"Well, *I* have. You're just too naïve and trusting.... Why, just the other day I caught one of the little Chinese girls crossing your name off the list for one of the best practice rooms and writing in her own instead."

I hope that wasn't Wendy, Gilda thought, noticing something annoyingly dismissive about Ms. Pickles's reference to "little Chinese girls."

"I don't care if you're in a piano competition, a beauty contest, or a tractor pull: people who *win* aren't afraid to use a little intimidation to get ahead."

"Listen to yourself, Mama. You're saying people should cheat to win?"

"Jenny, that isn't the point. For most people here, winning this competition is just something to brag about at the country club. I am a single mother, and we actually need the money."

"Wendy and I could use the money, too," Gilda interjected.

"Jenny, if your mother can do something to help give you a little edge, then so be it," Ms. Pickles continued. "You deserve a chance to win this, honey."

"But tarot cards, Mama? If you were setting out to humiliate me, then mission accomplished!" Jenny hitched up the bodice of her dress angrily. She looked close to tears.

"'Humiliate' you? Who is looking out for you except for me?"

"Me! I'm looking out for myself."

"Is that so? Well, your hooters are going to be looking out at the audience if you don't let me finish altering your cotton-pickin' dress!"

Gilda stifled a nervous laugh. The truth was, it was hard to maintain a sense of outrage at Jenny and her mother. A situation that had seemed terrifying minutes before now seemed utterly ridiculous and also somewhat sad.

"Who cares about my dress?" Jenny wiped her nose with the back of her hand. Black mascara trickled from the corner of her eye. "My concentration is totally ruined now."

Gilda no longer felt jealous of Jenny. At the moment, she actually felt sorry for her.

Applause vibrated through the wooden floor, followed by a pervasive silence that settled through the whole theater—a silence that seemed to last a bit too long. Was it close to Wendy's performance time? Was the audience staring at an empty stage, waiting for her?

Gilda abruptly rushed from the attic room down to the balcony level of the performance hall. As she peered down at the stage floor, she was relieved to see Wendy walking toward the piano, wearing her red silk dress.

Gilda caught her breath. Something was different about Wendy: she didn't slouch or shuffle her feet apologetically. She almost seemed to glide toward the piano and slip into her seat. Wendy closed her eyes to concentrate, and Gilda prayed that her best friend would be able to get through her music.

Then the atmosphere in the performance hall changed. The lights flickered for a split second, the temperature in the room seemed to drop, and people did not move or breathe as the first notes of the "Ghost Sonata" filled the auditorium.

49

The Ghost Sonata

As Wendy played, Gilda heard faint rustling sounds as the music students and teachers in the audience began to check their program notes and whisper to one another. This music was obviously not the Bach French Suite in G Major announced in the program notes. It was something modern—possibly contemporary—but who was the composer? Not knowing maddened them and piqued their curiosity. They leaned forward in their chairs and squinted at the ceiling. The rest of the audience sat very still with electric attention. *Everyone* listened.

In the front row of the theater, Mrs. Mendelovich clutched her fur stole and sat up even straighter than usual. She felt as if she might be dreaming. How could it be that she did not recognize Wendy's music? How could it be that she did not recognize *anything* about her own student? Wendy's posture, her gestures, her hair—everything looked different!

How long had Wendy been planning this, and why? Who had Wendy been studying with in secret, and where did this phantom teacher find such music?

Mrs. Mendelovich had to admit, somewhat grudgingly, that

this composition—whatever it was—suited Wendy's playing despite its outrageous departure from the standard repertoire.

But Mrs. Mendelovich had always thought of her piano students as her "very own children," and now she saw that she was not a mother at all, because her "children" had always been perfect. None of *her* students had ever run away from her, purposefully ignored her advice, or severely disappointed her. Mrs. Mendelovich felt betrayed.

She could have won, Mrs. Mendelovich thought, *but now she won't.*

As she heard her prize student drift further away upon waves of the unfamiliar music, Mrs. Mendelovich felt a new surge of loss. Wendy was more talented than she had understood. At the same time, Mrs. Mendelovich realized that she was saying good-bye.

Gilda observed the reactions of the judges. She couldn't see Professor Maddox's face clearly, but she noticed that Professor Waldgrave fidgeted: he tapped a pencil on the table, then patted his clothes as if searching for a lost weapon. Finally, he removed his glasses, wiped them off, then put them on again in a familiar gesture—as if seeing Wendy more clearly might help him understand the disturbing and inexplicable miracle of the music that now assaulted his ears. Next to him, white-haired Professor Winterbottom sat calmly with elbows on the table, his jowly cheeks resting in his fists.

Professor Waldgrave recognizes this music, Gilda thought. *He's hearing a ghost.*

As Wendy neared the end of the music, the storm outside

gathered intensity. There was a sharp snapping of thunder. A moment later, the lights in the theater went out completely. Wendy concluded her performance in complete darkness.

Warm applause combined with pockets of nervous laughter welled up from the audience. A moment later, the lights in the hall came on again, but both Professor Waldgrave and Wendy had disappeared.

50

"Curiosity Killed the Cat"

Gilda raced down the balcony stairs to the theater lobby just in time to see Professor Waldgrave hastily cloaking himself in a rain poncho and hurrying out the front door. Gilda instantly recognized the flat, outward-pointing feet, the hunched posture, the mournful *meow!* that surfaced from beneath his rain gear.

Gilda hitched up her trailing evening gown and did her best to chase Professor Waldgrave, who moved down Broad Street at a surprisingly fast clip.

"Professor Waldgrave! Wait!" Having left her jacket in the theater cloakroom, Gilda made a dramatic spectacle as she sprinted in her tiara, high heels, and sleeveless, sequined gown past a group of merrily drunk college boys.

"Let him go, luv!" one of the boys yelled. "Come to the pub with us!"

"Professor Waldgrave!" Gilda shouted at the top of her lungs.

To her surprise, Professor Waldgrave suddenly stopped and turned to look at her. He seemed stunned by the sight of Gilda charging through the rain toward him in her evening gown, as if she might be some apparition flying through the stormy air.

Gasping to catch her breath and shivering in the cold, Gilda finally caught up with him.

"Oh," he said flatly. "It's you."

"Professor Waldgrave... I need to know what happened to Charles Drummond."

The professor's face looked very white, as if no blood pulsed beneath his skin. For a moment, he seemed at a loss for words. "How—how did your friend know that music?"

Professor Waldgrave's cat peeked out from the neck of his rain poncho as if she was also curious about the answer to this question.

"Wendy knows that music because she's been haunted by the ghost of Charles Drummond ever since we came to Oxford."

Professor Waldgrave stared at Gilda thoughtfully, a sad expression in his eyes. He seemed to be trying to decide whether or not to become someone who actually believed in ghosts. "Come with me," he said, "and we'll talk."

Gilda walked with Professor Waldgrave to Holywell Street. When they reached his row house, Gilda felt a twinge of anxiety. *The only things I really know about Professor Waldgrave are that he's obsessed with his cat, he just walked away from judging an international piano competition, and he has some connection with a boy who's now dead*, she thought. Was it potentially dangerous to follow him into his darkened, cluttered house? On the other hand, Gilda was simply too curious to turn back, now that Professor Waldgrave was finally willing to talk to her. *I'm so close to discovering some crucial piece of information, I can almost taste it*, Gilda thought.

The room was filled almost completely by a grand piano barricaded with stacks of piano music, suggesting that nobody had played the instrument in a very long time. Gilda scanned the room for potential weapons, wondering if there was some object she could grab if she suddenly needed to defend herself.

"I'll put the kettle on," said Professor Waldgrave.

Gilda followed him into a small dining area that smelled of cat food. The table and chairs were stacked with music, scholarly books, student papers, and hundreds of pages of a typed manuscript.

"You'll have to forgive my clutter," Professor Waldgrave called from the kitchen. "I'm afraid academics like me have a habit of making every room an extension of the study."

"What are you writing?" Gilda was curious about the manuscript pages.

"A little book about the rise and fall of the piano as a status symbol in the middle-class home. Not the sort of book one would take on holiday to read at the beach."

"Oh." Gilda couldn't help thinking that Professor Sabertash's titles had sounded far more exciting.

Professor Waldgrave appeared, carrying two cups of tea. "Please sit down, if you can find a spot that isn't taken over by papers."

The teacups in Professor Waldgrave's hands shook slightly as he placed them carefully on the table. He removed a stack of books from a chair, sat down, and took a sip of his tea.

"*He* was here, wasn't he?" Gilda could no longer contain herself: her gut feeling that Charles Drummond had been in that very room was growing far too strong to ignore.

"Of course he was here," Professor Waldgrave replied. "I was his teacher."

"You *were*?!"

Sophia jumped up on the professor's lap and purred as Professor Waldgrave stroked her behind the ears. "I also killed him," he added.

51

Professor Waldgrave's Confession

As a boy, I was considered something of a child prodigy, and my teachers all anticipated a successful concert career. I attended the Royal College of Music in London and promptly won a series of concerto competitions. For a time, life and my career looked very promising indeed.

"Then, everything instantly changed. Almost without warning, a medical condition made it impossible for me to perform. No doctor could pinpoint the exact cause of the syndrome that made pain shoot through my fingers and arms whenever I touched the keyboard; all I knew was that I could no longer play. Naturally, I was forced to cancel my concerts. I assumed I would recover, but months and years passed without any improvement, and in the meantime, a fresh crop of young, talented performers had emerged from the competition circuit, ready to take my place on the concert stage.

"The unthinkable had happened: I had been completely forgotten before my performance career even got started.

"I had no choice but to turn to teaching. I was lucky to get a post at Oxford University, but in all honesty, I was always secretly bored by my students. *'Why would there ever be a future in this for you?'* I wanted to ask them. *'Why are you wasting my time?'*

"I also turned to writing about music, and before long, I was known as one of the most caustic music critics for *The Independent* newspaper.

"It was around this time that I began to perceive a flurry of interest in a performer I only vaguely remembered from my days as a student at the Royal College of Music—someone called Rhiannon Maddox. I had scarcely noticed her when my own star was on the rise. Now this Rhiannon Maddox—who had not been able to win even a single major competition—was becoming famous.

"She gave international concerts. She produced edgy music videos. She dyed her hair acrylic red or pink and wore ridiculous clothes designed by student fashion designers. She appeared in concert with Madonna and was photographed in silly, gossipy magazines like *Tatler*.

"I admit it; I resented her success, and I vented my frustration by writing scathing reviews of her concerts. What disturbed me was that nobody seemed to notice that she was merely a rather ordinary piano player and a very successful self-promoter.

"Then—everything changed. I stopped caring about Rhiannon Maddox's brilliant career because in a single day, my own life became far more interesting.

"It happened one afternoon, when an elderly woman brought her thirteen-year-old grandson to my studio to inquire about private lessons. My first impression was that, with the exception of his ill-fitting black raincoat, he had the rather ordinary, adolescent look of a boy I would expect to be interested in football instead of piano. On the other hand, he didn't have the nervous discomfort of a young person whose parents had forced him to attend piano lessons. He was very calm and in complete possession of his thirteen-year-old self. He actually looked as if he *wanted* to be there.

"'Sorry,' I told the grandmother, 'but I'm afraid I'm not taking new students at present.'

"'I've heard you would be the best person to work with a truly *gifted* student,' she said.

"I was skeptical about the probability that this boy was 'truly gifted,' but I couldn't help feeling flattered. 'May I ask who told you I'd be the best teacher for him?'

"'Charlie told me himself. He has an old recording of your Bach Preludes and Fugues, and he says it's his favorite piano recording, don't you, Charlie?'

"I admit it: I was hungry for flattery, and hearing this made me feel suddenly generous. 'Well, then,' I said, 'let's hear him play.'

"Moments later, I was offering to teach Charles at a minimal cost. I had assumed it would never happen, but by pure chance, I had actually discovered a genuine talent—a true 'diamond in the rough' that simply needed my help in order to shine.

"Each week, Charles Drummond turned up for lessons at my house, and each week, I became more amazed by my extraordinary student. In many ways, Charles was a normal teenager: he loved fantasy novels and mysteries; he loved exploring the outdoors with his pet dog and rowing down the Thames. His grades were good, but he said he hated school. Tragically, both of his parents had died by the time he was seven, and he lived with his grandmother in the tiny village of Binsey.

"But as we know, Charles was not at all ordinary. The most striking quality of his talent was an uncanny intuition—an almost psychic gift. Somehow, he seemed to know exactly how a composer would have wanted a piece to be played.

"'You should make this part lighter—more classical and less heavy,' I advised him once during a lesson on Mozart's Fantasy in D Minor.

"'No,' said Charles. 'It should be dark. He wants it dark in this section.'

"'What do you mean,' "he wants it dark?"' I demanded. '*Who* wants it dark?'

"'Mozart, of course.'

"'Charles, based on my extensive research into this era of music, I think I have a better idea than you of what Mozart would have wanted.'

"'He wants it the way I'm playing it,' said Charles stubbornly. 'He says that if there had been a grand piano like the one I'm playing under his fingers when he was alive, he would have used all of its abilities. He would make it sound heavier here.'

"'And how—may I ask—did a long-dead composer tell you these things?'

"'I can't tell you *how* I know,' said Charles. 'I just know.'

"And the thing was, I was convinced that he was absolutely right.

"So when I learned that my colleague Professor Winterbottom was organizing an international competition for young people to be held at Oxford University, I decided it was time to introduce Charles Drummond to the public. On some level, I suspected that once I shared my prize student with the rest of the world, he would no longer belong to me alone, but for the moment, Charles was mine. There was absolutely no doubt in my mind that he would win the competition.

"'Charles,' I said one afternoon following a piano lesson, 'we've never talked about your career plans. I think you could have a successful concert career.'

"'I know.' The boy never pretended to be modest.

"'What I mean to say is that you're good enough that you could actually become *famous* once people discover you. How do you feel about that?'

"'Okay,' said Charles, 'but I'm really a composer.'

"This surprised me because I hadn't seen any evidence that Charles was a composer. Charles had never shown me anything he had written. 'Have you actually *composed* something, Charles?' I asked.

"'I'll show it to you when I'm finished,' was his reply.

"But I heard nothing more about this invisible composition, and I thought no more about it. After all, I was keeping Charles quite busy preparing for the First Annual Young International Virtuosos Competition.

"Well, the day of the competition arrived, and after the first round, people were already talking about Charles, as I knew they would. Everyone wanted to know: *Where had this boy come from and with whom had he studied?*

"It was just as some parents of considerably less-talented children approached me to ask whether I might be taking on new students—a moment when I felt particularly pleased with myself,

I might add—that I glanced across the room and felt a sudden wave of nausea. In an instant, my perfect day was ruined.

"There—sporting a flowing gown made of gauzy green material and an absurd hairdo with tiny braids—was Rhiannon Maddox. I had heard a rumor that one of her latest ventures was positioning herself as a star teacher, a champion of young talent. And now she was hovering over my Charles like a sinister weeping willow.

"Why did Charles look interested in talking to her? I wondered. Why was he handing her a piece of paper?

"When the two of them disappeared together, I had to follow. I found them in a practice room. Charles was playing something I hadn't heard before—something haunting, dissonant, and genuinely beautiful. Rhiannon was listening with her eyes closed and a lit cigarette in one hand.

"'Have you heard this piece your student composed?' she demanded when she saw me staring.

"And here's where I made my biggest mistake. 'Of course I've heard it,' I lied. 'It needs a bit of work, in my opinion.' And in an instant I saw something in Charles's face change. He seemed to stare *through* me. We both knew I had lied. I knew I had lost his respect.

"'Come now, Charlie,' I said, simply wanting to get away. 'It's late.'

"'Remember what we talked about, Charles,' said Rhiannon. She handed Charles a small piece of paper as if passing him a secret note. He stuck the paper in his pocket, and this infuriated me. *After all*, I thought, *who is she to communicate in secret with my student?*

"Charles followed me sullenly to the car park. 'Charlie,' I said as we drove down the dark country road leading to Charles's house, 'your composition sounded interesting, but you should have played it for me first before sharing it with Ms. Maddox. She has some rather unorthodox ideas.'

"I remember how he stared out the window as if plotting some escape. 'She asked me to play it,' he said. 'She said I perform as if I'm improvising, and she guessed I would make a good composer.'

"'We can work on your composition after the competition is over, if you like,' I offered. 'Right now you should stay focused on your next performance. You really have a great chance of winning this.'

"'I'm going to play my *own* composition in the next round.'

"Well, I immediately suspected this must be the result of some sabotage on Rhiannon's part—retaliation for all those scathing reviews of her performances I had published. 'Charles, you know there are rules about what you can play in this competition,' I reminded him. 'Doing such a thing might disqualify you.'

"'Professor Maddox thinks I should perform it.'

"'Of course she does! If you get disqualified, one of her own talentless students will have a greater chance of winning. It's sabotage, pure and simple.'

"'She thinks I could *win* if I performed it. Besides, she also invited me to take some lessons with her in London. She could introduce me to people who will work with me on my composing. I don't *need* to win this competition; she could help me.'

"And then I knew that the worst thing I could imagine was

actually happening: the person I hated most was stealing my prize student. She would launch his performance career to the public and claim credit as his teacher. Without realizing it, I began to drive faster.

"'Charles,' I said, probably staring at his sullen profile instead of the road in front of me, 'I don't think that's a good idea. Professor Maddox actually knows very little about music. Her performances are wildly inaccurate and she has a chaotic approach to putting together concert programs. I think, at this very sensitive stage in your development—'

"'At least she *has* a concert career,' he retorted.

"And those were the very last words we spoke to each other, because when I looked back at the road in front of me, it was too late to avoid the oncoming van that had just veered into my path. The next thing I knew, I awoke in hospital with several broken bones. Charlie, I learned, had died instantly.

"The death was ruled a terrible accident.

"Days later, I inquired about a lost manuscript of music near the site of the accident, but nothing could be found. Until I heard it again today, I assumed the only copy had been lost forever."

52

The Aftermath

Standing next to his father in the lobby of the Sheldonian The-ater, Julian looked uncharacteristically stiff and uncomfortable. His father stood with his arm locked around his son posses-sively, offering a fierce, red-faced grin to the small crowd of people who approached to congratulate Julian on his perfor-mance.

"He played just brilliantly!" an elderly lady declared, push-ing through the crowd to gaze at Julian and his father with an appreciation close to reverence. "You must be so very proud of your son, Mr. Graham."

"I'm very proud, indeed!" Julian flinched as his father squeezed his arm a bit too tightly. "Back at home he's known as our local Liberace!"

Julian flinched. "I *don't* play like Liberace." He felt as if he were literally shrinking: in a split second, his father had man-aged to deflate him with a single condescending reference—annoyingly, the same reference Professor Waldgrave had used to criticize his performance in the first round of the compe-tition.

"Has your son been very gifted from a very young age, Mr. Graham?"

"I must say, he took to the piano quickly. This surprised us, you see, because he wasn't potty trained until age five."

Embarrassed, sympathetic chuckles rippled through the small gathering.

"Complete twaddle," spat Julian, wondering why he was never able to come up with a quick comeback around his father. He wished he could become invisible and slip from the room.

"Now, Julian, you know it's true," Julian's father insisted, warming to his audience. "I'm telling you; his mum couldn't find nappies large enough. In the end, she had to cut up our best white sheets and use them to cover his bum."

He just can't help trying to steal the show at my expense, Julian thought. *He's like some second-rate comedian. If it were anyone else, I'd come up with a scathing joke right now to put him in his place, but for some reason, I can't think of a thing to say.*

"Yes, you'd never know it now, but Julian was a rather plump boy in those days," Mr. Graham continued. "We thought his fingers would be too fat to tie his shoes, let alone play the piano. Of course, now he's all skin and bones...."

Stop talking, stop talking, stop talking! For once, Julian felt relieved when he spied Mr. Goodwin, his piano teacher, elbowing his way through the congested hallway toward him.

"Julian!" Mr. Goodwin embraced Julian briefly and slapped him on the back. "Just look at you—you already have a fan club! I thought I was trying to approach a rock star for a moment there. I don't know how you did it, but you amazed me this time! Very fine playing indeed!" He turned to Julian's father. "You must be immensely proud as well, Mr. Graham."

"Of course. It's like I always told Julian, 'If you spent half as much time practicing as you do goggling the young totties in town, you might come to something.'"

Much to Mr. Graham's satisfaction, this comment elicited more laughter, but for Julian, this was the last straw. "You never did tell me that, Dad," he muttered.

"Of course I did, son."

"What you told me was, 'Don't bother playing dead music on a dinosaur instrument.'"

Mr. Graham's face reddened. "I don't remember saying that. If I ever did, it was because you kept tinkering away at the ivories when there were real jobs to be done around the place."

Feeling increasingly uncomfortable as they sensed the personal conflict erupting between father and son, the group of well-wishers hastily extended their hands, offered congratulations, and dispersed.

"We know how boys his age can be, don't we?" A pleading tone entered Mr. Graham's voice. "Anything to prevent themselves from doing a decent day's work, right?"

"I know Julian worked very hard to perform the way he did tonight, Mr. Graham," said Mr. Goodwin, eyeing Julian's father with an expression of mild concern. "And regardless of the outcome of this competition, I believe he has a future as a musician—if he wants it."

I do want it. The new feeling of certainty surprised Julian. Admitting to himself that he actually wanted something—even something as uncertain as a music career—made him feel stronger for some reason.

"We'd best be shoving off now," said Mr. Graham, suddenly impatient. He turned to head for the coatroom.

Julian observed his father, who now stood in line looking very short and ordinary as he waited to retrieve his coat. *It's not that Dad isn't proud of me*, Julian reflected, *but I've finally realized something: he's also jealous of me.*

Anger and sadness combined with pity as Julian watched his father search his pockets for the ticket to claim his checked belongings. *There's a tiny part of him that wants me to fail*, Julian thought, *but I'm not going to do it. I'm not going to please him in that way.*

Wendy wandered into the lobby looking for Gilda and was astonished when complete strangers approached her wearing expressions of bright, eager curiosity. "I loved that piece you played!" they said. "Who composed it?"

Confused, fascinated stares met Wendy's reply. *A fourteen-year-old boy who had composed such music? Why had they never heard of him before?*

Within moments, Wendy found herself speaking to a young woman who wrote freelance articles for *The Oxford Times*, divulging the story of how she and her friend Gilda had discovered the Sonata in A Minor in the well near St. Margaret's Church.

Then, across the room, Wendy glimpsed Mrs. Mendelovich's frozen smile. As her teacher approached, Wendy felt as if she were awakening from the dream of her performance and facing an uncomfortable reality: Mrs. Mendelovich and her parents, who had seemed so small and far away just hours before, once again loomed in the present, watching her and shaking their heads with disappointment. How could she possibly explain herself? *"A ghost made me play the music,"* sounded ridiculous, even if she was now convinced that it was true. *But in the end, I also chose to play it because I wanted to*, Wendy reflected. *No matter what happens in the competition, that performance was totally my own.*

"Mrs. Mendelovich," Wendy faltered. "I—I'm sorry..."

"You look lovely, Windy," said Mrs. Mendelovich, silencing her student with a perfunctory embrace and an air kiss.

"Mrs. Mendelovich, I wanted to tell you—"

Mrs. Mendelovich held up a hand and shook her head. She clearly did not want to hear Wendy's explanation—at least not yet. "We weell talk later." She patted Wendy's hand in a manner that seemed to say, *Don't bother trying to explain; there's no point. It's over.*

Gone were her teacher's exuberant accolades, perfumed hugs, and promises of greatness. Wendy had always found these demonstrations of affection suffocating, but without them, she now felt as if she were standing alone, exposed on a windy plain.

Wendy watched her teacher breeze away from her and toward Ming Fong.

Usually, when Wendy played well in a competition, her parents treated her as if it were her birthday for that day. Sometimes they took her to a restaurant for her favorite foods. Sometimes the reward was a shopping trip or a wrapped present. Then there were the inevitable phone calls to friends and relatives to relive the honor of the experience.

Now, as Wendy left the Sheldonian Theater, she walked into a dark, silent street alone.

It's weird, she thought. *I honestly feel like I just gave the best performance of my life, but I've never felt lonelier. It isn't a completely bad feeling, but I have to admit—freedom is kind of lonely.*

Teacher's pet. She had always hated this label in school. She had always felt embarrassment at being singled out; how surprising that she now felt a strange grief at losing her "teacher's pet" role with Mrs. Mendelovich.

"Wendy! Wait up!"

With relief, Wendy turned to see Gilda running toward her in her sequined dress and tiara.

"What are you doing out here? Where's your coat?"

"Left it . . . in the theater." Gilda leaned forward and placed her hands on her knees to catch her breath.

"Where were you? Did you even see my performance?"

"Yes, and you sounded great! But where were you before the competition started? I looked *everywhere*!"

"Oh. Sorry. I just needed some time to myself away from everyone's nerves and everything, and I found this room backstage that nobody else knew about."

"Anyway, that doesn't matter now because I have *so much* to tell you." Gilda clutched her bare arms. Her teeth chattered, but she hardly noticed; she was so excited to tell Wendy about the final breakthrough in the investigation.

"Gilda, you're freezing. Let's get your coat."

"Just listen to this first."

"Don't tell me; you made up with Julian, and now you're in love again."

"Oh, *please*. Wendy, I've just been to Professor Waldgrave's house, and he told me everything! I know *exactly* what happened to Charles Drummond, and why his ghost has been haunting this competition!"

As Wendy listened to the story of the untimely death of the fourteen-year-old boy and the fate of the music he had written, she felt a strange feeling of release. A crucial piece of a maddening puzzle had finally fit in place, allowing her to see everything clearly. The music had finally been performed, and Charles Drummond had reached his audience. Still, her mind spun with bewildering questions about her own bizarre experience in Oxford.

"Gilda," she ventured as the two of them returned to the theater to find Gilda's coat, "with all the musicians around here, why do you think his ghost picked *me* to play that music?"

"I've been thinking about that, too," said Gilda. "And I really don't know. Maybe he just liked the way you play. Or maybe you were the only person who was willing to *listen* to him."

"I couldn't *help* listening to him."

"See? You *could* be a little clairaudient, Wendy."

"I don't think I want to be."

"I know it's scary, but if you learned to control it more, it could be a great skill to have for our psychic investigations."

"You mean, it would be a great skill for *your* psychic investigations."

"I think we solved this haunting together, don't you?"

"I guess. Except I was the one who was haunted, so that's kind of different."

"Can you imagine what we could accomplish back home? With your clairaudient skills and my psychic detective know-how, I bet we could solve things we've never even dreamed about!"

"We'll see." At the moment, Wendy simply wanted to sleep long and hard, without dreams of any kind. She wanted to go home and face her parents' prying questions, to play the piano and see her father tilt his head as he listened for mistakes, to hear her little brother's nonsensical chatter, to walk through clean rooms decorated with her mother's carefully positioned good-luck charms—the red frogs, the money plants, the mirrors. Whether or not they actually brought luck, they would feel familiar and safe, and for at least the first few days, she would be happy to be home, whether or not she was returning as a competition winner.

53

The Winners

Dear Julian,

It's six o'clock in the morning, and I'm peering through a bus window at the dark High Street, which looks cold and eerily still in the early morning lamplight. That's right—I'm writing to you from a bus bound for Heathrow Airport, which means that I'm already LONG GONE.

Why, you ask, am I bothering to write you a letter?

For one reason, and one reason alone, Julian. I simply want you to know that I've "moved on" completely. In fact, if we ran into each other on the sidewalk right now, I would probably give you a blank look as I searched my memory, trying to match a name with a face. "Jack? Jethro? Wait—don't tell me—your name is on the tip of my tongue. Jason! Right?"

Don't feel bad about this, Julian. It's just that I no longer spend time thinking of your smile (those initially cute but quickly manipulative dimples; those crooked teeth, so rebelliously free of an orthodontist's interference). No, Julian, you have been deleted from my brain as completely and abruptly as a lost homework assignment from an outdated computer. Let's face it: the bottom line is that we'll probably never meet again unless I decide to use you as a character in one of my novels, and that's just fine with me.

Well, okay, I'll <u>admit</u> that as I was packing my suitcase, I toyed <u>momentarily</u> with the idea of casually leaving you my email address, home telephone number, cell phone number, and street address—you know, just a few details in case you ever found yourself vacationing in the Detroit area and needed someone to help explain American rituals and customs. Luckily, Wendy talked me out of it. "Just let it drop, Gilda," she said. "I know you. If you even leave him your email address, you'll always be hoping for a message that might never turn up in your in-box, and you'll waste time writing him thirteen-page letters. Better to just keep the memories and move on with your life."

Well, I argued at first, but then I remembered that Wendy is the kind of friend who looks out for me at moments like this, just as I always try to do the same for her. I had to admit she had a point. After all, I'm not the clingy type, and I deserve a more mature relationship with less "faffing about" when it comes to romance. In fact, I'm not even going to <u>deliver</u> this letter, Julian. Just think of this note as a little psychic message from me to you—a message to say, "Good-bye, and thanks for all the good times." After all, the best part is that I'm going home with some good stories to tell. And don't worry, Julian, I would never embellish the truth!

So farewell, dear Oxford—city of "dreaming spires" and spurned love! Adieu to my brief love—the boy with the crooked smile.

With no regrets,
Gilda Joyce
Psychic Investigator

P.S. I suppose it's <u>possible</u> that we'll meet again someday in the future after we're both famous. If that happens, let's meet for a frappuccino after one of your concerts or one of my award-winning Broadway shows, okay? After all, we're both dynamic people with international careers. If nothing else, I'm sure we'll read about each other in the tabloids.

The Oxford Times
"Judges Face Discord in Selecting Competition Winner"

Fifteen-year-old pianist Julian Graham of Crawling has been declared the winner of Oxford University's Young International Virtuosos Competition. He will receive a prize of 5,000 pounds along with a potentially career-launching debut with the London Symphony Orchestra.

"I'm dead chuffed," was the winner's response to the news. "I'm in shock, really."

Judges acknowledged the difficulty of choosing a winner from among the ten finalists in this year's competition. "The environment was fraught with an unusual degree of discord and argument," commented competition founder and concert pianist

Eugene Winterbottom. "At midnight last night, I was certain that this would be the first year we would not be able to declare a winner, but thankfully, by morning, we had all come to an agreement."

Nigel Waldgrave initially favored the clean, accurate playing of pianist Ming Fong Chen, but Winterbottom countered that her performance was "unoriginal" and "completely derivative of the pianist Lang Lang."

Further complicating the decision-making process was a surprise musical selection by pianist Wendy Choy, who opted at the last minute to perform an unknown composition by the deceased young pianist Charles Drummond, who had once been a student of Nigel Waldgrave's.

"The performance was top-notch," Winterbottom stated, "but Miss Choy completely disregarded the competition guidelines for acceptable repertoire."

Nigel Waldgrave hesitated to comment on Wendy Choy's performance, noting that he had "strong emotions" associated with this music and the untimely death of its composer. He did not feel that he could judge its merits objectively.

Celebrated pianist Rhiannon Maddox disagreed with Choy's disqualification, almost withdrawing in protest at one point in the evening. "If we're committed to rewarding artistry in this competition, it seemed a travesty to disqualify this unique performance based on a technicality."

Although she failed to win the top prize, Wendy Choy's performance of Charles Drummond's Sonata in A Minor has generated a flurry of interest from Oxford musicians and concertgoers who are keen to know more about the haunting melody and distinctive, modern harmonies written by a young local teen whose life ended four years ago in a car accident. Perhaps most intriguing and bizarre are the claims by Miss Choy of the "paranormal" means by which she and her best friend Gilda Joyce, a self-proclaimed "psychic investigator," discovered the music.

"If I couldn't vouch for the authenticity of this music myself," Nigel Waldgrave commented, "I would have assumed this was merely an attention-seeking prank. As it stands, I have to acknowledge the possibility that these two girls had some psychic connection with a dead musician."

"This experience has changed me," Wendy Choy noted. "I didn't win the competition, but it made me see music differently.... I guess as something more interesting and mysterious than I realized."

Gilda Joyce, who also served as a page-turner for the competition, lamented her best friend's loss of the winning prize, but offered their investigative services to potential clients throughout the British Isles at "reasonable rates."

"Solving mysteries is what we do," said Miss Joyce. "And we're always willing to travel."